T0190737

Best Hex Ever

Best Hex Ever

A Novel

NADIA EL-FASSI

Dell
New York

A Dell Trade Paperback Original

Copyright © 2024 by Little Pink Ghost Ltd.
Excerpt from *Love at First Fright* by Nadia El-Fassi
copyright © 2024 Little Pink Ghost Ltd.

Published in the United States by Dell, an imprint of Random House, a division of Penguin Random House LLC, New York.

DELL and the D colophon are registered trademarks of Penguin Random House LLC.

Published in the United Kingdom by Del Rey, part of the Penguin Random House group of companies.

This book contains an excerpt from the forthcoming book *Love at First Fright* by Nadia El-Fassi. This excerpt has been set for this edition only and may not reflect the final content of the forthcoming edition.

ISBN 978-0-593-87179-9
Ebook ISBN 978-0-593-87180-5

Printed in the United States of America on acid-free paper

randomhousebooks.com

2 4 6 8 9 7 5 3 1

Book design by Virginia Norey
Moon and stars art: foxysgraphic/stock.adobe.com;
teacup: ylivdesign/stock.adobe.com; flower motif: Nina/stock.adobe.com

For Mama. Wherever I am, I carry you with me.

Author's Note

There are a few sensitive topics in this story, such as being cheated on in a past relationship (off page), loss of a family member (off page), growing up in a group home, and coming out to family members later in life (on page). I hope I have treated these topics with the care they deserve.

Best Hex Ever

Chapter 1

*I*t was a crisp autumn day in the last week of October, the kind of day that makes you want to curl up with a good book and a steaming cup of hot chocolate. Golden leaves crunched underfoot and early-morning frost clung to Serendipity Café's bright purple awning. It was Dina's favorite time of the year. The insufferable heat of late September had finally passed, when the air in the tube felt thick and glue-like, forcing her to spend most of her days performing cooling spells on her armpits.

There was always a change in the air when autumn came to London. For one thing, business at the café picked up, and right now every customer wanted a croissant with their coffee order.

Croissant magic was tricky at the best of times, but it was proving especially difficult during the morning coffee rush. Dina stared down at the mess of pastry and butter—no way was this salvageable. Pastry had never been Dina's forte. She tugged her mountain of curls into a bun and rolled up her sleeves.

Dina had just pulled out a new jar of her magic butter blend, ready to begin again, when Robin, her barista, called out, "Dina, where did you put the chrysanthemum tea blend you made last week?"

The croissants would have to wait.

She went out to the front, rummaged through her collection of teas and eventually lifted the tin of delicate dried blooms they were looking for onto the counter. Reluctant to return to the unfriendly croissants, Dina set about serving those who were just settling down at the tables and cozy armchairs of her café.

There was something different about Serendipity Café, a certain spark in the air that no one could quite put their finger on. It was a place where good things happened. Customers who dropped in to buy themselves a cappuccino would accidentally trip over the umbrella of someone at the table beside theirs, and that person would turn out to be the love of their life.

Dina loved how quickly the rumors about her café had spread: that if you bought a latte and a cookie on the way to a job interview, you'd get the job. She'd been particularly proud of that spell; it was one of her best. The special ingredient was a pinch of cinnamon and just a dash of calm. Like a hug with your loved one, or the feeling of kicking off your shoes after a long day.

The trick to Dina's spells was that she put her own memories and emotions in them, and then the spell would take it from there, mimicking her feelings in the person who ate or drank whatever she had made. A confidence charm to help someone get a job didn't give them artificial confidence, it just gave them a little magical push to find that confidence in themselves.

The spells didn't last forever, of course. No magic did.

Even so, Dina had to make sure that she kept her magic secret. After all, she couldn't have all of London knowing she was a witch.

As the city frosted over, customers would be flocking in through the doors, searching for comfort and a good cup of tea. A particular favorite was Dina's special chai blend, full of warming ginger, clove, and nutmeg, and just a sprinkle of that feeling you get when you rub a cat's soft, warm belly.

All around the city, coats were being pulled out of the backs of cupboards where they'd spent the year gathering dust and moth holes, radiators groaned to life, and people began searching for that special someone they could snuggle up with once winter really settled in.

Dina was far too preoccupied to even think about the start of cuffing season. She'd been on a couple of dates in the last year, one man and one woman, and only one of them had gone vaguely well. The guy had been a walking red flag, while Maggie—the insanely hot yoga teacher Dina had gone out with a few months ago—had been lovely, kind, and smart. Dina knew that she could have had something real with Maggie if she'd given it a chance, but she hadn't wanted to hurt her. So, she'd left before things could get any worse.

Thankfully, the busy autumn season at the café was enough to take her mind off romance; Dina had sworn herself off dating for the foreseeable future. It wasn't worth the pain it would cause herself and others. Besides, business was booming, and she had to finish making another batch of her ever-popular "Cozy & Calm" candles before they sold out again.

"Robin, could you take these to table four please?" Dina said, handing her colleague a tray bearing two slices of her apple and blueberry pie and two mugs of the Serendipity house tea blend. The couple sitting there had been regulars at the café for a few months now, coming here every Wednesday to study together.

At least that's what Dina assumed they were doing, with their heads bent down over their respective laptops. Every now and again, the man would reach out for his partner's hand and they would just sit like that, in perfect companionable silence. *That's what I want*, Dina thought. Could she have that one day? Lately, even the idea of a happily ever after felt unattainable.

"Yes, boss." Robin smiled, knowing full well how much Dina hated being called "boss." Robin had been at the café for a couple of years, working shifts in between the spin classes they taught near Blackfriars station. They had walked in one day, only moments after Dina had placed a job advertisement for a barista in the window. Dina had taken in Robin's dark green mohawk and effortlessly cool eyeliner, watched how they straightened one of the picture frames on the wall absentmindedly, and had known that they were the perfect person for the job.

Dina didn't have much time to do anything but work today, not that she minded. Serendipity, with the buzz of its coffee machine and the warm scent of pastry, was her happy place. She'd founded this business herself—with only a little help from her magic—and every time she saw a customer return after their first visit her heart thrummed with joy.

This morning, however, Dina was acutely aware that it was only Robin and herself working in the café, and they were vastly outnumbered.

Time-slowing spells tired her out, so she tended to save them for the lunch rush. The coffee machine was being temperamental again, and Dina had already had to give it a thump (said thump may have contained a spark of something extra) to get it working again.

She was just finishing up the latte art—a cat on a broomstick on one and a ghost on another; it was spooky season after all—when the door swung open wildly in the wind, leaves swirling in the doorway, knocking an evil eye charm off the wall, which fell to the ground with a clatter, smashing in half.

Dina sucked in a breath. She recognized a bad omen when she saw one.

The door slammed shut, the small bell above tinkling belatedly. A man stood in the doorway, picking a stray leaf off his sweater.

The first thing Dina noticed was his nose. It looked a little crooked, like it had been broken but hadn't healed straight. And then his size. Not only was he tall, he was broad enough to take up the entire narrow entrance. That sweater, fluffy as it was, wasn't hiding the muscles rippling underneath as he bent down to pick up the broken evil eye. What was a man with a body like that doing with tweed elbow patches and wire-rimmed glasses? He looked like a professor who moonlit as a cage fighter.

Dina swallowed, acutely aware of her dry mouth. Dark curling hair, a groomed beard—it was like he'd walked straight out of her daydreams and into her coffee shop. The evil eye was right; she was doomed.

"Sorry, this fell off the wall," he said in a low, honeyed voice.

Don't flirt with him, Dina, she told herself, tucking a stray curl behind her ear. When his eyes met hers, they were brown as caramel.

"Thanks," she said, taking the charm from his outstretched hand. Their hands brushed as he placed the halves in her palm, a rough calloused touch. Dina quickly pulled her hand away. The henna spell she'd crafted last night when she couldn't sleep was beginning to come alive and draw love hearts up her wrist.

"It's a nazar amulet, right?" he said matter-of-factly. "Like your necklace." He nodded toward Dina's throat, where a hamsa with an evil eye set in the center rested. Her fingers reached up for it, and she felt the blush rising in her cheeks. She had no business letting a strange man—albeit a very attractive strange man—do this to her.

"Similar, yes. They're both protection from the evil eye."

"Should I be worried that it broke when I walked in?" He smiled, a mischievous glint in his eye.

"No, it's fine, I break my pendants all the time," she said, fiddling with her hamsa necklace. "It means it worked."

"So it protected you?" The man leaned forward, resting his forearms on the counter, his voice husky. Dina could smell his cologne—cedar and something citrusy.

"It protected me." It was odd. They were in the middle of her busy coffee shop, yet Dina felt like they were the only two people in the room. She hadn't met someone so interested in her evil eye before, but he was looking at her with a calm, knowing inquisitiveness that sent shivers rippling down her neck.

She glanced down at the broken pendant on the counter. When it broke, had it protected the café, Dina, or this man? Either way, when she glanced at him, she felt unmoored. That was a bad sign. She couldn't let his evident sexiness distract her.

"So"—she cleared her throat, willing the blush to fade from her cheeks—"what can I get you?"

"I'll have an Earl Grey, and one of your croissants."

"Any milk or lemon?" Look at her, keeping it super professional. She was definitely not staring at his flexing bicep as he pulled his wallet from his back pocket.

"Just black, thanks."

Dina was about to duck under the counter to grab the jar of loose Earl Grey (she'd foraged the bergamot herself on a trip to Italy), when she heard a loud crash from one of the tables.

"Oh, I'm so sorry," a customer said, looking down at two cups of spilled coffee that had smashed on the floor. Dina smiled at the customer and was about to go and grab her mop from the store cupboard when she heard an awful rattling sound, followed by a pop. This wasn't exactly unexpected—bad luck had a way of following Dina around.

"Coffee machine just broke!" Robin shouted.

Dina inhaled deeply, her hand curling into a fist. She glanced up at the handsome stranger, who she would probably never see again. His gaze was already on her.

"Robin, can you man the till? I'll sort out the machine and spill," Dina called. She walked away before the man could say anything else—anything that might make her turn around and do something foolish.

The coffee machine just needed a little elbow grease, she thought—and by "elbow grease," Dina meant another punch of strong magic. Soon the spill was mopped up, the hot drinks replaced.

As Dina looked up, she saw the stranger leaving the café, sipping his Earl Grey. In another life, perhaps.

"Oh, I love a man in a turtleneck, it makes them look so studious." Robin was standing beside her, grinning. Dina swatted them with a tea towel, and they both got back to work.

Chapter 2

*S*cott Mason ran a hand through his hair and tried very hard to think about work. He had to approve the exhibition posters, write his speech for the opening gala, and go to the archives for research. He had to think about anything other than that barista, who'd looked like she'd walked straight out of his daydreams and into reality. What idiocy had compelled him to leave the café before getting her number? Damn, he should have offered to get down on his knees and clean up the spilled coffee if it meant he could have continued speaking with her. He didn't even know her name.

Scott sat in his office in the British Museum and stared at his laptop screen. His office was crammed full of as many books as it could hold—some left over from the curator who had worked here before him—and the towering stacks had a tendency to fall on him when he least expected it. There was a radiator in the corner that occasionally let out a metallic grunt but never actually seemed to warm up, and a family of pigeons had set up roost right outside his window. His desk chair creaked whenever he sat down, and the desk itself was stained with a century of ink spills, but now that he had hung up some postcards and prints from his travels and the previous exhibitions he'd curated, it was starting to feel like home.

Each time Scott had taken a sip of the delectably sweet Earl Grey tea from the café, his mind had strayed back to the barista. She'd reminded him of those Grecian goddess statues, all voluptuous curves and soft open features; those mahogany curls flecked with purple, eyes such a deep brown they were almost black. And those lips . . . "kissable" didn't even begin to cover it.

He'd gone on a few dates since he'd moved back to London, mostly through the apps, and there was nothing wrong with the women he'd met up with. They'd all been attractive, intelligent, and funny, but something just wasn't clicking. It wasn't that he was still hung up on Alice; more that after being in a long-term relationship for a while he was bloody tired of going over the same first-date questions again. *What do you do for work? What sort of stuff do you do on the weekends?* All of these dating apps, and none of them could tell you anything about how chemistry worked in real life. It grated on him.

Scott hadn't been able to get himself out of that funk. Until now. That barista had lit up something within him, like a ray of sunshine finally breaking through the clouds after a storm. She even had him thinking in cheesy similes. For the first time in ages, his body—his senses—felt awake. And he *wanted*.

This was Scott's first year as the curator of the permanent collections, and he couldn't help but feel that apart from Dr. MacDougall, who had stuck her neck out to hire him, some of the other curators and board members looked down their noses at him. Not all, mind you. It just happened to be the most powerful ones.

He'd done his best not to get distracted all afternoon. Dr. Jenkins and Dr. Garcia, two curators who far outranked him in seniority, weren't pleased with his plans for the summer and autumn exhibition schedule. They had shuddered when Scott had dared to utter the phrase "interactive exhibition." To them, a museum was not a place for children to learn about embalming mummies, or for anyone without a PhD to have access to the round Reading Room.

He remembered how shocked some of them had been when he'd explained that their idea for an exhibition based around the ancient sewage systems of Mesopotamia wasn't likely to draw in big crowds.

Again, his mind was pulled back to the smile of the barista, the way she had blushed and touched her neck when he'd drawn attention to the hamsa necklace she wore. Maybe he should go back and offer to buy her a new amulet to replace the one he'd broken? Was that too much? He didn't want to come on too strong.

Although their interaction had only lasted a moment, it had been delightful to talk about his passion for historical objects with someone else, especially anything related to talismans of luck or good fortune. Eric—Scott's best friend—was always happy to listen but didn't really reciprocate his interest. Alice had never been keen to talk about Scott's work with him, and when she had, it was always to sneer that he could have made more money doing anything else. How many times had he explained that becoming a curator was not something a person did for money?

When he'd first unpacked his work boxes in this office, he'd found a photo of Alice and him from their first trip to see the northern lights in Norway years ago. They looked happy in the picture, but he didn't feel the same pangs in his chest when he looked at her face anymore.

There was still anger, and there would be for some time, but it had dulled around the edges. Any love Scott had felt for Alice faded in his years abroad and hadn't returned with his arrival home. It certainly helped that she'd gone off to live with what's-his-face in the United States. At least he didn't have to worry about bumping into her at any of their old haunts.

Without a second thought, he'd crumpled the photo and thrown it in the bin. Good riddance.

$\mathcal{S}$cott checked the time, realizing he'd been daydreaming for longer than he'd thought and it was time to go and meet Eric. Into his rucksack he threw his laptop, a few snack bars—Eric tended to get cranky if he hadn't eaten enough—and a book on the mythology and traditions of pre-Islamic North Africa; just some light reading for the train journey.

He locked his office door with a large iron key that looked like it belonged in a medieval monastery.

His phone beeped with a text from Eric saying: **See you at the boathouse, prepare to get your ass kicked.**

We're rowing in a double today, you moron, Scott replied.

He hurried through the atrium, noticing in his peripheral vision that a couple of women were not so slyly trying to take a picture of him. It was possible they recognized him from the September page of the "Curators Against Cancer" naked calendar he'd done last year, though thankfully that had sold out pretty quickly and now he didn't need to flush with embarrassment every time he passed the gift shop.

It made him a little uncomfortable, but he tried not to let it bother him. Scott had always been averse to attention, ever since he was a kid. Of course, it had come from a different place back then. There had been a lot of "Where are you from originally?" questions when he was at school, from teachers and other kids. It was that *originally* that annoyed him. Partly because of the thinly veiled othering, but also because he didn't even know.

Scott had been adopted when he was ten years old. Before that, it was all short-term foster homes and the group home that he'd stayed at in between. His memories from the time before he moved in with his amazing mums was a bit of a blur. No, that was a lie. He remembered it all; sometimes it was just easier to forget.

Once, Scott had considered doing one of those spit-and-send heritage tests, but then Eric, who worked for a big-money tech firm, had shaken his head and suggested that Scott's information might be used for things he wouldn't necessarily approve of, so he'd dropped the matter.

Scott waved at the ticket sellers as he made his way around the east side of the Great Court, the glass roof letting in the last of the afternoon sunlight, bathing the atrium in a buttery glow.

"Ah, Dr. Mason, just the man I was hoping to bump into." It was Dr. MacDougall, the museum's head curator. A short, stout Black woman with a crop of salt-and-pepper hair, she always seemed to be dressed in an effortlessly chic suit with a chunky necklace.

"Dr. MacDougall," Scott said, smiling.

"You look like you're hurrying off somewhere."

"Ah yes, sorry. On the way to the boathouse."

"Well, I won't keep you, but I do have good news. Your proposal for a global tour of the Symbols of Protection exhibition? The board loved it."

Blood thrummed in Scott's ears. He wanted to jump up and down but he also wanted to go and hide in a cupboard. This was a huge deal—career-changing.

"Really? You're serious?"

"As the plague." She laughed and patted his arm. "But we can celebrate in a few weeks, at the internal launch."

"Agreed. I'll buy you a martini."

"It's an open bar, Scott, but I'll hold you to that. And I know it's a quick turnaround, but as you said in your pitch, the majority of the artifacts for this one have just been sitting untouched in our archives. It's time they saw the light." She gave Scott a toothy smile and patted him on the arm before saying goodbye.

He couldn't believe it. They wanted his exhibition to go on a global tour. When Dr. MacDougall had first hired Scott as a curator nearly a year ago, he'd just been thrilled to be here. But then he'd been sent the full list of the artifacts in the archives.

It was when he'd spotted the medieval Norwegian troll cross pendant, and a few minutes later found a cornicello dating back to the 1500s made from pure amber, that he'd known he had something remarkable on his hands. All these objects, most of them stolen by the British Museum in the past few centuries, had been stored in near-perfect condition in the archives, ignored because of their perceived lack of value. They weren't expensive or all that rare; they were amulets and dried herbs glazed in resin and small statues to gods and goddesses that people would have carved themselves and kept in their homes. But to Scott, these small lucky trinkets were his lifeline.

Scott had always wanted to believe in magic. In a universe where if you wished hard enough, and if you did all the rituals in the right order at the right time, things would go the way you hoped. He'd found a book on ancient world mythology in the school library when he was still living in the group home. He could still picture each page, even now.

It'd had a whole chapter on lucky charms from around the world. He'd read that if you kept an acorn in your pocket—as long as it was one you'd found on the ground and hadn't plucked directly from a tree—it would offer you good luck. Scott had kept an acorn in his pocket for weeks, rubbing it with his fingers until it shone. And when he'd found out he was being fostered with the Marini family, he'd thought it was proof that his luck really had turned. And it was all because of the acorn.

But the Marini family hadn't wanted to keep him, and so

back to the group home Scott went. He'd tried again, with the ankh symbol, with juniper berries, with a wishbone, a clover, a horseshoe, a jade pendant, and a copper penny. None of them had worked. No one had wanted him. It wasn't until years later, when Scott had entirely given up on lucky charms, that he was adopted by his mums. On the car ride home with them, after they'd stopped for an ice cream at the park, Scott had noticed a small ladybird sitting on his finger, and he had wondered for a moment if perhaps lucky charms worked after all.

All these years later, Scott had found hundreds of these charms, amulets, and talismans hidden away in the archives, and he wanted to share them with the world. The Symbols of Protection exhibition was going to begin its tour at the British Museum, and then, hopefully, it would tour the world. And the brilliant part was, as it continued on its tour, the charms and amulets would be dropped off, and exchanged for others, as they were returned to their home countries to be kept and displayed by their own museums and cultures. It was a new era for the British Museum, one that was trying—at least in some small way—to apologize for its past. And Scott would be a part of this; his exhibition would be a part of it. He couldn't wait to tell Eric.

Scott fell in behind a large tour group and it took longer than expected to extricate himself. He was going to be late and Eric was going to try to shove him in the river as punishment.

With a fair amount of speed, weaving between slow-walking tourists—Scott could not abide them when they strolled off the escalator at a snail's pace—he made it to Waterloo, catching the fast train to Barnes Bridge. He could already see Eric carrying a pair of oars across the bankside as he walked over the footbridge to the boathouse.

Eric looked up and saw him, taking the time to rest the oars against a wall before giving him the finger. Scott looked down at his watch. Twenty-five minutes late. Not unforgivable.

"I'll buy you a beer after" was the first thing he said to Eric. Apparently everyone was getting drinks today.

"You owe me at least two beers and some chips. I had to get the trestles out of the back cupboard, the very spider-infested cupboard, and you know how much I hate it in there."

"Two beers, chips, and I'll be the trestle chaperone for the rest of the month."

Eric pretended to consider the deal.

"Done. Go get changed. We have some last-minute wedding prep to get done tonight, so I can't stay too long."

"Anything I can help with?" As the best man at Eric's upcoming wedding, Scott wanted to be as helpful as possible. That was much easier now that he was actually living in the same country and city as Eric, instead of gallivanting across the world for other museums.

Scott and Eric had first met when they were staying at the same hotel in Iceland, both on their gap years. Someone had rung all the rooms at two in the morning to let them know that the northern lights could be seen, but only Scott and Eric had heeded the call. In their haste to see the lights, neither of them had bothered to put on all their layers.

They'd stood outside in the freezing cold, both stunned into silence by the ethereal beauty of it all—completely at peace. After that, they'd stayed in the hotel bar drinking hot cider to warm up, and before Scott knew it they'd been best friends for over a decade.

Over the past couple of years, since the breakup with Alice, their friendship had struggled, and Scott knew he was to blame. When a job offer to work on a collection of artifacts from Petra in Jordan had come up, Scott had taken the chance to flee. He'd left his entire life in London, left Eric, left his mums. It was as if all he'd cared about was getting as far away from his feelings as possible.

But now he was back, his heart somewhat healed, and Eric was about to get married. He hadn't even met Immy until he'd moved back to London less than a year ago, though he knew from their first meeting that she was perfect for Eric.

His friend waved a hand, interrupting his thoughts. "You okay?"

"I'll tell you about it in the boat."

The boathouse was theirs to enjoy on Wednesday evenings. The other regulars tended to live locally, and would take their boats out at lunchtime, and the schools that used it for practice were normally done by four o'clock.

Scott and Eric hauled their double over their heads and carried it down to the river bank. The water that splashed them as they lowered the boat was ice-cold—Scott thanked god that he had remembered to wear an extra-thick pair of woolly socks in his Wellington boots.

They sank into their routine of setting off with quiet ease: feeding their sculling oars through the oarlocks, Scott holding the boat steady while Eric clambered into the bow seat, Eric doing the same for Scott in the stern position.

Scott reluctantly tugged off his wellies and folded them into the little hold area of the boat, strapping his feet into the boat shoes, not relishing the bite of cold he could feel even through his socks.

The low-hanging late-afternoon sun bathed their backs in warmth as they pushed off from the riverbank and made their way under the shadow of Barnes Bridge. A train rattled overhead and droplets of dank bridge water rained down on them.

Scott had rowed this route hundreds of times, and yet every time it was a different experience. The slightest change in weather could be felt on the water, the city around him constantly shifting. He loved the way his muscles fell into the rhythm of each stroke, and how his breathing synced with Eric's as they feathered each oar into the water, heaving against the current. There was no space for his brain to worry; there was barely enough time to let his mind wander back to the barista from this morning, and her beautiful brown eyes.

The river exhaled around them, and soon they were past the other boathouses, past all the buildings and fancy Victorian mansions that lined the riverside. Soon, it was just trees painted in autumn shades of orange and deep pink, and the sunset reflecting on the water.

"You're being weirdly quiet," Eric said after a while.

"Sorry, I'm just distracted."

"Work stuff?"

"I guess. I had some good news today—my exhibition might have that global tour I was telling you about. There's still a ton to do to get it ready in time for a winter launch here but nothing I can't handle."

"So that's not what's distracting you then?"

"Honestly?" Scott admitted. "I met someone this morning."

Eric let out a whistle. "I thought you'd sworn off dating?"

"That was the plan. But then I went into this café near the museum earlier, and there was this barista and, well, I can't get her out of my head," Scott said as they paused for a rest, letting their momentum carry them along.

"Did you get her number?"

"No, but I think I came on too strong anyway."

"I find that hard to believe," Eric retorted. "What did you do, ask for her hand in marriage within five minutes of meeting her?"

"Nothing that bad. I just started talking about how cool nazar amulets are, and I got a little overexcited. She did seem interested too, she was even wearing one—but then I walked out before even getting her name."

Eric laughed. "If she was into it, then you probably weren't coming off too 'crazy professor.' This is exciting! You just need to go back there and try again. Maybe make a joke, then ask for a cup of the weirdest, most flower-infested tea they sell. I'm telling you, women love tea with flowers in it, don't ask me why. That'll be sure to win her over."

"I'll try it next week and let you know how it goes." They had a long weekend ahead of them, with Eric and Immy's wedding happening on Sunday.

As they turned the boat around, Eric reached out and squeezed Scott's shoulder.

"I'm glad you're finally ready to meet new people. You really had me worried there for a minute, after . . . you know . . ."

"You can say her name," Scott said.

"Well, after Alice. It's good to see you getting your mojo back."

"I will pay you fifty pounds to never utter the word 'mojo' again."

"Done and done. Shall we do some sprints to warm back up?"

Scott groaned. Eric loved to torture him with sprints.

Scott made it home an hour or so later, calling his mums to let them know he would be with them before seven tomorrow evening, in preparation for the wedding weekend. It had been too long since he'd been home, and he could hear their dog, Juniper, barking excitedly on the other end of the line every time they said Scott's name.

He hung his keys on a hook at the door, kicking off his trainers that smelled of river water.

Scott's footsteps echoed through the mezzanine apartment; the floors were too polished and bare. The whole flat still felt new and foreign. It had come already furnished when he'd rented it, but the furniture was dull and generic and made him feel like he was staying at a hotel.

Wasn't that the whole reason he'd come back to London—to get away from that "hotel" feeling? He'd been so scattered after the breakup. The pain from being cheated on had overwhelmed him, and all he'd been able to think was *Get out.* He'd made a home with Alice, or at least he'd thought he had, and then all of a sudden he'd been unmoored again. Scott had worked in museums all over the world, studied with the most incredible professors and curators, but every night he would go back to whatever hotel or short-term rental he was in and just wait for the night to pass so he could get back to work. For years he'd thrown himself into his travel and studies, but after a while the homesickness was too much to bear. He needed his friends, his family. He wanted . . . he wanted to love someone again.

This apartment would do for now, but after the wedding he'd start looking for something with some more character. Maybe somewhere a little nearer to his mums, so that he could visit them more often now he was back in the UK. He had missed them both.

At the very least, he needed to buy some rugs—anything would be better than these shiny gray tiles. Maybe some paintings for the walls too, and a pet. A dog would be good—he'd always been more of a dog person, and perhaps he could persuade the museum to let him bring it to work.

Scott had filled the empty shelves with all of his books, which brightened the living room; each of them was a little bit of himself. Scott had even added two of his childhood books on ancient Rome and ancient Egypt to the shelves. They were two of the first books his mums had given him once he'd moved in— two of the first books that he'd owned and hadn't needed to return to a library—and he'd devoured them. They were probably partly responsible for his whole career choice, now that he thought about it.

Scott briefly went out to check the balcony, and saw that all the stale bread he'd left out for the pair of robins he'd seen two days ago had been eaten. He put a few more crumbs into a bowl for them and resolved to buy a bird feeder.

After inhaling a quick dinner and standing in the shower for as long as it took to ease his sore muscles, he slumped into bed. His dreams were filled with the barista's face, and the scent of Earl Grey tea.

Chapter 3

T he evil eye pendant falling to the floor had only been the start of it. As morning turned into afternoon, Dina had found herself surrounded by bad omens on all sides.

A customer had opened their umbrella while still inside the shop, then Dina had accidentally knocked over the salt as she was clearing a table. With the pendant, that made three omens in one day. The last time Dina had had this many bad omens in a day she'd failed her driving test. Though that was possibly more to do with the fact that big machines and magical beings don't tend to pair well together.

The face of the man from this morning kept popping into her head, almost unbidden. The way his smile had been a little lopsided, the way his eyes had burned into hers when he'd asked about the evil eye amulet. Clearly, she'd been reading some kind of flirtation into the encounter, when he was probably just one of those nerdy hot-professor types who made women swoon wherever they went. She wasn't swooning though, was she?

Shaking her head, Dina realized she needed to get this man out of her mind and do something about all the weird magical energy in the café this afternoon. She texted her mother, Nour. She replied almost immediately, as if she had anticipated Dina's message, which she probably had since she was a divination witch. Cleansing spells were an important part of her mother's divination, so Dina always asked her for tips when it came to this kind of thing. In fact, Dina asked her mother for witchy tips about everything . . . well, almost everything.

Nour instructed Dina to burn some sage. Not wanting to set off the fire alarm, she decided to add a little of the sage oil she'd made last autumn to the cleaning spray she used, making the entire shop smell like a fragrant herb garden.

Dina made use of the peaceful afternoon crowd of readers quietly sipping her hallowed hot chocolates (the marshmallows were in the shape of small ghost pumpkins) as they escaped into a good book, to head outside into the crisp air and add a few new items to her chalkboard menu on the pavement.

Pulling out a stick of lilac chalk, Dina added "besotted briouats" to the list, followed by "rosy-cheeked ghriba." The briouats—melt-in-your-mouth filo pastry filled with honey and almonds—were heavenly, even without the spell that made you feel like you'd been kissed on the forehead by a loved one. The ghriba, decadently soft sugar cookies with rosewater essence and lemon zest, were laced with a spell to warm up the fingers and toes.

About an hour before closing, Immy and Rosemary—Dina's closest friends and the nearest things she had to sisters—swished into the shop, each carrying several bags of books from the bookshop around the corner.

Immy had recently had her blonde hair cut into a short bob in purposeful defiance of her soon-to-be mother-in-law, who had suggested that a bride always looked best with long hair. Rosemary, on the other hand, was a walking Pre-Raphaelite painting, with bright ginger hair that was plaited down her back, and a billowing green dress. If it weren't for the vintage cat-eye glasses perched on the end of her nose, you wouldn't know she was from this century.

Although their appearances were wildly different, both Immy

and Rosemary were horror authors. Immy wrote sci-fi horror filled with tentacled aliens and strange sentient spaceships, while Rosemary was more of a gothic-haunted-house kind of girl.

If Dina was honest with herself, she'd always been a little too scared to read Rosemary's books. At least with Immy's writing there was an element of detachment, as she was never going to be the only astronaut left fighting an alien species, but Rosemary's horror was the kind that would have her casting protection wards around herself as she went to bed.

Dina, Immy, and Rosemary had known each other since their early twenties. Rosemary had been completing half a year in England as part of her literature degree from Princeton, Immy was on the same course, and Dina had been at bakery school.

They'd met for the first time at an *Addams Family* movie night at the Prince Charles Cinema—costumes mandatory—when the three of them had all decided to go as Cousin Itt, complete with top hat and sunglasses. The costume choice had made it difficult to watch the movie, so they'd slunk out and ended up walking across central London before getting wine-drunk in Ye Olde Cheshire Cheese pub. Dina remembered immediately feeling like she'd met her people. They'd been inseparable from then on. Even though Rosemary had had to go back to the United States, the three of them spoke constantly and visited whenever they could.

Immy and Rosemary were the first people Dina had ever revealed her magic to. One night, the three of them had been sitting on the floor of Dina's kitchen, eating a lemon meringue tart she had made, when her witch's intuition signaled that now might be a good time. After telling them her secret, she had levitated mugs of hot chocolate to them, just in case they thought she'd gone insane.

The night had been full of revelations, as shortly after Dina revealed she was a witch, Rosemary explained that she could, on occasion, see ghosts. Immy couldn't believe she was the only non-magical person out of the three of them.

When Eric had proposed to Immy, she'd asked Dina's permission to reveal her witchcraft to him. She hadn't been sure at first; it was a big part of herself she'd be entrusting to another person. But after looking at Eric's cards, and reading his tea leaves on the sly, she knew he could be trusted. Also, she enjoyed his company; he had a witty sense of humor and clearly worshipped the ground Immy walked on.

Dina had made a show of the reveal by making them a "happy engagement" cake that let off small fireworks in their living room when they cut the first slice.

Now, Immy pulled Dina into a hug over the counter, enveloping Dina in her clean linen scent.

"Missed you," Immy mumbled into her hair.

"Missed you too, even though I saw you yesterday."

Immy grinned. "I was talking to those pains au chocolat, but yeah, you too."

Dina turned to Rosemary, who had popped around the counter, and they beamed at each other, falling into a hug. For such a short woman, Rosemary packed a seriously powerful hug.

"I wish I could live in this shop," she groaned as she squeezed Dina. "Even the air tastes like cake."

Dina smiled. "I hope you're both hungry, since we're about to eat ungodly amounts of pastry."

"I've been fasting since this morning," Immy said gravely. Beside her, Rosemary rolled her eyes and mouthed the words *We had pizza an hour ago* at Dina.

Immy and Rosemary headed back to the kitchen while Dina tidied the counter. She was glad for the distraction of these two loud, glorious women. They were probably the only people capable of getting the interaction with that guy from this morning out of her head.

"Would you mind serving the last few customers so I can get started on the baking?" Dina asked Robin.

"Sure, if you promise to save me some pastry cream," they said, winking.

The lunchtime rush had passed, and now there were only a few regulars hanging around in the hour before closing. There was an elderly couple doing the crossword puzzle together, though they would occasionally ask the pair of students studying beside them for help if they couldn't figure out one of the clues. A few customers were seated by the windows, sipping their drinks and looking outside at the blustery autumn weather. At least it was cozy in here.

There was also a couple that Dina remembered seeing before, although last time they'd been strangers sitting at different tables. If Dina remembered correctly, they'd both had the same order: a mocha with extra chocolate on top and a sugar-sprinkle doughnut on the side. It warmed her heart to see that all it had taken was the same order in her café to bring these two people together.

Usually, Dina would spend the quiet afternoons working on her recipes for the month ahead. She liked to tie in her baking with the seasons, and sometimes she needed to practice the more complicated recipes. She might be a kitchen witch, but even Dina knew that practice makes perfect, especially when dealing with pastry.

For spring and summer, Dina baked delicate and light pastries fragranced with rosewater, meskouta orange bundt cake, and delicate raspberry macarons. When strawberries were in season in early June, she made airy fraisier cake. For autumn and winter, Dina worked with heavier ingredients: thick, dark chocolate, cinnamon, cardamom, gingerbread, and pumpkin. As the days grew colder and the light dimmed earlier and earlier, people started to crave that feeling of warmth and comfort. And

Dina would give that to them, even if only for a short while. One special bake for this season was a ginger and persimmon cake, yellowed with saffron strands, which Dina had bought on her last trip to Morocco, and fresh vanilla pods, their sweet scent so potent that it wafted across the café.

This was in addition to all the regular pastries and cakes she had on offer, which were all recipes her mother had taught her to bake. The cake made with dark honey from the Atlas mountains was an all-time customer favorite. Dina had imbibed it with a very specific spell, one that kept customers coming back for more. She'd crafted it from a childhood memory of a time that she must have fallen asleep on a car ride home, and although she was a little too big to be carried, she remembered her father lifting her into his arms, her mother closing the car door softly so as not to wake her, then carrying her upstairs and tucking her into bed.

When she'd been fashioning the spell for the first time, it had occurred to Dina that one day your parents put you down and they never picked you up again, and so she'd made the honey cake to recreate that feeling of childhood comfort. That sensation of someone taking the utmost care of you, holding you close, was a feeling that many in the rushing city of London didn't experience often.

Sometimes she wondered if she was really in the business of café ownership, or if she was more of a fairy godmother in disguise. Undeniably, the magical pastries were great at keeping customers coming back for more, so that was a bonus on the businesswoman side of things.

Today she wouldn't be prepping her winter recipes, however. Today was all about Immy's wedding pastries. Instead of opting for a cake, like a normal, sane individual, Immy had decided— Eric had had no say in the matter—that she wanted either apple pie or cinnamon buns. She just wasn't sure which one.

And so, being the best maid of honor in the world, Dina had promised she would bake both for Immy to choose between. Dina's friends had practically begged to help her make the two recipes. The wedding was this weekend; Dina was planning to take whatever ingredients she needed to the old manor house where Immy and Eric were tying the knot.

Dina made her way back to the kitchen, where Immy and Rosemary were helping themselves to hot chocolates with whipped cream. Immy was telling Rosemary all about her planned honeymoon to Australia, and all the massive spiders and snakes she was hoping to see. It lifted Dina's heart to see the two of them making themselves at home in her kitchen.

The kitchen in the back room of Serendipity Café wasn't exactly roomy, but between the shelves of colorful jars and tins and the old industrial baking ovens, it had a cozy warmth that Dina loved. It was one of her favorite places in the world.

"All right," Dina said, lifting mixing bowls onto the marble counter, "you're both going to want to put some aprons on." She nodded her head toward the rack of pastel-pink and green aprons hanging on the wall, and snapped her fingers, two aprons flying across the room to land in Rosemary and Immy's hands.

"Finally, I get to witness Dina's magical baking process." Rosemary smiled, rolling up her sleeves and displaying her heavily tattooed forearms.

"I hope it lives up to expectations." Dina grinned back. She looked over at Immy. "Are you sure you don't just want a simple frosted vanilla wedding cake, Immy?"

"Not happening. Remember"—Immy narrowed her eyes—"that you made a blood oath to do whatever I want when I made you my maid of honor."

"All right, bridezilla," Rosemary said.

They pulled on their aprons and Dina went into her pantry to hunt for all the ingredients they would need.

"So, what's your process then?" Rosemary asked, standing ready with Immy at the kitchen counter.

"First, we get out all the ingredients," Dina called. She rummaged around for enough mixing bowls, as well as fresh unsalted butter, flour, cinnamon, yeast, vanilla pods, and sugar. She'd peeled, cored, and sliced the Bramley apples earlier, so for the apple pie it was simply a matter of cooking the butter, brown sugar, and apples on the hob while they prepped the shortcrust pastry. "And now . . . I get to boss you around my kitchen for the next two hours."

They gossiped as they worked, Dina stepping in to add a pinch of cinnamon and star anise to the sweet apple mixture that Rosemary was in charge of stirring.

"Who's going to help you do this on the weekend?" Rosemary asked, noticing that Dina had her hands so full that she had charmed a clementine to peel itself in mid-air.

"Oh, she'll have help," Immy muttered, an oddly maniacal gleam in her eye.

"What the hell does that mean?" Dina said. "Did you hire extra staff? Honestly, Imms, I don't need the help, and it'll be easier if it's just me because then I won't need to hide my magic."

The bride-to-be only grinned mischievously.

"It's not staff, don't worry about it."

Dina was worried about it, but she could tell that whatever plan Immy had up her sleeve, she wasn't about to reveal it. Dina flashed Rosemary a *Do you know anything about this?* kind of look, to which her friend shook her head.

The apple pie was ready first, since the dough for the cinnamon buns needed proving and Dina's proving oven was out of whack. Electrical appliances and magic often did not see eye-to-eye. They stood around the pie, the crust perfectly golden, and each grabbed a fork.

"Fucking hell," Rosemary said, taking a bite. "This is better than my dad's. Don't tell him I said that."

"It is insanely good . . ." Immy began.

"But? I sense a 'but.'" Dina waited.

"But I think it's not quite right for the wedding. And Eric and I had cinnamon buns on our second date."

"That's decided then—cinnamon buns it is!" Dina clapped her hands, flour going everywhere.

Dina wished she could spend every day baking with friends; it was a joy unlike any other. She hummed under her breath as she rolled out and began kneading the proved dough for the cinnamon buns. Usually, this was when Dina would lace a spell into the bake. For something like a cinnamon bun or a muffin, she might put in that feeling you get of wrapping yourself in a soft, woolly blanket. Baking magic worked best when it was peppered throughout the process.

Today was different.

"Immy, tell me about the first time you knew you loved Eric." Dina had heard this story many times, but she needed Immy to tell her now, so she could let the story flow through—turning it into a spell, into a feeling that could be baked into the buns.

"It was our third date, we were meeting near the entrance to Hampstead Heath to go for a walk, and it was fucking freezing that day. I remember waiting for a while, because I got there disgustingly early, and when he turned up he saw me shivering and he blew on my hands until they warmed up and bought me a tea. And on our next date he brought me gloves so my hands wouldn't get cold. And then I knew I was head over heels for him."

"Ugh, that makes me feel so single. When will men learn that women don't want grand gestures, they want someone who cares about them keeping their hands warm," Rosemary groaned.

As Immy spoke, Dina had taken that memory—Immy's feeling of Eric caring about her, the sensation of cold hands warming up—and turned it into a spell, kneading it into the dough. As they continued to prepare the cinnamon buns, Dina prodded Immy to tell them other things she loved about Eric, to recount other treasured memories, and she put them into the dough too. Anyone eating these cinnamon buns would be filled with a deep sensation of love all around them. It wasn't a love spell, because those simply didn't exist—magic could create a false sense of love, but never the real deal. Dina had learned that the hard way. No, this spell would just make people look at Immy and Eric and think, *Wow, they really love each other.*

Beside her, Immy and Rosemary worked together to make the cinnamon-sugar paste for the buns.

"Does it need more cinnamon?" Immy said, frowning over the mixing bowl.

Dina ran a finger through the mixture and popped it in her mouth. The whipped buttery sugary goodness met with the soft earthiness of the cinnamon.

"No, it's perfect."

Once everything was in the oven, they sat around drinking more hot chocolates, and chatting about Rosemary's horror novel that was soon going to be made into a movie. The air in the kitchen was soon filled with the delicious scent of baking buns, spiced with cinnamon and clove.

Dina had made an extra batch. None of them waited for the buns to cool down before they tucked in.

Immy's eyes began to water as she took a bite.

"Dina, these . . . Your magic . . . How did you . . . It's like you put me and Eric in them. I don't understand."

Dina went over and gave Immy a flour-covered hug.

"I'm glad you like them, love."

"Mmmfckinggood," Rosemary mumbled from the other side of the counter, mouth full of cinnamon bun.

Dina had bites of a bun too, but she mostly liked to watch as the magic took hold of her friends as they ate, the frown lines disappearing from their foreheads, the way they sighed contentedly.

"You're a damn good kitchen witch, Dina. Can you start posting these to me weekly, please?" Rosemary begged.

They continued snacking until none of them could manage another bite. Dina gave them both bags full of pastries and cakes to take home, knowing that Eric would be grumpy if Immy came back from the café without a selection of baked goods.

Dina pulled each of them into a tight hug at the front door of the café.

"Thanks so much for being my baking guinea pigs," she said with a smile. At least she wouldn't have to wait long to see them—Immy's wedding was only a few days away.

"Will you do me a favor?" Immy said, leaning in close.

"Anything."

"Would you check the, um, tea leaves or the cards or whatever you normally check, to see if the wedding will go all right?"

Dina got it. It was a lot of stress hosting a wedding, and all Immy was asking for was a little peace of mind. Dina was overdue a reading anyway.

"Of course." She smiled. "I'll text you what they say."

"Okay, but if it says there's going to be some kind of Red Wedding situation then I just don't want to know."

"Duly noted."

*C*losing the shop on her own was a nightly ritual. Not that she didn't trust Robin to do it, but it was much easier—and more efficient for both of them—if she had the quiet to focus her mind on several cleaning spells at once.

Robin would be in charge of the café for the next few days while Dina was in Little Hathering, the village north of London near where Immy's wedding would be taking place. It helped that it was the same village where Dina's parents lived.

Dina pulled her jacket tight as she locked the shop door behind her, taking a deep inhale of the crisp evening air. She whispered a protective warding spell as she turned the key in the lock. Sometimes Dina cast in English, other times she fell into Darija or French, whichever felt right in the moment. And this wasn't a malignant spell—Dina didn't do those. It was simply a spell that would incline any potential burglars away from the café, making it look entirely uninteresting and definitely not the sort of place where cash was stored overnight.

The sun had mostly set, and the leaves swirled around in the autumn breeze as Dina made her way to the station. The trip home was thankfully uneventful, although Dina did use an itching spell to make a man vacate the priority seat that a heavily pregnant woman was too polite to ask for. Dina got off the tube at Putney Bridge and walked down the riverbank to absorb the last of the sunlight.

There were a few rowing boats out on the river, their oars pooling the water around them in small circles. Dina never felt the magic of the city more than she did when she was beside the river. It was as if all of London existed in the swell of every small wave.

Or perhaps it was the river itself. The way it twisted and turned through the city, always flowing. It had been there since before London was anything more than a few mud huts cobbled together on marshland, and Dina had no doubt that it would be there when London was no more. Just the kind of melodramatic thoughts she tended to have when she was tired and wandering home. It was all the water—it brought out her pensive, melancholic tendencies.

As always, Heebie Jeebie was waiting for Dina, yowling something awful the moment she stepped through the door.

"I missed you, you tiny menace," Dina said, cradling the rotund cat in her arms like a baby, a position Heebie would sullenly endure for the unspoken promise of treats later.

Dina had meant to get a black cat when she'd gone to the cat shelter a few years ago; she loved the way they looked like little pockets of midnight. But then she'd heard a grumpy yowling coming from a small cage near her feet.

"That one's just come in, the vet reckons it's a feral one. No microchip," the man who worked there had said. Dina had crouched down and locked eyes with the cat, who was mostly black but with a golden crescent shape on top of her head and a creamy white belly. Heebie, who hadn't even had a name then, had bumped Dina's outstretched knuckle with her head, and Dina had felt the warmth of the cat's cheek and known instantly that she had found her familiar.

If she had been feral once, Heebie Jeebie was the opposite now, eating small pieces of cheese from Dina's hands as they sat on the kitchen floor. Dina ruffled a spell up between her fingers, and all the lamps switched on in her flat, their warm pink glow helping her settle in for the evening.

But she couldn't settle down just yet. She'd promised Immy a reading. Dina thought she may as well do two—one for Immy and Eric's wedding and one for herself. Even after the magic-pastry tasting, the omens from earlier in the day still nagged at her, like a belt strapped too tight.

There was only one thing for it: divination. This might be her mother's kind of magic, but Dina had her own special way of doing it. She flicked on the kettle, watching the steam curl. Then she slipped into her pajamas and brewed herself two cups of lemon verbena tea, sweet and comforting. Her favorite herbal tea of all time. In Darija it was called louiza, and her mother swore by it for healing anxious minds. Tonight, it would have another purpose.

Dina needed to read the leaves; she needed to understand the meaning of the omens she'd witnessed today. She settled on her green velvet sofa, Heebie busy grooming herself on a cushion beside her.

Dina turned off most of the lamps with another flick of her fingers and lit a white pillar candle on the table in front of her. Witchcraft was always done best by candlelight.

For Immy's reading, Dina took a couple of sips from the tea, keeping her mind on her best friend and her fiancé, envisioning the wedding ahead. When she looked at the leaves, everything seemed as she'd expected. Two strong lines of tea coming together, with a smaller circle at the bottom. The wedding would go well; Immy and Eric's connection was strong. She texted Immy to that effect.

Now, Dina settled in to do her own reading, taking a few deep breaths in an attempt to clear her mind.

As Dina drank the tea, she focused on the day just past. The fallen amulet, the salt, the umbrella all replayed in her mind, but her thoughts kept twisting back to the man she'd served. His forearm as he'd leaned on the counter, the slight break on the bridge of his nose that had never properly healed. The deep golden brown of his eyes. A flicker of heat shot through her at the memory of his rough hands against hers. He had lit a fire in her that she didn't want to interrogate.

She sipped the last of the tea and placed the cup down on the table. Tasseomancy, the art of reading tea leaves, was one of Dina's strongest magics—she quite often had to stop herself from reading customers' fortunes as they left the shop.

Every witch had different magical strengths. Dina's had always been baking and brewing—anything that involved mixing spices and herbs in a kitchen. If her magic was a scent, it would be freshly baked brownies.

Her mother was more of a seer; she read tea leaves, fortunes, sometimes she could even read the stars in the night sky. She had an uncanny way of predicting what the lottery numbers would be, though she had never once seen fit to cash in.

Dina scooted forward until she was looking down at the tea leaves from directly above. That was an important part of the reading. You had to read from an aerial viewpoint, because the center of the cup represented the "now," with the edges curving around it representing the "near future" and the "far future." If your view of the leaves was skewed from an angle, the entire reading could go awry.

Once, Dina had read the shape of a wand in Rosemary's tea leaves before a date she'd arranged. The wand signified an exciting new beginning, and Rosemary had gone on the date sure that it would end well. She'd come back an hour later, a mess of snot, tears, and smudged mascara, saying that her date had seen her in the café and done a one-eighty. Dina hadn't seen a wand, but a dagger. After that she'd been sorely tempted to take a dagger to the idiot who had stood up Rosemary, but after a night of ice cream and watching old Hollywood musicals she'd let her murderous intent go.

Now, Dina craned her neck to read the leaves sogging at the bottom of her cup.

Three leaves in the center, with the root of their shared stem branching out to the left in a wing-like shape. Two other leaves curved together in what could be the bottom half of a heart, or a V-shape. And then at the top, a single leaf curled in on itself in a near-perfect spiral.

Dina didn't like what she saw. She knew instinctively what the leaves were telling her, but she didn't want to believe it. She made her way to one of the many bookshelves that adorned the walls of her small flat. Flipping through the pages of her worn tasseomancy dictionary, her heart beating a little too fast, Dina looked for other options, other signs that would point to a different future.

"Why do they always have to be so dramatic?" Dina muttered as she read the portent defined in her dictionary: *Romance is on the horizon; it will only end in disaster.* Honestly, it was as if these dictionaries were meant more for Roman emperors in danger of being stabbed in the back than for coffee shop owners.

Dina slammed the dictionary shut and reshelved it. Slumping back on the sofa, she pushed the cup further away from her so she wouldn't have to look at it anymore. Heebie, sensing her mood, crawled onto Dina's lap and peered up at her with a worried expression in her eyes.

"Romance is on the horizon . . ." Dina muttered aloud, stroking behind Heebie's ears. "Maybe I'll meet someone at the wedding?"

Even as she said it, her mind was wandering back to the man from the café. No, forget him. He was just a guy passing through who she'd probably never see again. Besides, she wasn't open to dating anyone seriously. And even if she was, she was *far* more likely to go for a woman than a man.

The second part of the reading was, unfortunately, very easy to understand.

Call it a sixth sense, clairvoyance, or even just that feeling you get deep in your bones—Dina already knew that the bad omens from today all pointed in one direction: the hex.

Insidiously weaving its way back into her life, leaving misery in its wake.

Chapter 4

The hex had been the worst mistake of Dina's life. She could trace its origins back to when she was only thirteen, and feeling the first flutterings of love. And something else that wasn't quite love but left her blushing and tingling in strange new places.

Her body had woken up for the first time that summer, her senses eager to explore. Her magic, too, had come into fruition. Oh, she'd been able to do spells before then. Small ones, like turning a light on and off, and levitating a feather or a pen in the air. But this magic was stronger, wilder.

It came with her first period and tossed her as if she were a single swimmer on the open sea, lost in its current. Her mother had helped her navigate it, teaching her the different forms of witchcraft, letting Dina learn which ones suited her most. She taught her how her magic would change each month along with her cycle, and how she would be at her most powerful a couple of days before her bleed. Something about the pain of premenstrual cramps added to the potency of a witch's magic.

Dina had been able to perform magic in a way that astounded her at first. She had summoned a spirit of luck the day before her yearly school exams, just because she could. She was a reckless teenager, and her crush on Luke Montgomery had only made things worse. Luke was the guy that every single girl fancied.

Dina hadn't been one of those girls, not at first. She'd played it cool, staring at the back of his head in maths class and admiring his tanned forearms in PE. But then he asked to borrow a fountain pen and she lost all her remaining chill, melting into a spluttering, bumbling mess.

That night, Dina did something she really shouldn't have. She waited until her parents were asleep, and snuck into the living room where her mother kept her spell books. She knew she couldn't cast a love spell—all the books on witchcraft she'd read made it quite clear that that was impossible. But what about a fate spell? A spell to draw herself and Luke together, until eventually he would *have* to fall in love with her. Teenage Dina was too naïve for her own good.

The spell had a lot of components. A red rose petal harvested during a full moon; a white candle, left outside all day to soak up the sunlight; a piece of paper with Luke's name on it; and finally a spoonful of honey, poured onto the candle, to bind him to her. It would take time to prepare, and thankfully the summer holidays were just around the corner.

Dina spent most of her holiday preparing for the spell in secret. When the first week of the new school year came around, she was ready. Except, when she saw Luke again, he'd grown some peach fuzz on his upper lip and wouldn't stop talking about his video-game kill ratio. Whatever ounce of infatuation she'd had for him over the summer had dissipated almost immediately.

Dina remembered hiding away the candle and the rose petal in her drawer, and not thinking of them again until she met Rory.

If Luke had been a teenage infatuation, Rory was the first real love of Dina's life, and had inspired the realization that Dina also desired women.

Dina had met Rory when they were both nineteen, fresh out of sixth form and straight into bakery school. Dina knew she wanted to open a café, and although she was already a talented baker, even without the assistance of her magic, she was sure there was so much more she had to learn. Rory wanted to be a pastry chef and had dreams of moving to Paris. She had a short black bob that curled a little at the ends, and eyes so green they looked like moss after the first spring rain. Dina suspected that there was a witch in Rory's family line, as now and again a spurt of magic would flash around her, before fizzing into nothing.

Dina remembered the tanned skin of Rory's forearms as she kneaded dough beside her in the student kitchen, the way desire had bubbled up within her. They'd started dating, and Dina had fallen head over heels for Rory within two weeks. She was young, she had no guards up, no expectations. She only knew that she loved Rory and wanted to be with her. She was a little foolish.

As can often happen in relationships between two women, things got serious fast. Dina would spend multiple nights a week at Rory's flat, baking and fucking until sunrise.

Rory was the first person outside of her family and close friends that Dina told about her magic. One evening they were alone in the library, reading about the colonial history of chocolate, when Dina used her magic to heat up their paper cups of cold tea. The more she showed Rory her magic, the more Dina mistook the expression on her girlfriend's face as delighted awe—when, in fact, it was shock.

When Dina scored highly on her tarte tatin recipe, Rory sneered that she'd only got that score because she'd cheated with magic. In the weeks that followed, Rory would blame Dina for every low score she received, every time something went wrong with a recipe.

She should have realized what was happening. Her witchy instinct had sent her flickers of warning that telling Rory about her magic wasn't a good idea, but she'd resolutely ignored them. She should have walked away then with a bruised heart, and not waited around for a broken one.

They agreed to take a break over the Christmas holidays, to see if they could salvage their relationship in the new year. Dina was hopeful—they still spoke every day. Dina had gone home to her parents, Rory to her family in Dorset.

She'd even revealed to her parents that she was dating someone named Rory.

"Oh, I knew it! You're glowing, just look at you," her mother had said, pinching Dina's cheeks. "It's good to have a man in your life, habiba. I like the sound of this one—Rory. A good name."

Dina was ready to blurt out that she was in fact dating a woman when her mother said, "Maybe one day I can be a grandmother." She said it with such hope in her eyes, and Dina was struck by the realization that if she came out to her parents now, she'd be crushing that hope. So she kept her silence. Her mother wasn't exactly traditional, she was a witch after all, but she had been raised in Morocco in the sixties, not a place with a booming queer community. A comment here and there from her mum had suggested to Dina that she was very happy for *other* people to be queer, just not her daughter.

As that holiday had worn on, the stream of text messages from Rory had slowed to a trickle, until one night Dina woke up to a text that said: I'm not sure I want to do this anymore.

Dina couldn't bear it. She needed Rory. A memory from years before resurfaced, and she dug through her childhood drawers to find it. The rose petal, now dried between the pages of a book, the candle charged by moonlight. The scrap of paper.

Sitting on her bedroom floor, Dina scribbled Rory's name on the paper, lit the candle, and performed the spell. Nothing happened immediately, though Dina felt the spell take effect. It was as if she was suddenly able to sense Rory at the periphery of her mind, an invisible string connecting them. The fate spell had worked. She saw a text on her phone from Rory: **I'm on my way, baby, I've missed you. It'll take me a couple of hours in the car.**

An hour later, Dina felt something strange down that string, and her heart jumped to her throat, as if she were suddenly inside a falling elevator.

A call came in a moment later, from Rory's phone.

"Is this Dina?" a man's voice on the other end said.

"Yes, is everything all right? Where's Rory?"

"Rory's okay, but she's had a bit of an accident on the motorway. We're taking her to hospital now."

"Oh god. Fuck. Can I talk to her?"

"I'm sorry, but she's unconscious at the moment." The paramedic gave Dina the details of the hospital they were taking Rory to, and she ran to her car immediately. She wouldn't remember much of the drive or arriving at the hospital—it was one big stressful blur. All she could think was that she could no longer feel the tether between herself and Rory—how much danger was Rory in?

It was the early hours of the morning when Dina was finally allowed to see Rory. She looked so small in that bed, the clinical lights making her skin even paler than usual. One side of her face was bruised, her lip scratched. The doctors explained that Rory had been speeding down the motorway and the car had slipped on ice. *She was speeding to reach me faster* was all Dina could think, guilt seeping through her. What had she done?

Dina sat by Rory's bedside and cast a small healing charm on her. It was the least she could do. When Rory awoke, she didn't smile at Dina. She just stared at her with bitter accusation in her eyes.

"You did something to me, didn't you?" she said. "With your magic."

Dina wanted to deny it.

"It was a small spell. To . . . to bring us back together."

"How fucking *dare* you. Jesus Christ, Dina. It was like I was a puppet, watching myself texting you and calling you "baby" again, and jumping in that car. I didn't want to do it. I kept try-ing to stop, but I wasn't in control of my body, *you* were."

"I'm so sorry," Dina sobbed. "It wasn't meant to be like that."

"Oh? And what was it meant to be like then? I could have died. All because you couldn't let go. We were over. Whatever this was"—Rory gestured between them—"it was finished months ago, you just couldn't see it. I was trying to let you down easy."

"I never wanted to hurt you. I just love you so much."

"Forcing people to do your bidding isn't love," Rory spat. Something had loosened inside her, Dina could feel it; a low vi-bration growing. Whatever magic had been dormant in Rory was now stirring. And it was angry.

"You know what, Dina? I hope one day this happens to you, so you can understand what you did to me. Everyone who loves you will be hurt, do you hear me? Everyone who loves you will be hurt, just like you hurt me."

Like an icy shroud, Dina felt the curse settle onto her shoul-ders in that moment. Rory hadn't intended it, but her raw, un-trained magic and anger had combined into an unshakeable force. A hex had knotted itself to Dina's soul, and it had re-mained there ever since.

When she finally arrived back home the next morning, her mother tried to ask her what had happened. Dina grumbled something about a breakup and told her parents to leave her alone. She desperately wanted to tell her mother. She wanted to say, *Fix it, Mama, fix my mistake.* But every time she came close, she remembered that there was no way she could tell her only part of the truth. Nour would need to know everything about the relationship, including the fact that Rory was most definitely not a man. Dina had just lost Rory; she couldn't lose her mum too.

All these years later, and the hex's oily shadow still clung to Dina. It showed no signs of weakening. Every single time she felt a relationship was going well, the hex would find a way to fuck it up, hurting the people around her.

Once, Dina had been dating a guy for a few months—a head chef at a London restaurant. On the same evening that he'd told her he wanted to introduce her to his parents, his oven glove had caught fire—one that Dina had bought him—inflicting burns across his hand.

Another time, Dina had been seeing a woman called Eliza. She was one of those amazing people who never ran out of energy, and even dragged Dina on hikes every weekend. They'd been walking up Box Hill when Eliza had shared that she might be falling for Dina. A second later, Eliza had tripped, hitting her head against a rock that was nestled in the grass. The dark irony of it hadn't been lost on Dina.

One perverse trick of the hex was that the more Dina liked someone, the more it tried to hurt them. She'd tried everything to fight it. Cleansing spells on herself, unbindings. It didn't matter what she did, all of her romantic relationships were doomed to fail.

She'd pretty much stopped dating, only allowing herself a

one-night stand here and there so that she didn't turn into a nun. She could never let herself fall in love again; it was too dangerous.

But here were the tea leaves, and the message was clear: *Romance is on the horizon.*

Well, maybe it was all right if it was just romance. Romance didn't *have* to mean love, did it? And how bad could it be, really, to never let herself get close enough to love someone again?

Dina asked herself that question a lot these days. Sometimes she looked in the mirror and saw that same young girl who had fallen in love with Rory looking back at her, with her frizzy hair and plumpness that threatened to spill out of whatever clothes she was wearing. Some days it took a lot of time to find ways to love herself again.

She fell asleep that night ruminating on the tea leaves' prediction, and spent the following day at home, preparing and packing for the weekend, throwing all kinds of outfits in her bag to change into as her mood suited her.

She fished around in her wardrobe for the bridesmaid's dress that Immy had bought her a few months ago. A dark forest-green brushed-velvet dress that molded to Dina's curves—what she lacked in the boob department she made up for in ass. Dina Whitlock never traveled light.

She had a train to catch. Dina gathered her bags, and tucked a soft blanket into Heebie's travel carrier, along with the toy pumpkin filled with catnip that was theoretically meant to keep the cat calm while traveling.

She put a spell on her plants to stay watered while she was away. Dina had a lot of plants, so the spell took some time to settle onto the leaves, coating them in a glistening dew that would remain there until she returned.

Dina threw a few spell candles and herb pouches into her bag, though her mum would no doubt have enough for both of them—it was more of a safety blanket to have them with her. Heebie had already curled up inside the cat carrier, kneading the pumpkin, and would soon be asleep. Brewing a quick hot chocolate in a travel flask, with an added spark of comfort magic to keep her going until she was home, Dina locked up her flat.

Chapter 5

King's Cross St. Pancras was gloriously quiet in the evenings after the rush-hour crowd had all passed through. Halloween decorations and early sparkling Christmas lights lit Dina's way through the station, and she delighted in listening to the music a teenager was playing on the free piano in the walkway. The way his fingers moved over the keys, the song echoing around them, was its own kind of magic.

Sitting down in a four-seater, Dina laid Heebie's carrier beside her and tried to settle. It was just under an hour to Little Hathering. Immy's wedding was taking place in a country house nearby.

Gradually, the train began to fill, and Dina let the sound of the other passengers wash over her. She was just about to crack open a horror novel—one of Immy's recommendations—when she heard a click. A very familiar click, followed by a scrabbling.

By the time she looked down it was too late. Heebie, by some unearthly power that only cats possess, had unlocked her carrier and zoomed off down the carriage.

"Fuck." Dina groaned and hauled her ass up to chase the cat. This was so unlike Heebie, who had never attempted to escape her carrier. She was surprised she even knew how . . . well, not that surprised. Heebie was a familiar after all.

"Excuse me, sorry, excuse me," Dina muttered as she wove around other travelers trying to find their seats. Every few seconds she caught sight of Heebie's black tail, swishing around the passengers' heels.

Then she couldn't see her anymore. Dina's heart thrummed anxiously in her chest. She could compel Heebie to her with magic, but if Heebie had run away she might not respond to it. And she didn't want to get caught doing magic in public either. There was also the small matter that Dina's magic never quite worked how she intended when it came to animals.

The last time she had tried magic on Heebie, the cat had ended up talking in a high-pitched baby voice, constantly demanding treats, tuna, or pets. Thank god that spell had only lasted a couple of nights.

Then Dina heard a familiar meow, and she pushed past a family of four to find Heebie contentedly licking her paws and resting in the arms of a tall dark-haired man who was studiously tickling her under the chin.

"Heebie, what are you—" she began to say, but her thoughts dissipated as the man looked up. It was the same man from the café, with his strong nose and lopsided smile. The man she had so easily fallen into conversation with; the man who had taken her breath away.

His eyes widened as he recognized her.

"Hello again," he said, his voice smooth as honey. "Is this cat yours?" Heebie's purr switch was turned up to maximum; she clearly liked this guy. And she generally wasn't a fan of men, so that was saying something.

"She is. I don't even know how she . . . Heebie, come here," Dina said, partly out of breath and partly shocked to silence. Of all the trains in London, he was here, and Heebie was in his arms. This wasn't exactly an ill omen, but she sure as hell didn't know what to make of it.

Dina reached out to take Heebie from him, but the cat hissed, digging her nails into his very nice jumper.

"Hmm. Clearly you've made quite the impression," Dina said.

He shrugged. "I'm more of a dog person really, but I like this one. She's very round."

"I hope you aren't calling my cat fat?" Dina flicked up an eyebrow.

"Wouldn't dream of it. Listen, shall I just bring her back to where you're sitting? I haven't booked a seat anyway."

Dina had to agree this made the most logical sense, but she couldn't shake the knowing glint in Heebie's eyes as the man carried her back to Dina's seat. As if this was all part of her master plan.

She also couldn't help but glance at the man's stature as he cradled Heebie in one hand, holding his bag with the other. His chest was so broad he took up the whole aisle, and he had to stoop a little as he lowered himself into a seat so as not to head-butt the overhead luggage rack.

Dina noticed all of this with complete detachedness, of course, and it definitely didn't give her butterflies.

Only once he was sitting down opposite Dina did Heebie deign to re-enter her cat carrier, falling asleep almost immediately.

"So, you're more of a dog person, huh?" Dina asked, narrowing her eyes at him. "That's highly suspicious. Everyone knows that cat people are the best people."

"If you say so." He smirked. It set Dina's pulse racing.

Now, sitting opposite him, she could get a better look at his features, and she was trying very, very hard to ignore the fact that he was fucking gorgeous. A heavy brow, those eyes that she couldn't bear to hold contact with for too long, a perfectly wonky nose, a lopsided smile, and a jawline that could cut glass peppered with a trimmed beard.

He had a few lines on his forehead that spoke of days spent in the sun without sunscreen, and he was perhaps in his early thirties? He wasn't wearing his glasses now, but Dina thought no glasses suited him just as well.

"I never got your name, at the café," he said, as if she needed reminding of their interaction yesterday. She carefully folded her hands under the table, just in case the henna there decided to start acting up again.

"It's Dina," she said, her mouth feeling dry. "And you are?"

"Scott. Scott Mason." He reached a hand across the table to shake hers, and Dina put out a hand. As they shook, she noticed that his hand enveloped hers entirely, and it sent a delicious shiver careening through her. Who knew shaking hands could be so hot?

It was nice, pretending to flirt with a stranger. Because she was only pretending, she told herself. Then she remembered what the tea leaves had said. *Romance is on the horizon.* She quashed the thought.

Outside the train, the London suburbs whizzed by in a blur. The apartment blocks turned into houses, those houses into cottages surrounded by green lawns, and then the countryside unfurled around them, filling the windows with views of heathered fields and woodland and sleeping sheep.

"So, what made you open a café, Dina?" Scott asked.

"How do you know I own it?" she countered.

"I just assumed, I guess. The whole place—it . . . it looks like you. If that makes sense."

Somehow, it did.

"I opened it to make people happy, really. I wanted somewhere that would feel like an oasis for people in the city—you know, when you're out and about having a long day and you just need somewhere to sit and exhale and switch off with a good cup of tea for a while. And you work at the museum, don't you,

Scott?" Dina couldn't help it. She liked the sound of his name on her lips.

"What gave it away—was it the elbow patches?" He chuckled, a deep rumbling laugh.

"Unfortunately, yes, dead giveaway."

"Ah well, it's the only uniform they let curators wear, so you'll have to get used to it." He looked at her from beneath those dark lashes and heat licked at her spine. *You'll have to get used to it.*

"Is that what you do then?"

"I'm a curator. I haven't been there for long. I'm trying to bring a bit more of the modern day to the museum."

"In what sense?"

"An interactive tablet here, an exhibition focusing on ancient Islamic art there. But mainly I'm attempting to sort out the way the British Museum handles artifacts they not so secretly stole from the Middle East during the Second World War. I want— I really want—to return what we can. Or at least create an exhibition that travels on a permanent basis around the museums of North Africa and the Middle East."

"That's really admirable," Dina said, and he smiled shyly. "You're doing a reverse Indiana Jones."

"I'll tell my boss you said so the next time she thinks I'm acting too old for my age."

Scott shifted in his seat, his leg briefly brushing her knee under the table. Heat flared at the touch. She shouldn't be letting this man—this stranger—get her so riled up. *Stick to talking, Dina, and quit staring into his eyes.*

"What did you do before being a curator?" she asked, definitely not staring into his dreamy eyes.

"I traveled, working for different museums around the world. I"—he ran a hand through his dark hair—"I hadn't been back to England for a while."

"But now you're back, you're planning to stay?"

He smirked. "I think I will."

The train pulled into a station deep in the countryside, and Dina realized that they had already been talking for nearly half an hour. She was running out of time to drink her hot chocolate, so she might as well share that and some of the ginger and persimmon cake she'd brought with her.

She pulled off the cup that was attached to the top of the flask and opened it up. Chocolate-scented steam rose into the air.

"That smells lovely," Scott murmured, his eyes closing a little. Hot chocolate often made her feel the same. Like she was wrapped up in a cozy chocolate-scented blanket. She needed the calming magic that was brewed into this right now though, because each glance from Scott sent a buzz reverberating through her whole body.

"Would you like some?" she asked.

"If you have a spare cup, I wouldn't say no."

Dina didn't have a spare cup, but that's what magic was for. She stuck an arm in her bag, which was not quite a Mary Poppins bag but was known to rustle up pretty much whatever she needed in the moment if she thought hard enough about it. Her finger hooked on the handle of a mug. She popped it down on the table and realized in horror that the mug said "World's Best Cat Mum" on the side, complete with a set of pawprints.

"How self-congratulatory," Scott teased.

Dina ignored him, because he was definitely not funny *and* handsome, and poured the hot chocolate into both mugs. It frothed a little on top, just as she liked it. But no hot chocolate was complete without marshmallows. She dug her hand back into the bag, pulling out a sizable handful of pink and white mini marshmallows.

As Dina passed Scott his mug, their fingers touched. The

henna on her wrist flared to life again, and Dina quickly pulled her hand away. *Note to self, no more magic henna around Scott.*

Unaware of her turmoil, Scott leaned back in his seat and sipped the hot chocolate.

"You made this?" he said in a soft tone.

"Mmm. It's a secret recipe, which I'm taking to my grave." She slurped at her drink and caught Scott watching her intently as she licked some melted marshmallow off her top lip.

"You missed a spot," he said. "May I?"

Dina nodded.

He reached out and stroked her upper lip with his thumb, his eyes boring into her all the while. She absolutely did not catch her breath as his hand moved gently across her face. She didn't inhale his bergamot and cedar scent. And when Scott pulled his hand back and licked the marshmallow off his thumb, Dina definitely didn't flush all over. It was just warm on this train.

Unfortunately, the train chose that moment to announce that they would shortly be arriving at Little Hathering station. She didn't want this journey to end.

Dina put away the empty hot chocolate mugs and began to arrange her things to depart. Scott did the same, getting up and wrapping a scarf around his neck. Apparently, Dina could be jealous of a scarf.

"You're getting off here too?" she asked.

"Yeah, visiting my mums."

"Would you mind?" she said, pointing at her bag on the rack above. With Heebie, who was now whining in her crate, unsettled by the movement, she had her hands full.

When he reached up, the top of his shirt lifted and she glimpsed a dark-haired snail trail and heavy, packed muscle. She looked away, blushing. He could pick her up like she weighed nothing.

They got off the train together and stood on the windy platform. The cold had picked up, and Dina's breath steamed as she exhaled. She was home.

"You know, since we're both here for the weekend, perhaps—" But Scott never got to finish what he'd been about to say, because an older woman started calling his name from the station exit.

He smiled. "That's my mum."

Dina looked up at Scott—it was hard not to, since he towered above her, taking up most of her field of vision. Maybe she should give him her number? But then the whole interaction yesterday replayed itself in her mind. The bad omens at the café. The fallen hamsa when he'd entered. The tea leaves. It would end in disaster—that's what was predicted.

Dina could see how it would all play out: the dating, the sex—which would be phenomenal, she had no doubts about that—and then Dina would fall hard, because she always did, and the hex would hurt Scott just as it had hurt those before him.

She looked down at herself, seeing her bushy hair flying out in all directions, her ill-fitting jeans, her top that had a coffee stain on the bottom. There was no way he'd been flirting with her; she must have misread the signals. Not when she looked like this.

If she offered him her number, she'd only be embarrassing herself. She wasn't ready for more embarrassment, and certainly not for more heartbreak.

"It was nice to meet you. Bye." She spoke with as cold a tone as she could manage, and walked away, Heebie yowling in her carrier all the while. Then she hurried out of the station, careening down the hill into the center of the village. She only looked back once.

Chapter 6

*W*ell, folks, the idiot award goes to Scott Mason for the second time in one day. How—how could he have messed it up *again*? Scott stood on the train platform, watching as Dina *literally* ran away from him, wondering what on earth he had done wrong.

He thought they'd been getting along really well. Dina was wickedly funny, and she'd warmed up to him after he'd complimented her cat. Well, Heebie was a furry little angel so he hadn't been lying. And he'd seen the way she'd looked at him from underneath those long, dark eyelashes. His mind raced back to when she'd licked some marshmallow off her lip. Just the thought of her tongue parting her lips, firmly licking, the brush of his thumb on her mouth, was making him hard. Maybe he had come on too strong.

Or maybe she just isn't into you, his traitorous brain thought. He was, after all, out of touch with the dating game. He had no way of knowing now, anyway. Dina was long gone, though he swore the scent of her spiced orange perfume still lingered in the air around him.

Scott had been about to ask if she wanted to get a drink, since they were both going to be in Little Hathering that weekend. What were the chances of them meeting twice in two days, anyway? A younger, more naïve Scott would have believed it to be serendipity.

Dina had obviously sensed that he was about to ask her out, since she'd upped and left before he'd even finished his question.

Ah, well. This weekend wasn't about him anyway. It was about Eric and Immy's wedding, visiting his mums, and going for walks with views that weren't encumbered by skyscrapers. Scott didn't have much time to ruminate on Dina, because his mum was waiting for him in the parking lot of the station near her bright yellow Beetle.

"Scott! Darling!" Helene shouted, waving over the small crowd of people who had gotten off at Little Hathering, her strawberry-blonde hair tied up with an elaborate headscarf.

Scott laughed and bent down to give his mum a hug. He remembered when he was little and he'd hugged her, he'd only come up to her waist. Now, each hug was a bear hug, his arms wrapped all the way around. But hugging his mum tonight, he couldn't help but think that she felt smaller than she used to, more fragile.

"It's good to have you home," she whispered, stroking his hair. "Now, are you going to tell me who that lovely lady was that you were talking to on the platform?" She grinned mischievously, patting his arm as she tugged him along to the car.

"No one. Just someone I sat next to on the train." He had never been good at lying to his mum, even if this technically was just a shade of the truth.

"Mmm-hmm, sure." She winked, before launching into an update on what they'd been up to. The wonderful thing about his mum Helene was that when Scott wasn't up to talking much, she could carry the conversation for both of them.

"Alex has been painting the garden shed, a color called Majorelle blue. It's quite something! And the neighbor was complaining about our sunrise meditation again, but honestly, if he doesn't want to see my lady bits he can just avoid peeking out his curtains at five in the morning."

Scott listened to his mum nattering away as she sped around village corners, telling him all about the improvements they were making to the house, and the different kinds of birds she'd spotted at their bird feeder. Retirement suited her.

Both of his mums had been morticians, but you'd never guess that if you met them. Both sunny and bubbly, they loved to regale people with the story of how they met, their scalpels touching as they both sliced up the Y-incision of the same cadaver at mortuary school.

Scott looked out the window as Little Hathering passed them by. He could understand why his mums loved it here. It was adorably quaint, and each shop on the high street had curved glass windowpanes and hanging lights. As it was so close to Halloween, most of the shopfronts were artfully decorated with grinning pumpkins, cinnamon broomsticks, and cardboard cut-outs of cackling green witches stirring their cauldrons.

Little Hathering was the sort of place where you would find bunting all year round, and the sort of place Americans would think of if you described an English village. It looked straight out of a romantic comedy—the kind his mums loved and made him watch whenever he came to stay. But as they passed through the streets, he couldn't help but look out for Dina's silhouette, or Heebie off on the run again.

As they pulled up outside his mums' house, Scott noticed Eric's silver Audi was parked outside.

"Eric's here?"

"Oh yes, did I forget to mention? He brought over your wedding suit."

The scent of fresh apple cake wafted over as soon as Scott

entered the house, Juniper racing up to him on her short little legs.

"Hi, gorgeous girl." Scott scooped the perfectly rotund corgi into his arms, scritching her between her ears as she furiously slobbered all over his face. Scott noticed the fur around Juniper's nose was a shade paler than when he'd last visited, and guilt streaked through him.

"I've been telling her you were coming home all day. She's been so excited," chimed Alex, who pulled Scott into a long hug the moment he put the dog down.

"Hi, Mama," Scott said, burying his face in Alex's graying curls.

"You look hungry—have you eaten?" She tugged him through the narrow hallway, family photos lining the walls—far too many from Scott's awkward teenage years—and into the kitchen.

Eric was sipping tea from an enormous clay mug and waved hello as Scott entered.

He grinned. "I'm not here for you, just the cake."

"I'd expect no less," Scott replied, cutting himself a hefty slice. Helene's apple cake was perfectly spiced with cinnamon and nutmeg. He thought about asking her for the recipe—maybe he could give it to Dina. If he ever saw her again.

"Look at you both, eating cake in the kitchen. I've missed it." Helene smiled as she walked in, pressing a kiss to Alex's forehead as she poured herself a cup of tea.

He'd missed this when he was traveling for work. The simple joy of sitting with his mums and his best friend in their warm, cozy kitchen. Alice hadn't liked coming to visit his mums much; she'd said that the bright colors they'd chosen to paint their house gave her a headache. It was a little like being inside a coloring box at times, but he loved it. It was the first real home he'd ever had. He remembered realizing that his mums didn't like Alice either, though they hadn't been too forceful about it, believing Scott was happy. He wished he'd listened to them.

Scott glanced over to the fridge, which was cluttered with a random assortment of fruit-shaped magnets, each one holding up a postcard he'd sent. Ouarzazate, Lima, Kirikiriroa, the list went on. Had he really been gone so long? At the time he'd just needed to escape England; he hadn't wanted to see his mums, hadn't wanted to admit that they'd been right about Alice all along. But now Scott realized he'd let the pain from his breakup seep into this part of his life too, affecting his relationships with the people he loved the most. He could still repair things, he hoped. He would try.

"I wish I could stay longer," Eric said, breaking Scott out of his self-imposed guilt trip. "But Immy has me on flower-arranging duty before we head out later. Which reminds me"—Eric nudged Scott—"come out to the Roebuck later? A few of Immy's friends will be there, kind of breaking the ice before the wedding, you know."

"Sure, sounds good."

"And listen," Eric said, pulling him into the privacy of the hallway, "there might be someone there I'd like you to meet. Immy's maid of honor. She's . . . let's just say I think you're going to get on well, that's all." Scott didn't like the mischievous glint in Eric's eyes.

"This better not be a matchmaking scheme," he warned.

Eric held up his hands. "Honestly, mate, I think you just need to get laid." He clapped Scott on the back.

"I see. You just want to play wingman. I'll see you a bit later then," Scott said, pulling Eric into a quick hug before he left.

After that, the evening sped by. His mums had a load of DIY tasks they needed his help with—mostly putting up shelves and dismantling old furniture. He felt again that he'd wasted time not visiting them while he'd been with Alice. They weren't getting any younger, and every meal, every evening together, felt more precious to him than it ever had before. The same went for Juniper. The fur around her nose was whiter than when he'd last seen her, and she napped more than she used to. Scott took her out for a walk around the local park; she was always overexcited in the first few minutes, eagerly sniffing every corner of the street—her territory—with the enthusiasm of a hound on the hunt. They spent a few minutes beside the "magical pie bush," a small shrub that Juniper had once found an entire pie in, and now had to check on every walk in case the bush manifested any more delicious snacks for her.

After that, he ended up clearing the garden shed of spiders, his mums' mortal enemies, and decided to pop to the shop to fill the fridge.

"Are you sure?" Helene said when she spotted him taking the shopping list off the fridge. "Weren't you meant to go to the pub to meet Eric and Immy's friends?"

"Yeah, I just feel wiped out. A long day at work and all that."

"Well, make sure you at least wrap up warm." She smiled and settled onto the worn sofa beside Alex to watch their evening soap opera.

As Scott walked through the quiet village streets, he thought about how easy his mums made being in love look.

Even when he was a boy, they'd always been like this, and unlike many of his friends' parents they hadn't fallen out of love as the years went on—if anything they were more in love now than ever. They still bought flowers for each other, most of the time picking up two of the exact same bouquet. Scott had lost count of the times he'd come home to visit and found them dancing to the radio in the kitchen.

He wanted a love like that.

Maybe he should have gone to the pub tonight to meet Immy's maid of honor. Maybe Eric was right, and all he needed was to get laid. But his mind kept crawling back to Dina, her cackling laugh and the worry he'd seen in her eyes when she'd thought Heebie had run away from her on the train, quickly followed by relief when she'd seen Heebie in his arms. He wanted to see that relief in her eyes again, that happiness. He wanted to be the one to cause it.

He didn't want to meet another woman, not tonight anyway, with his mind full of Dina. Next time he wouldn't mess it up. He'd say all the right things. Fuck, he wished he could see her again . . .

Chapter 7

The house knew she was coming. The back of Dina's neck prickled with a magical awareness as she turned onto Cypress Street, huffing under the weight of her bags and Heebie's carrier.

"I need to stop feeding you so much cheese," Dina muttered to the cat. But as they neared the house, the weight of her bags slowly became lighter—the house had a habit of doing that, stretching its magic across the street, like a mother bird protecting the young in her nest.

It knew when Dina walked up to the front door. The brass door knocker, shaped like an evil eye, blinked once at her—or was it more of a wink?—and swung open.

"Hi, House," Dina said, patting the door lovingly as she stepped inside. The floorboards creaked happily. The house was delighted that one of its people was home.

From the outside, 2 Cypress Street looked just like any other country Victorian terraced house. But the moment you stepped inside—and the house decided that it knew you well enough or trusted you—it would shake off its glamour like a shabby coat and reveal itself.

Dina kicked off her shoes, slipping into a pair of house sandals. The house was very picky about no one dirtying its floors.

The house hadn't been created using her family's magic. Dina's mum had suspected it was a spirit tied to the earth here, and over time it had slowly joined with the house until they were one and the same. If you treated the house badly, you could very well end up with a serious unwelcoming poltergeist situation. But the house loved them, and loved their magic.

"Mama! Baba! I'm home!" Dina called out.

"Coming, habiba!" Her mother's muffled voice came from upstairs. Dina bent down and unlocked the cat carrier, letting Heebie sway out and stretch before scurrying off to eat from the food bowl that the house would have put out for her. The house always spoiled Heebie with fresh tuna, no matter how many times Dina had told it not to.

Dina dropped her bags at the entrance, and when she looked back, they had vanished—probably in her room already, the clothes neatly folded in her old chest of drawers.

The front room had a cozy, cottagey feel, with a warmly lit hearth and worn armchairs that were a delight to sink into. If you opened up the curtains, instead of seeing Cypress Street, you'd be greeted with a view of the verdant green valley in Wales where her father had grown up, complete with grazing cows. That was her father's favorite room.

As Dina walked down the hall, the floorboards seamlessly transformed into blue and white tiles beneath her feet. She found herself standing in the heart of the house: a riad with a bubbling mosaic fountain, vines twisting up the walls and, above her, fuchsias blossoming in terra-cotta pots and miniature date trees coiling around the pillars. It was more of a garden than a room, really. The ceiling was open to the night sky, burnished stars in an inky darkness.

It wasn't the real sky of course, but the house's magic was powerful. Dina could even hear crickets chirping in the distance and the cinnamon scent of the earth in Khemisset, where her mother had grown up. She exhaled deeply, the feeling of being home sinking into her bones.

She headed into the kitchen, copper pots hanging from the ceiling, pots of fresh basil lining the windowsill—something her mother had done since she was a child, because it kept the spiders and mosquitoes away.

On the stove, a pot of harira was bubbling away, a wooden spoon stirring the soup, held up by the house's invisible hand. Dina snuck a spoonful; it was perfectly delicious, the lamb melting in her mouth. This was the sort of food that went straight to your soul. The house preened in satisfaction as she went for a second bite.

A tortoise hobbled slowly toward Dina, and she bent down and gave it a gentle pat on its shell. Her hand slipped straight through and grazed the floor, because the tortoise wasn't technically there, being a ghost and all. Still, it was a very affectionate ghost, and it liked to follow Dina around when she came home to visit.

"Mama, where are you?" Dina shouted.

"Ay! Coming, coming," her mother's disembodied voice shouted back from one of the rooms on the upper floor of the courtyard. Dina headed up the spiral staircase situated in one corner of the riad, and found her mother in the family bathroom, hurriedly scraping bleaching cream off her (now very blonde) mustache.

"Mama, what are you doing?" Dina said, standing in the doorway with her hands on her hips. Dina's mum jumped out of her skin.

"Tfoo, I thought you were downstairs! Don't make me jump like that, I'll get it in my eye," she tutted, pulling Dina in for a tight hug with her free arm.

"You know I have a spell for that. You don't need to use that stuff, it's toxic."

"Ah well, I forgot. And last time I tried it myself I had MORE hair coming out, so I'll stick to bleach, waha?"

Dina's mother washed her face in the sink and dried it off with a towel Dina handed her.

"Okay, now let me look at you," her mother said, taking Dina's face between her hands. "Mm-mm. A bit of stress, yes . . . but you're glowing! What's happened?"

"Mama, are you reading my aura again?" Dina sighed.

"What! Can't a mother know how her daughter is feeling? *Especially* when that daughter doesn't call to say hello anymore." Nour Whitlock, everyone—the original, trademarked Drama Queen.

"I called you twice last week," Dina replied. Her mother sniffed, feigning hurt. She had a penchant for dramatics, a wickedly fierce sense of humor, and people-watching skills that would be the envy of any MI5 operative. She was a five-foot-two-inch bundle of concentrated chaos, with a short crop of henna-red hair and a piercing gray gaze. Dina got her mahogany-colored eyes from her dad.

"Are you staying next week? We won't be able to have a proper catch-up, what with the wedding this weekend," Nour said, handing Dina a pot of homemade beeswax and chamomile makeup remover that she had made herself. Taking off their makeup and doing their skincare routine together was something that Dina and her mother had always done, as soon as Dina had shown interest when she was younger. It was a very special kind of magic, this ritual between a mother and a daughter.

"I'm staying until Tuesday morning, then I need to get back to the café. Robin can't top up anything with magic, so I need to be there."

Nour tutted. "You never give yourself a break from work. But I am proud of you, habiba," she said, patting Dina's hand. "Tonight, you'll let me do some henna on you, hmm? I've been working on a henna spell that will give you luscious hair and glowing skin, and I thought you might want it for the wedding."

"Always happy to be your magical guinea pig, Mama." Dina smiled, feeling the calm settle into her bones in the way it only did when she was home. Dina and her mother spent the next few minutes part-catching up, part-bickering in the way that only mother and daughters could do, until the sound of the front door opening called Dina's attention away.

"Dina, you home?" her father called.

"I'm here, Baba. One second!" She patted the remnants of her moisturizer into her hands and went downstairs to greet her dad.

Robert Whitlock was in the kitchen, putting away bottles of orange juice, while the house levitated the used shopping bags into a holder above the sink.

"There's my girl," her father said, giving Dina a warm hug. "You look well, hayati."

It was always endearing to hear her father speak Darija. With his Welsh accent, Robert couldn't quite sound out some of the pronunciation, but that never stopped him from trying. When she was little, Dina had told him that she was his hayati, his life, and he had called her that ever since.

"I bumped into the bride-to-be on my way back from the shops. She said to tell you to come down to the Roebuck when you're ready. They're having drinks," he said, the corners of his eyes crinkling. He had more gray hairs than the last time Dina had seen him.

"Great. But I should probably eat something first." As if on cue, an egg timer in the kitchen went off, the house's way of signaling that dinner was ready.

The three of them—four if you counted the ghost tortoise—sat down at the dining table, which the house had decided was now a shade of forest green. Dina's father served up the harira, while her mother set out small plates of zaalouk, shlada, and khobz on the table. Her mother held the basket of bread and muttered a spell. When Dina broke apart the khobz, it was warm and steaming and smelled mouth-wateringly good.

Her parents asked her all the usual questions: how was the café doing, was she tired of London life yet, and where was Heebie? The cat had probably gone off and found a bed to crawl under the duvet of, and was no doubt deeply asleep.

Dina's father held her mother's hand across the table, smiling at his wife as she chatted away. She noticed that he was careful to tiptoe around asking Dina any questions about her love life, though her mother clearly had no such qualms.

"Have you been on any dates lately? Met any handsome young men you want to introduce to us?"

Dina loved her mother, but she sometimes thought that Nour was best loved in small doses.

"No handsome men, I'm afraid," she lied, "but if I meet any you'll be the first to know."

Dina was relatively open with her parents when it came to her love life, but that came with caveats. She would tell them about first dates with men, especially the ones that went wrong, but discussion of Rory, and any other woman she might be dating, was off-limits.

As dinner turned into dessert—a sweet apple Pwdin Eva with heaps of cream that her father had baked that afternoon—Dina found her thoughts straying back to Scott Mason. To his chiseled, bearded jawline and his deep rumbling laughter. To the way he'd held Heebie in his arms. Maybe they should have swapped numbers. Maybe one drink would have been fine.

Dina looked down at her hands, the henna twisting into a thorned vine before her eyes, suffocating itself. The hex, making sure its presence was known, no doubt. She reprimanded herself.

Dina Whitlock would be taking a break from dating for the foreseeable future. Or until someone came along who was safe for a quick fling. Scott Mason was not fling material.

Once she'd eaten, Dina changed into the classic Friday-night pub outfit: jeans and a nice top. She found Heebie asleep in a pile of freshly washed and dried linens, now covered in cat hair, and she gave the purring cat a kiss on her cold little nose before heading out.

Chapter 8

It was that perfect kind of October night, with a waxing gibbous moon and a crisp chill that made you walk a little faster to keep warm, and your breath came out in puffs of steam. Fairy lights twinkled in the windows of the pub as Dina approached.

The Roebuck was one that conjured many embarrassing teenage memories for Dina, mostly because it was the only pub that had served underage kids, provided they didn't order anything stronger than a fruit cider or mulled wine.

The inside seemed to have been designed to feel as warm and cozy as possible. Brass sconces on the walls bathed the room in a golden glow, and a fire crackled in the wide hearth. It smelled like worn leather, beer, and cedar.

It wasn't the kind of pub that had awkward bar stools where you spent all night fidgeting to find a comfortable seating position; the Roebuck was the kind of pub that wanted you to stay a while. Each seat was an armchair, worn and homely. The owners were a married couple in their sixties—the Hollands, Dina remembered vaguely. They offered her good-natured smiles from behind the bar as she entered.

She spotted her friends on the twin sofas by the fire and made her way over. Immy was sitting on Eric's lap and waved, but as soon as Rosemary noticed Dina she hopped out of her seat and came bounding toward her, letting out a squeal loud enough to frighten the locals at the next table.

"You better save me from them, they're too loved up." Rosemary grinned, tackling Dina with a wonderfully aggressive hug.

"Shocking, almost like they're getting married in a few days."

Rosemary looked grave. "I know, it's sickening. Let's get drunk. Can you believe I've never had mulled wine?"

Dina gasped in mock horror. "We need to remedy that immediately."

They hovered by the bar, Rosemary giving Dina the lowdown on the rest of Eric and Immy's friends who were by the fire. Some she'd met before, but she didn't recognize a lot of Eric's workmates.

"I've been told that Eric's best man was meant to be coming, but then he texted Eric saying he's still running errands for his parents so he might not make it." Rosemary sipped her mulled wine, her eyes rolling back in pleasure.

"Who runs errands at nine P.M. on a Thursday?" Dina said.

"Indeed," Immy replied, sidling up to them. She was wearing one of her signature classic horror shirts, this one depicting the hand-swallowing chest cavity scene from *The Thing* in pretty graphic detail.

For a brief stint during the wedding-planning stage, Immy had been convinced she wanted a horror-movie-themed wedding. Thankfully, Eric had called in a favor from Dina and Rosemary, and they had talked her out of it. Now, Immy and Eric were getting married at Honeywell House the day after Halloween, with a dense forest as a backdrop. It was brilliantly spooky, and Dina couldn't wait.

"You have your maid-of-honor dress, right? It arrived in the post?"

"Yep, and it's been rehemmed. How are your parents holding

up?" Mr. and Mrs. Partridge were notorious traditionalists and were having a hard time stomaching the idea of their daughter having a humanist wedding, sans church.

"You mean after all the threats that I'll go to hell and that my marriage won't be blessed by God? Oh, they're just dandy." Immy grimaced.

"Well, just say the word, I've got a subduing spell I can use on them for the ceremony. They'll be calm and happy, but most importantly, lacking in opinions."

"Wait, is that a real thing?" Rosemary asked. She almost looked like she wanted to pull out a pen and take notes.

"Yeah, but I wouldn't use it lightly."

"How come?" Rosemary said.

"If I make the spell too potent, they'll just fall asleep for days."

"I'll let you know. Hopefully we won't need it," Immy said.

They made their way over to the group by the fire, the heat turning Dina's cheeks a pleasant pink. Eric bear-hugged Dina, grinning ear to ear.

"You're like a lumberjack with that beard," Dina remarked, nodding toward Eric's reddish-haired chin.

"Not my fault. You've got to tell Immy to get her lumberjack fantasies under control." He laughed heartily. Dina smiled, so glad that her best friend had found someone like Eric.

Seeing them together, and the way that Eric looked at Immy when she was breaking down the plot of a new horror idea she had, was enough to make a skeptic believe in true love.

Nevertheless, when Eric and Immy had first become serious, Dina had made it clear that Eric would pay if he ever hurt her friend. Thankfully, it didn't look like it was going to come to that.

The hours passed quickly, spent chatting with her friends and drinking more mulled wine, the edges of the pub beginning to blur merrily.

Every once in a while the pub door would swing open, a flutter of crisp air sweeping leaves onto the cobbled flagstones, and Eric would look up, fully expecting to see his mysterious best man. But whoever he was, he never turned up.

*T*ime flew by in the way that it always did when Dina, Rosemary, and Immy were together, so when she looked down at her phone she was shocked to find it was already close to midnight.

"I'd better go. My mum said she wanted to practice a new henna spell on me," Dina whispered to Immy and Rosemary.

"What kind of spell?"

"Luscious hair and clear skin, I believe."

"Ooh, I'll take some of that!" Immy exclaimed as she hugged Dina goodbye. "See you tomorrow! Tell your mum she can't lie in!" Dina's mum practically had three daughters—Rosemary and Immy had spent so many nights staying at the family's house when they'd all been studying.

Dina waved goodbye to the rest of the group, fist-bumped Eric, and stumbled out of the pub.

Okay, so she was a little drunker than she thought. Turned out two glasses of mulled wine and a white wine spritzer when you didn't drink all that often could make it quite difficult to walk in a straight line.

Dina decided to take a different route on her walk home, mostly because she wanted to go past a house that always had the most fantastic Halloween decorations.

Each year it surpassed itself. This time round, Dina spotted the green halo of light in the sky from two streets over. When she finally made it outside the house she had to stop and marvel, leaning against an icy street lamp. It was so quiet here; she was so used to the background hum of London that she only noticed it when it was absent.

This year, instead of opting for many smaller spooky decorations, they had opted for two giant ten-foot skeletons, which Dina was pretty sure you had to get shipped over from America. British people never went this hard for Halloween. Their usual limit was a couple of carved pumpkins filled with plastic candles on the doorstep.

Dina never bought sweets for trick-or-treaters herself, partly because she lived on the third story of her apartment building, and partly because she spent each Halloween dancing naked around a fire with Immy and Rosemary, a tradition they'd begun a few years ago.

The two skeletons were positioned to look as if they were gardening, one paused in the movement of pushing a large papier-mâché lawnmower, the other pruning an apple tree with a pair of giant cardboard pruning shears. They were lit from below by two green tinted lights, which bathed the entire house in an eerie lime glow.

A church bell echoed in the distance, breaking Dina out of her tipsy stare. She'd probably been ogling that house long enough (she was lucky no one in the neighborhood watch had called the police), so she turned on her heel to head home.

Unfortunately, as she did so, her heel caught on an uneven bit of pavement, sending her flying. She smacked onto the ground, the air pushed from her lungs with force. She tried to move, immediately feeling a bruise blooming on her elbow and a smear of blood on her chin. It didn't hurt yet but she expected it would soon. Where was her damn witchy intuition when she needed it?

She tried to stand, her ankle twisting uncomfortably under her, and groped dizzily for something to grab a hold of to haul herself upright.

"Here, take my hand. Are you all right?" a voice said from above her. Dina looked up, but her eyes seemed to be playing tricks on her because there seemed to be two Scott Masons standing in front of her.

"Do you have a twin?" she asked, but her voice sounded slurred.

In response, both of the Scott Masons wrapped an arm around her waist and lifted her up. She was vaguely aware how nice it felt to have their arms around her, warm and solid.

"Smell like pine," she mumbled.

"I smell like pine?" She heard him chuckle.

"Pine and soap and dog."

"Ah well, that'll be because of Juniper, who needed an extra late-night walk and is being a very good girl right now," Scott said. Dina tipped her head down and woozily noticed a small round ginger and white corgi waiting patiently at her feet, tongue lolling out of its mouth.

"Hi there, Juniper," Dina said. Then she felt Scott's warm touch, his rough palm holding the back of her neck, tilting her face up toward his.

"Dina, look at me. Are you hurt? Your chin has a little bit of blood on it." He seemed concerned, his brown eyes boring into hers, but she wanted to tell him she was fine, except for the swarm of butterflies in her stomach. Damn the mulled wine.

"You *are* a dog person!" was all she managed to say, and Scott huffed a laugh in reply.

"Yeah, I'm a dog person. Dina, listen, I think I should call an ambulance, you might be concussed."

The idea of a concussion jerked her awake, though her limbs were still feeling a little floaty.

"I think I might be, yeah." She groaned. "But I don't need an ambulance. Can you just take me home? My mum can do first aid."

Dina inhaled, smelling Scott's warm scent, and suddenly her head was very heavy and she needed to lean it against his chest.

"You're very warm. And big," she slurred, vaguely aware that she was saying something she should probably be keeping to herself.

"Oh yeah?"

"I don't normally get held by men, only women. And no one has held me in a long time."

Scott was silent for a moment, his warm body tensing slightly.

"I didn't realize you were—"

"I'm bi," Dina added.

Why had she said that? He probably hadn't even been about to ask that. It's not like Scott needed to know who she was attracted to. So why did she want him to know?

Thoughts were swirling around her head and the bump on her chin was starting to ache. All she wanted was to rest her head against Scott's chest and have a nap. Just a small one. She let out a long breath.

"Don't fall asleep, Dina. Can you tell me where you live?" Scott said, his breath on her cheek and in her hair. What would happen if she leaned up and pressed a kiss to his lips?

"Stay awake, sweetheart. Tell me where to take you," Scott said, one arm tucking under Dina's legs and lifting her up into his arms. He cradled her like she weighed nothing. Dina just about managed to mumble her parents' address before she slumped into unconsciousness.

Chapter 9

*O*nce Dina was in his arms, Scott twined Juniper's lead around his wrist and felt around Dina's head for any lumps and bumps; she seemed to be fine, just dazed. Her breath smelled quite strongly of spiced wine though, which Scott suspected might have been the cause of the dizziness rather than a concussion. He was surprised by how relieved he was that she wasn't badly hurt. Just a scrape under the chin and a bump on the elbow by the looks of it.

She looked, quite frankly, adorable in his arms. And she fit perfectly, like she was meant to be there. Dina had tucked her head into his collar, smooshing her face up against his neck. From this angle, he had a fantastic view of her cleavage, but Scott was a gentleman so was trying very hard not to ogle. He figured Dina would be mortified to know that he'd had to carry her home. And that she'd told him he smelled of pine and soap and dog.

Juniper trotted happily beside him on the pavement, her little paws trampling the dried leaves underfoot. He'd decided to take her to the pub with him, to use as an excuse in case he wanted to duck out early. He'd been on his way there when he'd bumped into Dina.

Scott had passed Cypress Street earlier on his walk, and

thankfully Dina had specified it was the last house on the right before she'd fallen asleep.

From the outside, Dina's family home looked surprisingly normal. *What were you expecting?* he asked himself. He knocked on the door using the hamsa door knocker. Her family must be into protective charms too.

He heard a shuffling, then the door opened, revealing a woman who looked like an older version of Dina, albeit a little shorter and rounder, a silk wrap around her head.

"Dina fell over. I think she's okay," Scott said hurriedly, as he saw the woman's—presumably Dina's mother—face grow pale. Then she looked up at Scott and held his gaze just long enough that it started to feel uncomfortable.

"So it's you," she mumbled, and then beckoned them in. "Bring the dog too!" she called over her shoulder as she hurried Scott into a small sitting room where a fire crackled in the hearth.

"Put her down here, I'll go fetch my kit. I'm Nour, by the way," Dina's mother said, indicating a sofa piled high with fluffy cushions. Scott laid her down as delicately as he could, making sure to rest her head against one of the pillows. His arms felt strangely empty without her there.

While this was happening, Juniper had managed to detach herself from the lead, which shouldn't have been possible without Scott noticing, and was now letting out little snores from a dog bed in the corner of the room. Weirdly enough, the dog bed looked oddly similar to her bed at home.

Dina's mum returned in a panicked flurry, crouching down beside her daughter. She had a small bag with her, presumably the "kit" she had gone to retrieve. She pulled out a small tin and rubbed some salve into the cuts and bruises on Dina's chin and elbow. Then, she uncorked a small vial filled with an amber liquid and tipped the contents down Dina's throat. This wasn't like any kind of first aid he'd ever seen.

A moment later Dina opened her eyes, blinking slowly.

"I feel like someone stamped on my head with steel-capped boots," she groaned.

"That's what you get for drinking too much," her mother replied, but not in a mean-spirited way. "You're lucky this young man and his dog brought you home safely," she added, brushing a stray hair out of Dina's face.

Dina looked up at Scott then, her dark eyes focusing, drinking him in.

"Scott?" she said, sounding a lot more like herself already—no more slurred speech.

"Hi. Juniper fell asleep in your dog's bed. I hope that's okay."

"We don't have a dog," Dina's mother chuckled. "Would you like some tea? You both look like you need it."

"Tea would be lovely," Scott said, wondering why they had a dog bed but no dog.

And then it was just the two of them, alone.

"It would be you, wouldn't it. My knight in shining armor." Dina smiled, patting the sofa next to her. Scott sat down, with just enough space between them that he was acutely aware just how easily he could pull her onto his lap, her legs cradling his thighs.

"How are you feeling?" he said.

"Rough. Could you hand me that ice pack?" she asked, nodding toward the coffee table. He passed it to her, momentarily wondering where on earth it had come from.

Dina moaned with pleasure as she held the ice pack to her head, her frown smoothing out. All Scott could think was how much he wanted to hear her moan like that again. *Get yourself under control man,* he chastised himself.

"So. You again," she said with a smirk.

"Me again."

"Are you stalking me or something?"

"Last I checked I *saved* you when you fell over on a dark street at night, and now you're calling me a pervert?"

"Hmph. I would have been fine," she replied, sounding a little unconvinced. "About the train earlier, I—"

"Tea's ready," Dina's mum called out just before she stepped into the room, carrying a tray of tea and a plate piled high with all manner of biscuits. Dina rolled her eyes at Scott.

"Oh, you're already looking much better!" Dina's mum said. "But you should still have some of this." She poured out three cups of tea—chamomile and honey, Scott reckoned.

Scott took a biscuit from the plate that Dina's mother was holding out to him.

"I've never seen one like this before."

"You've never seen a biscuit before?" Dina grinned. "It's a gazelle horn biscuit. Mostly almond and sesame seeds."

Scott took a bite. "You're selling it short, this tastes heavenly," he said, eating the whole horn in two bites.

"They're Dina's favorite," her mum said, her eyes roving over him appraisingly. "So, how do you know my daughter, Scott?"

Dina and Scott spoke at the exact same time.

"We met on the train."

"I went to her café."

"Is that so?" Dina's mum said, quirking an eyebrow.

"What Scott meant to say is that he had the audacity to topple my evil eye amulet from the wall at the café yesterday," Dina said.

Nour mocked being horrified at this.

"And then we bumped into each other again on the train here," Dina continued.

"So that's why you were all in a huff when you got home," Nour remarked.

"I was *not* in a huff," Dina said icily.

"And then you bump into each other again. Three times in such a short span, what a coincidence," she said, as if it wasn't a coincidence at all. "Well, Scott, I was about to head off to bed before you brought Dina home, so I'll say goodnight. We need our beauty sleep for the weekend we're about to have."

"Goodnight," Scott said. Dina's mum smiled at them both with a knowing expression and left them to it.

Now that they were alone again, Scott felt a sense of tension return to the air. Christ, the way Dina was looking at him from below those thick eyelashes of hers was not helping.

"So, what's happening this weekend?" he said, his voice sounding rougher and lower than he'd intended. Something about the way that Dina was sitting, holding her teacup in both hands, her legs criss-crossed, made his hands ache to hold her again.

"A wedding," she almost whispered.

"You don't say." He laughed. What were the chances?

"Why are you pulling that face?"

"Well, it just so happens that I too have a wedding this weekend." He saw the realization dawn, her eyes widening.

"No."

"Yes."

"You're Eric's best man, aren't you?"

"And I'm guessing your Immy's maid of honor?"

Dina slammed her teacup down on the table.

"Fuck."

"Indeed."

"How have we never met before?" she asked.

"I was away. Different museums, different countries . . ." He trailed off. He didn't want to be the kind of guy who went off on a thirty-minute narcissism session talking all about his travels as if he'd been on some kind of extended gap year.

"And you were meant to come tonight, weren't you? But you were running errands." Dina nodded at Juniper, snoozing away, who had now been joined by Heebie. Heebie normally hated dogs, but she seemed to have curled up quite amicably beside the corgi and was now licking between Juniper's ears.

"I just . . . didn't feel like going out tonight," Scott admitted.

"After I ran away from you at the train station," Dina whispered back.

"That might have had something to do with it."

"Let me explain, I—"

"You don't owe me any kind of explanation, Dina. Really you don't. I didn't—I don't expect anything of you." Scott put his empty cup down on the tray. "I think I'd better go."

"Scott, please . . ."

He scooped up Juniper, who snuffled in her sleep like the big furry baby she was, and headed toward the door.

"Please thank your mum for the tea and biscuits; they were lovely. I'm sorry if I made you uncomfortable—that wasn't my intention."

They were going to have to spend all weekend together, at the very least, so he thought it best to leave things amicable. And from the way she'd run away from him earlier, it was clear she wasn't interested in him, right? Had things changed since then? Right now, surrounded by a house that felt so much like Dina, it squeezed at his chest a little. He needed to get out.

"Scott, just wait a second, please." Dina jumped out in front of him as he approached the door. Her hair was a mess, mascara smudged, and she'd never looked so beautiful. "I ran away from you because I was, well, I'm not looking for anything right now. And I haven't been serious with anybody in . . . a while."

"You did mention that when I was carrying you earlier."

Dina's face blanched. "Oh god, I hope I didn't say anything else too embarrassing."

"Only that I smell like pine. And that I'm warm and big." He smirked as Dina groaned.

"Please try and forget anything I said. Blame it on the wine."

As if he could ever forget a second of it.

"Dina, it's okay," he said. "We can just be friends—friends for the rest of the wedding weekend."

She smiled and his heart tripped.

"Friends would be good. Goodnight, Scott." She went up onto her tiptoes and planted a kiss on his cheek. Her lips were soft and warm and he wanted nothing more than to turn his face and meet her lips with his.

"Goodnight, Dina," Scott said, and he shut the door gently behind him. This was going to be a long weekend.

*G*etting Dina and her mother into a car was a trying experi- ence for all involved. Nour had lost her sisters in a car accident when she was younger, and so had spent the past forty- five minutes adding protection spell after protection spell to every inch of the car. Dina, a little more pragmatic than her mother, had been busy undoing her mother's henna magic all morning.

She had woken the house up with screams at 6 A.M. when she'd discovered that her mother's spell had changed her hair to a mermaid-blue color overnight. After the initial shock, the whole bright blue hair look had kind of grown on her, but she wasn't convinced it would be the best look for the wedding, so she had begun the painstaking process of charming it back to its original aubergine brown with flecks of purple.

Finally, they were in the car, and heading off to Honeywell House, where they'd be spending the weekend. Immy and Eric were having a relatively small celebration, with around thirty guests.

Honeywell House was a National Trust property deep in the gentrified Hertfordshire countryside. Eric's parents had actually got married there, and although Immy was vehemently opposed to following tradition, once she'd seen the place she had fallen in love. The phrases "definitely haunted" and "cabin in the woods" had been thrown about.

As they drove down twisting country roads, Dina found herself growing apprehensive. The way things had been left with Scott last night—the spark of longing she had felt pulse through her as she'd kissed his cheek . . . She had butterflies in her belly. And what kind of grown woman experienced butterflies, for crying out loud.

They passed through an archway of low-hanging tree branches, the sunlight piercing through and scattering on the road ahead. The leaves were already turning a blood orange shade, and next month they wouldn't be there at all.

Nour poked her head around from the front passenger seat. "Are you excited to see that handsome man this weekend?"

"How do you know Scott's going to be there? Were you snooping, Mama?"

"No—and I knew you thought he was handsome!"

"Mama!"

"Oh, pssh. I just have a feeling in my bones about this weekend, that's all," Nour said, her eyes glinting with mischief. In Dina's experience, her mother's "feelings" always had a tendency to come true. *Romance is on the horizon.*

"Who is this handsome man we're speaking of?" Robert Whitlock asked, his eyes remaining on the road.

Dina sighed. "Scott Mason. He's actually Eric's best man."

"Is he now?" her dad said, sounding amused.

"I didn't know that until last night. So, yeah."

"Well, if your mother likes him, I like him," he said, giving Dina a smile in the rearview mirror.

"Thanks, Baba. But it's not like that."

"Oh, please! Robert, take my word for it, they're practically in love," Nour said, which earned her a swat on the arm from Dina. She had just met Scott, for goddess's sake—she wasn't in love with him!

"Mama, are you going to tell me what you foresaw for this weekend?"

Nour smirked. "Where would be the fun in that?"

The cobbled country road wound abruptly to the right, and Honeywell House came into view, surrounded by tree-lined hills and, behind it, an imposing forest. Although it was a clear October day, clouds hung low around the mansion, creating long shadows that moved about the hills.

"Well, it's certainly . . . striking," her dad said.

"I wouldn't get married there," Nour muttered under her breath.

"You two eloped, of course you wouldn't get married somewhere like this," Dina replied.

Her mother looked over at her dad and she could practically see the hearts in her eyes.

"And I would do it again in a heartbeat," Nour said.

Robert reached out and caught his wife's hand, kissing it delicately, and whispered, "Cariad."

Dina wanted a love like her parents had: unflappable, unscathed by time.

They drove down a long gravel driveway lined by stoic, serious evergreens. Honeywell House looked formidable at first glance, like a determined old tyrant lording itself over the landscape, but as they approached, Dina could understand why Immy had fallen in love with this place.

Ivy clung to the sandstone battlements, and stern gothic windows flanked the medieval arch of the front door, complete with a wrought-iron handle. Small faces were carved into the stone cornices, and the wicked face of a green man grinned down at them from above the main door. It certainly had a haunted feel about it, and Dina wondered if she might spot a ghost looking down at them from an attic window.

Behind the house the land fell away into dense forest, tall pines blocking out any autumn light. Wonderfully spooky.

Immy and Eric must have heard them pulling up, because the front door creaked open ominously to reveal them standing there, like the lord and lady of the manor.

Immy came running up to Dina.

"Don't you just love it?" she said, gazing up at the stained-glass windows.

"I do. The wedding photos are going to be epic!" Dina squealed, squeezing Immy's hand.

"Maybe if we're lucky we'll spot a ghost in the background when we get them developed. Or Rosemary will see an actual ghost!" Immy said, and Dina knew her friend was being one hundred percent serious.

"Fingers crossed."

Eric waved Dina hello as he helped her parents carry their bags through the front door. Immy looped her arm through Dina's and pulled her across the threshold into a side room where the walls were covered in taxidermised deer heads. Their glassy stares followed them across the room as Immy and Dina sat down in a cozy corner.

"Where's Rosemary?" Dina asked.

"Off on a walk around the house. She wanted to see if all the ghost stories about this place are real."

"Of course she did."

"Anyway, I hear you met Scott last night," Immy said, winking ominously.

"Ah, you heard about my little fall, did you?"

"I did—glad you're all right by the way, but I want to know all about it. Eric told me you met each other before, on the train? Why didn't you mention anything?"

"Number one, I didn't know he was Eric's best man at the time, and number two, this is your wedding weekend. I didn't mention it because nothing of interest happened."

"Nothing of interest, huh? That's not what I heard. You do remember that I'm the bride, and you have to follow my orders. I demand you give me all the juicy gossip."

Dina couldn't argue with that.

"There's not much to tell really. He came into my café Wednesday morning, the hamsa fell on the floor—"

"Oh dear."

"Right. And then we met each other again on the train, and yeah, that time it wasn't so bad, and then he helped me home when I fell over." Dina shrugged, attempting to keep her cool. And failing—the image of Scott's happy trail when he'd reached for her bag in the train had scalded itself into her mind.

"Hmm. Remember what you always tell me about the power of three in magic? Seems *pretty interesting* that you met Scott three times in two days, don't you think? Immy smiled, a cunning gleam in her eye—Dina wasn't sure she liked where this was headed.

"Do you think there could be something there?" Immy asked.

"I don't know," Dina said, telling the truth. "But I can't date, you know that."

Immy and Rosemary knew about the hex, though sometimes Dina suspected that Immy was tired of hearing her talk about it. She seemed to believe that Dina should just come clean to her mum about it. Immy thought that Dina's parents would welcome their daughter's sexuality, but Dina knew it wasn't that simple. The hex was the one thing she and Immy couldn't see eye to eye on. Case in point, she clearly didn't believe in the dangers enough to stop playing matchmaker between Dina and Scott.

"You don't have to date him—just, you know, have some fun

this weekend! You need it. And you know what they say about the best man and the maid of honor . . ." Immy waggled her eyebrows suggestively.

Dina didn't have time to whack the future bride over the head, because at that moment Immy's dad, Tony, popped his head round the door to hustle Dina and Immy to the Reading Parlor, where all the wedding guests would be meeting.

"It was Colonel Mustard in the library with the candlestick," Dina whispered morbidly to Immy as they walked through the gothic black-and-white-tiled hallway, their steps echoing.

The Reading Parlor was far too large to be called cozy, and yet somehow it managed to be. A fire crackled in the blackened stone hearth and thick forest-green drapes fringed the floor-to-ceiling windows, which let in the gray afternoon light.

Every space on the wall was filled with bookshelves. Dina could have easily spent hours in there, just picking one book up after another, alternating between reading and dozing in one of the grand leather armchairs. She would have been particularly suited to the life of a Regency gentlewoman.

Of course, all thoughts of celibate bookishness fizzled away the moment she locked eyes with Scott, who was seated in one of said armchairs, lounging in a way that should have been criminal. And—goddess help her—he was wearing a shirt with the sleeves rolled up, truly the sexiest thing a man could do.

Dina inhaled sharply, desire fluttering through her. Scott smiled, as if he was so happy to see her, and she felt the blush rising in her cheeks.

Maybe it was the setting, or maybe it was her Jane Austen obsession, but this felt distinctly like that moment in the 2005 *Pride and Prejudice* movie when Darcy and Lizzy danced together for the first time, and everyone else in the room disappeared. Now, it was just her and Scott, the rest of the room falling away.

Dina blinked and looked away. She saw her mum chatting with Immy's father, while her dad was admiring a row of books that contained old naval charts. Two women were sitting in a corner of the room, Juniper on the sofa between them, snoozing away. They must be Scott's mums. This was going to be a complicated weekend.

In a flustered haze, she made her way over to Eric's parents, a rather stern pair, and greeted them politely. Mr. and Mrs. Hawthorn never gave anything away in their expressions other than mild distaste. To Dina, they seemed like physical manifestations of the English stiff upper lip.

"Mum, did you know Dina owns a coffee shop near your office? You could drop by some time," Eric said as he approached, clapping Dina on the back. She thanked him with her eyes; no one knew better than Eric what kind of people his parents were.

"Is that so?" Eric's mother, Patricia, replied, picking lint off her tweed blazer. She looked like she ought to be off hunting foxes for sport, Dina thought.

It was, frankly, a miracle that Eric had turned out as down-to-earth as he had. He had never batted an eyelid at Immy's less-than-Queen's-English accent, or her writing profession, although his parents certainly had.

Dina remembered Immy calling her crying after she'd been introduced to Eric's parents, and how they had berated her writing career, telling her that unless she changed her tune and started writing Booker Prize–winning novels, she might as well give up her writing dreams. When Immy had told them that she wrote horror novels they'd reacted even worse, spouting some nonsense about how women weren't good horror novelists because of all their hormones.

Dina couldn't remember the last Booker Prize–winner she'd read, but she devoured every single one of Immy's novels. And not just because Immy was her friend, but because they were genuinely some of the scariest novels she'd ever read. So scary that Immy had created a red-flag ranking system for Dina so that she knew how likely each book was to keep her from falling asleep that night.

The reminder of how Eric's parents had treated her friend made it difficult for Dina to resist dropping a curse on them. Just a little one. But she resisted all the same, because she was a good witch.

"I hear you've already met my best man." Eric nudged Dina, steering her away from his parents.

"News travels fast." They walked toward the hearth where Scott was bending over, adding extra kindling to the fire. Sweet saints in heaven, how had she not noticed his tattoos until this moment? The rolled-up sleeves displayed the dark lines and geometrical shapes that traced their way from his wrist to his elbow. *He looks like a lumberjack holding all that firewood*, she thought, as her brain short-circuited entirely. She didn't even realize Eric had left the two of them alone, she was so preoccupied.

"You're looking better," Scott said, chucking a final piece of wood onto the fire. Dina wasn't sure if it was the fire or the heat between her legs, but for a second she was struck dumb.

"Much better, thanks," she finally managed to choke out.

They stared at each other, neither one speaking. There was almost too much to say. The kiss she'd planted on his cheek hovered between them, unspoken. It had just been a kiss, she told herself. A kiss between friends.

"Is your speech prepared for the rehearsal dinner then?" Dina said, forcing herself to break eye contact to stare at one of the deer heads on the wall. The way that Scott was looking at her with his honey-brown eyes made it difficult to concentrate on anything. Small talk would help. Surely.

"Oh, it's ready," Scott said, grinning cheekily. "Soon everyone will know about Eric's diary entry from when he was fourteen, where he detailed the traits of his perfect girl."

"You're kidding."

"I wish I was. Don't worry, Eric gave me approval to read it. You'll be surprised: He basically describes Immy."

Dina looked over at the pair. Eric was planting a kiss on Immy's nose, then whispering something that made her tip her head back and cackle with laughter.

"Actually, that doesn't surprise me at all." She smiled.

She suspected she could talk with Scott for hours and never get bored, but she didn't get the chance, as he was pulled way into a chat with the other groomsmen. Dina felt a shiver of desire as she saw how Scott towered over the other men. Apparently she had a thing for tall men now.

A short while later, Immy and Eric were showing people where their rooms would be, with the help of a very eager steward called Martin.

"Shouldn't I be doing this, as the maid of honor? You should be relaxing before the big day," Dina said to Immy as they walked out the main entrance of Honeywell House and round to the right.

"It's really more of a small-to-medium day when you think about it. Besides, I wanted your room for the weekend to be a surprise." Immy wiggled her fingers like a movie villain.

"Why do I feel like I'm walking into a trap?" Dina muttered, as Immy pulled her toward the edge of the woods.

"I don't know what you're talking about," Immy replied.

As soon as they entered the forest, Dina felt something stirring in her magic. Normally it lay dormant within her until she needed it for a spell. But now it was thrumming in her blood, reacting to this place. The trees were tall and thick, little sunlight made it to the forest floor, and the narrow pebbled path they walked along twisted out of sight ahead of them.

"There's something here," she whispered to Immy.

"Like magic?"

"Yeah. Like, I don't know how to put it—like this is an old and powerful place. Like the land itself is breathing."

"Ooh, I'm going to write that phrase down for my next book," Immy said, pulling her phone out of her pocket.

As Immy slowed down to make her note, Dina walked on, feeling the power of this ancient wood flooding through her. She felt as if she were walking into the mouth of a great, slumbering goddess. But it didn't scare her; it wasn't meant to. It was just nature, older than history, older than bone.

The path curled around to the left, revealing a small cottage in the dappled light, dwarfed by the surrounding oaks. The lights were on inside, illuminating the ivy and wisteria vines that had twined themselves around the outer walls of the cottage. The windows were sashed in dark green wood, complete with window boxes filled with daisies. Daisies that Dina was sure shouldn't have been able to grow in such little light, but this wood seemed to play by its own rules.

"It's the Honeywell hunting lodge," Immy said, catching up with Dina.

"Looks like a fairy-tale cottage," Dina replied. "I love it."

Immy beamed. "I knew you would. Now, don't get mad at me, but that's not the end of the surprise."

Dina cautiously followed Immy to the house, where she unlocked the quaint wooden door with an almost medieval-looking key of wrought iron. *I really have fallen into a fairy tale*, Dina thought.

The inside of cottage was exactly how Dina had pictured it: a small kitchen with cream wooden cabinets, a red tiled floor, pots of fresh herbs by the window. Mint, rosemary, and sage—all good for luck and protection. Copper pots and pans hung from hooks on the wall over a bright red Aga, gently warming the cottage against the chill of the woods.

"Adorable," Dina said.

"Just you wait. Come and look over here." Immy pointed out the cream sofa that faced a hearth that was currently unlit.

Picture frames hung above the fireplace showing a mouse and its family in their underground house—delightful little watercolor paintings.

There were three doors leading off from the heart of the house, which Dina assumed must be the bedroom and bathroom and perhaps a closet? This felt like the sort of cottage perfectly sized for one person. And ideal for one witch.

"How come you aren't staying here?" Dina asked. "It feels like the perfect little honeymoon spot."

"Dina, please." Immy rolled her eyes. "This is far too cutesy for me. Our bridal suite has a stag's head above the bed and this big copper bathtub that I've already had sex in twice. There's no way I'm swapping that."

"Well, I'm not about to complain. This place is heaven."

"I knew you'd like it. And here's your room."

Immy opened the door to a beautifully cozy little room with pale pink walls and a tall wooden double bed covered in all manner of cross-stitched cushions. Dina threw herself onto the bed, squealing as she fell into the heap of pillows.

She heard a sound coming from outside, so she went to look out the window.

Her mouth went dry.

"Immy, why is Scott chopping wood behind my little house for the weekend?"

"About that . . ."

"Immy . . ."

"Don't murder me, I'm getting married."

"What have you done?"

"Well . . . technically this isn't going to be only *your* cottage for the wedding. Scott will be staying here too."

"On second thought, murder feels like the right response to this *flagrant matchmaking*."

"It's not . . . We're not . . . okay, well, maybe a little bit. The truth is—and you know I love you so please don't get mad— I thought that maybe Scott might be a good fling for you. He's exactly your type, and I thought you might want something to take your mind off everything."

"And what does Scott think of all this?" Dina realized she was trembling. Not from anger; perhaps more the intense apprehension of living in such close quarters with Scott. They would have to share a bathroom, sweet heavens.

"I think we're about to find out," Immy said, nodding toward the door.

A moment later, Scott walked in, his hair a mess, carrying a bundle of freshly chopped firewood.

"You," Scott said, his mouth turning up at the corners. "What are you doing here?" He looked over at Dina's pile of bags.

Dina glared at Immy, who was unabashedly waggling her eyebrows at them both. That woman had no shame.

"I suppose we're both staying here then," Scott said, dropping the logs down on a curved brass log holder by the hearth.

"It would appear so," Dina replied, doing her best to act cool despite feeling quite the opposite. What if he heard her snoring? These walls didn't exactly look thick.

"Well, if we're going to be roomies for the weekend, do you want to help me light the fire?" Scott offered. Dina turned toward Immy, but her friend was already out the door.

"See you both shortly for the rehearsal dinner!" Then she waved, pulling the door shut behind her.

Silence hung between them like a declaration. The way Scott

just stood there, looking at her. Like he was waiting for her to say something, to make the first move. And she wanted to. But if she did, and it didn't work out, they would ruin the wedding weekend. She was the maid of honor, he was the best man; they were going to have to be in close proximity a lot.

"We should set some ground rules, while we're here," she said.

"Okay. What do you have in mind?"

"No bathroom hogging, unless one of us wants to have a bath."

"I don't remember the last time I had a bath anyway," Scott said.

"What?" Dina was outraged. "You don't have baths? How—how?" She couldn't comprehend it.

"I don't know," Scott replied sheepishly. "I just never know what to do when I'm in them."

"I could show y—I mean, I could tell you what you need. Bubbles. Books. And candles." Heat pulsed around Dina's body. Had Scott heard her slip up?

"I'll take your word for it, Dina." Oh no, how was she meant to focus when he said her name in that soft, deep voice of his. "What's rule number two?"

"Hmm. No snoring, the walls are thin."

"I don't snore, but how can you be so sure that you aren't a snorer?" Scott grinned.

"I most definitely am not a snorer. If you hear me snoring you can come into my room and throw a pillow at my head, that's how sure I am."

"Right, so rule number two: Scott can go into Dina's room at night to throw pillows at her when she inevitably snores."

"You're twisting my words."

"You said it, not me."

What an insufferable man. She couldn't get enough of him.

"What do you need to light the fire?" she asked.

"Matches, if you can find some," Scott replied, his voice husky. He was standing closer to her than she'd realized, his warm breath on her face and neck sending shivers to all the right places.

Dina broke away first, stalking to the kitchen, hunting for matches, for anything that would stop her running across the room and flinging herself into Scott's tattooed, muscled arms.

There were no matches in the drawers, but she did find a fire striker and a piece of flint at the back of the pantry. She could just light the fire with her own magic, of course, but she wasn't about to show Scott her magic.

She walked back to the fireplace, taking a moment to admire the way his back muscles rippled under his clothes as he laid out the kindling.

She crouched down beside him, inhaling his woodsy scent, the smell of the forest on his clothes and skin. It made her head spin. It made her want to do dangerous things.

"I've actually never lit a fire like this before," she admitted, holding up the flint and the fire striker. It wasn't a lie; the hearth at home was always lit by the house itself.

Scott met her eyes, a flash of hunger.

"Let me show you." His hands enveloped hers. "All you need is a little bit of pressure. Right here."

Holding her hands inside his own, Scott struck the flint, holding them close to the kindling. A spark flew out, a small orange glow appearing in the hearth.

"Now you try," he said, releasing her hands. Dina could feel his breath on her exposed shoulder, the heat of his body surrounding hers.

She struck the flint, once, twice, until finally she managed to send a flick of fire toward the hearth, landing on dry wood.

"Good g—job." Scott said, his voice gravelly in her ear as he praised her. All she had to do was turn her face, meet his lips with hers. . . . No, fuck. What happened to being no more than friends?

Dina stood abruptly, taking a step back from Scott and the heat of the fire.

"Do you need the bathroom? I was going to have a shower. I smell like car," Dina said, speaking way too fast.

"The bathroom is all yours," he replied, smirking slightly.

Dina all but ran to her room, leaning against the door until she heard Scott close his own bedroom door behind him. She could hear him moving around in his room, even with the bathroom between them—the walls really were thin. Christ, that'd been close.

Dina unzipped her suitcase and swore. She was going to shout at the house when she got home. It had a tendency to meddle in things it did not understand—*because it was a house*—and this was evidently one of those times.

When Dina had been packing her outfits for the weekend back at her London flat, she had definitely *only* packed her comfy pajamas. She remembered putting her penguin pajama trousers and fluffy socks into the weekend bag, and yet they were nowhere to be seen. Instead, there was a skimpy pair of cream silk pajamas that she had left at her parents' house years ago. Not something she would have packed—not in a million years.

The rest of the bag was filled with her usual travel items: empty jars for collecting herbs, a bottle of anti-hangover honey, and at least two romance novels, with one final unexpected addition. A book of Rumi's love poetry. *Real subtle, House, real fucking subtle.*

Dina made a mental note to fiddle with every single picture frame so they were just a little off-center. The house would hate it, and it was no less than it deserved for being such a meddlesome matchmaker.

Dina grabbed her washbag and stripped off, wrapping herself in a towel and checking the coast was clear before locking herself in the bathroom.

There was a deep porcelain tub, and a bright copper shower head. Someone had hung a hand-tied bouquet of eucalyptus and fresh mint in the shower, and the fresh scent reinvigorated Dina as she inhaled.

She pulled her homemade shower gel out of her washbag. It was a mixture of argan oil, rosewater, clary sage, and royal jelly that left her skin feeling soft and supple.

Dina let the water flow over the back of her neck and down her back, revelling in the warmth, feeling it loosening her muscles. She was acutely aware that Scott was only one room away. Her mind strayed to the memory of his muscled forearms, covered with tattoos. She wanted to trace over them with her fingers. His mischievous grin when he'd joked about coming into her room at night, the way he had smelled like wood and moss and sweat. Her hand found its way between her legs. Maybe she just needed to get this out of her system.

Dina rested her head back against the cool tile, wondering what it might be like if Scott came into the bathroom now. Would he pull back the curtain, see her naked?

Would he peel off his clothes, revealing the hard, packed muscle underneath? She knew instinctively that he wouldn't be clean-shaven. His chest would be covered in curls of dark brown hair that she wanted to knot her fingers in.

He'd take off his glasses, placing them ever so gently beside the sink. He'd climb into the shower, the water cascading down his skin. Dina's fingers drew circles around her clit, finding a rhythm that made her body flush. She bit back a moan as the pleasure intensified.

What would Scott do, once he was in the shower with her? She knew what she would do. She'd wrap her legs around him.

He'd open her up and she'd be ready for him. So ready. His cock would be so hard he'd be desperate to be inside her. He'd push his tip inside, then plunge deep.

Dina's hand moved faster, and she pushed her fingers inside her. Her mind was full of him. In her fantasy, Scott was inside her while her fingers were clawing his back. As he thrust inside her, he planted kisses along her neck, sucked at her bottom lip.

The orgasm washed over her, sweet and delicious. She couldn't help herself, and a whimper escaped her lips as she came. She sighed deeply.

Dina finished her shower and spent some time combing through her hair while it was still damp, coiling argan oil and hair mousse through her curls.

She would do her makeup in her room, once she'd cooled down and could think straight. She felt a sudden need to look stunning tonight. She wanted to feel Scott's eyes on her from across the room, stripping her naked with his stare.

Dina slipped out of the bathroom and nearly walked directly into Scott. Well, fuck. He was shirtless. She definitely hadn't been wrong about his body. His wasn't the chest of a man who spent endless hours in the gym or kept to a strict diet. Scott's muscles were heavy, densely packed. His shoulders were broad and rounded with thick cords of muscle. He looked like some kind of Scottish war hero or Greek god.

Dina was definitely staring and she didn't give a fuck. She had been right about the hair too. A mass of dark brown—almost black—hair peppered his chest and trailed down his stomach to the V-shape of his hips. He was wearing navy suit trousers and dress shoes, already half dressed for the rehearsal dinner. She wanted, if she was honest with herself, to get on her knees and take him in her mouth. Dina had never felt like that before, and certainly never with a man.

She'd always found it easy to love a woman's body, with its curves and dimples and soft places made for kissing. With men it was always trickier; she rarely liked their personalities enough to even see them without their clothes on. But Scott was different, more vulnerable and attentive, plus Dina just had a feeling that he would know his way around her body, that he could make her come again and again. Clearly, the orgasm in the shower had done nothing to alleviate the heat she felt between them.

"Sorry, I thought you were done. I left my deodorant in there, but I can come back." He said, his eyes darkening as he took in Dina, skin still damp, wrapped in a towel. She had just come thinking about him in the shower and was sure it was written all over her face.

"No, no. I'm done, bathroom's all yours." She smiled shyly and dripped her way to her room. She was sure she could feel Scott's eyes following her there. Dina closed herself in her bedroom and fell back on the bed, not caring that she was going to make the sheets damp.

Had that just happened?

Part of her, a big fucking part, wanted to open the door and jump on Scott right now. But she'd made a promise to herself. No romance. No dating. Not while the hex was still in her life. She'd just have to be on her best behavior around Scott. After all, how hard could it be not to sleep with someone?

Chapter 11

Scott was trying very, very hard not to think about sleeping with Dina. And he was failing, miserably. Had he left his room to go to the bathroom shirtless on purpose? Well, that was beside the point. Dina's reaction, the way she'd stilled, her eyes mapping his body, drinking him in. It had given him a hard-on that had been reluctant to go down even after a quarter of an hour.

The bathroom still smelled like her soap, even with the window open and the steam spilling out. Something fresh and sweet, but earthy too. If she'd still been here he might have pulled her to him. He was sure if he bent down to tease her hair away from her collarbone he would catch that scent on her skin.

Here I go again, thinking about sniffing her collarbones, he thought. *Congrats, how very Hannibal Lecter of you Scott.*

Try as he might, he still couldn't get over their interaction by the fire. The way her hand had felt so small and delicate in his. He'd nearly slipped up, nearly called her a good girl. He wanted to praise her, ideally with his mouth between her thighs. All Scott could think about was saying it, whispering it in Dina's ear as she took him inside her. Christ, how was he meant to get through this evening?

Even if he wanted to, he wouldn't ask her out again. They had agreed to be friends for the weekend. Just friends. Friends who wanted to rip each other's clothes off with their teeth.

Scott stared at himself in the mirror, contemplated trimming his beard again even though he had done so only this morning. Hairiness appeared to be in his genes. As he dressed, he remembered Dina's transfixed expression, pupils dilated, as she'd seen him shirtless. She hadn't seemed disgusted by his chest hair, not as other women he'd slept with had been. He imagined Dina tangling her fingers in his dark curls and felt heat bloom inside him.

Sucking in a breath and steeling himself for the evening ahead, Scott opened the bathroom door.

"Are you wearing cologne?" Dina asked, though he couldn't see her, as she was around the corner in the kitchen area.

"I am. Is it too much?" Maybe she had a sensitive nose.

Dina ducked her head around the corner. "No. I like it." She smiled, and he couldn't help but imagine what her ruby-red lips would look like wrapped around his cock. *Get it together, Scott, you have to spend a whole evening with her.*

"What do you think?" Dina said, twirling around before the fireplace. Teasing him. Driving him insane. She was wearing a navy velvet dress that clung to her in all the right places, emphasizing her full hips and ass. The dress was artfully styled to slip off her shoulders, and her collarbones seemed to be glimmering in the firelight.

You look perfect, he wanted to say. *No one in the history of the world has ever looked so good in a dress. Please take it off.* But Scott didn't say any of those things.

"You look beautiful, Dina," he said, his voice coming out hoarse. She stopped still, taking him in, then stepped closer. He couldn't help himself; he reached out and tucked a stray curl behind her ear. For a moment, her lips parted and her head tipped up toward him, as if she were contemplating kissing him. But then she stepped back, putting distance between them.

"We should go, or we'll be late," she said quietly. Scott nodded and walked to the front door. Disappointment surged through him. *Friends don't kiss*, he reminded himself. The air around them felt full, brimming with unsaid words and unspent touches.

Chapter 12

Martin, the all-purpose butler and weekend chaperone, directed them to the aptly named Green Room, where dinner would be eaten. Dina glanced up at Scott, and found him studying her with a guarded expression. Laughter from the room ahead called their attention away.

The Green Room had been lavishly decorated for the dinner, and Dina was reminded again just how rich Eric and his family were. The huge vaulted room was flooded in the warm glow of tens, if not hundreds, of candles—not a single one of the electrical lights was switched on.

Candlesticks of polished brass lined the center of the long table. Thick, bone-white pillar candles glowed in copper sconces on the walls. A chandelier of twinkling crystal scattered rivulets of light across the room, like light refracted through a diamond.

Almost immediately, Dina and Scott were pulled apart, as Dina's parents wanted her to introduce them to more people and Scott was roped into helping Eric's great-aunt find her seat.

"So, how's the Hunting Lodge treating you?" Immy said, sidling up to Dina. "Has the Hunting Lodge made you blush yet?"

"The *Hunting Lodge* has been a perfect gentleman," Dina replied through gritted teeth.

"Well, he can't keep his eyes off you, that's for sure," Rosemary added, joining them. She was wearing a beautiful polka-dotted dress that flared out below the waist.

Dina looked across the room and locked eyes with Scott, who was currently surrounded by a gaggle of aunts, standing at least a head taller than all of them. One of them had reached up to squeeze his bicep and Dina felt a flare in the pit of her stomach.

"We're just friends," she said.

"I wish I had a friend who looked at me like he wants to rip my clothes off." Rosemary grinned.

Dina felt a wave of desire wash over her and longed to throw her arms around Scott's broad shoulders. His voice when he'd praised her earlier by the fire had just about sent her off the edge. She wanted him. Badly. Her pussy was slick with it, but she tried to push her focus away, at least for tonight.

"For tomorrow night . . ." Rosemary began, leaning in conspiratorially. "What time should we start?" Rosemary hadn't been to one of their Halloween rituals since she'd lived in England, and Dina had added a few more magical components to it over the years.

"We'll escape just before midnight to make sure the moon is still full. Immy, you said my mum arranged this all with Honeywell House. Will they have a bonfire for us?"

"Yeah, in the north field. I told Martin we were going to be dancing around naked and he appeared visibly unwell," Immy cackled.

They took a turn about the room, smiling at guests, like three female leads in a Jane Austen novel. A lot more of Immy and Eric's friends had turned up later in the afternoon, and the room was alive and buzzing. A few of Immy and Rosemary's horror novelist friends waved them over.

"We need your opinions on something," Ash said, sipping

from a cocktail. "Deep sea horror. What's the scariest thing you can think of?"

Dina, being a thalassophobe, shuddered at the thought.

"The Mariana Trench," Immy said. "Those cliff edges inside the water where it's darkness all the way down. So. Much. Potential."

"Seconded," said Jeremy, an editor at a film magazine.

"I've read that there's a church in Austria that's completely abandoned, and over the years it's been covered with water so now it's at the bottom of a lake, and you can only find it if you go looking," Dina told the group.

"I've never heard of it. You're sure this is real?" Rosemary said, pulling out her phone. "Oh my god, Dina's right. It's the fucking sunken place. Okay, Dina wins because that is absolute nightmare fuel."

"What's nightmare fuel?" Eric said, wrapping his arms around Immy and planting a kiss on the top of her head.

"Dina is regaling us with stories about creepy underwater churches," Immy replied, leaning back into Eric's hug.

"I would expect nothing less." Eric grinned. "But I've been told by Martin, who seems very stressed, that we all need to take our seats for dinner."

Dina glanced down at the place cards arranged on the table. Immy had seated Dina next to her and Rosemary, and directly opposite Scott. No surprises there. Eric was sitting beside Scott, and opposite his wife-to-be.

Dina was about to sit down when a deep voice behind her rumbled, "Please, allow me."

Scott was standing behind her, close enough that she could smell his moss and sea salt cologne and feel his breath on the back of her neck.

"A consummate gentleman," she joked. "I guess chivalry isn't dead." She could have sworn his pupils dilated as she turned and looked up, feeling the heat of him so close to her.

Scott pulled out the chair, and when Dina sat down, he slid her closer to the table. As he did so, he bent close.

"That dress really suits you," he said, low enough that only she would hear.

In his mouth, the compliment sounded positively filthy.

Scott took his seat and she felt his eyes on her, hungry. His hair, curling at the ends, fell across his face in the most flattering way. Dina wanted to run her fingers through it. She kept glancing his way all through the first two courses.

"What do you do then, Scott?" Dina's mother launched into conversation with all the subtlety of a nuclear missile. Of course, trust her mum to be asking about his job, just to make sure he was adequate material. Dina's father met her eyes over her mother's head, and he smiled apologetically.

"I'm a curator at the British Museum."

"And what do you curate?" Nour pressed him. Thankfully, Scott took it in his stride.

"Well, at the moment I'm working on an exhibition about symbols of protection from around the world—symbols used by ancient mystics. Did you know that mistletoe was used by ancient Celts to protect their livestock? It's fascinating."

"Always useful if you want to snog a sheep too," laughed Eric.

"Oh, Nour knows all about symbols of protection," Dina's father said, as Nour nodded sagely.

"I noticed that, actually. You had the hand of Fatima on your front door."

Nour beamed. "Well, you can never be too careful. Dina has lots of them in her very successful café too, as you know," she continued, purposefully turning the conversation to her daughter. Trust her mother to make sure all potential suitors knew how successful she was.

Is that what Scott was to her then—a potential suitor? Damn those tea leaves and their accurate predictions.

"How did you two meet, if you don't mind my asking?" Scott said to Dina's parents. He was handling their matchmaking like a pro, and somehow that made her like him even more.

"We were both in the same halls at university, but I was too shy to talk to her." Dina's father looked at his wife. "But I'd seen her around and would smile at her whenever I got up the courage. We'd never spoken though. Then, this one time, I was at the library searching for a book. I was walking through the stacks, looking for the last copy of this text on impressionist art, when I finally found the shelf. Only, the book wasn't there. So I was looking around and I saw her"—Robert took Nour's hand and planted a kiss there—"and she was sitting in a nearby cubbyhole with—you guessed it—the book."

"Did you speak to her then?" Scott asked.

"I had to. She was so much lovelier up close, I must have seemed like a right buffoon trying to get my words out."

"It was very endearing." Nour smiled, patting her husband's hand.

"We got chatting, and we were there for hours."

"The librarian had to kick us out because they were closing," Nour added.

"Then we sat on a bench outside, even though it was November and freezing. And then she told me to give her my hands."

"That's so romantic, Nour," Immy sighed.

Dina felt her gaze straying to Scott, who was staring down at the table, studiously avoiding eye contact. As if he were arguing with himself about something.

Hearing her parents' perfect love story jarred harshly with

her own tragic love life. Dina suddenly felt short of breath. The air in the room was too close, it moved through her lungs like glue, and the warmth from the candles and people around her pressed in.

"Excuse me," Dina muttered, pushing out her chair. Rosemary reached out to squeeze Dina's hand as she stood.

"You okay?" she whispered.

"I'm good. Just need a minute."

As soon as she stepped out of the Green Room, the chill of the drafty hallway raised goosebumps on her skin. But she needed more. She needed to see the sky overhead. She needed proper fresh air.

Dina marched down the hall and slunk through the heavy front doors of Honeywell House. The driveway and open fields unfolded before her, and she exhaled deeply.

The moonlight sunk into her skin, refreshing her. The moon looked full, but it wasn't quite yet. Most people would find it hard to tell the difference—visually it was barely noticeable. But Dina could feel it in her bones. As if her magic was a vibration, and the moon was a tuning fork. The pitch wasn't quite there, but it would be tomorrow night. For Samhain. For the full moon ritual. She longed for it, for the sense of power it imbued in her.

Right now, memories of the hex rose unbidden. Rory in the hospital, Eliza in the hospital. All these people she'd cared for. All of them hurt. But if she was careful, Scott would be fine. Even if she did kiss him, that didn't mean anything. She could kiss someone without developing feelings, right? Maybe just a weekend fling? Just to get it out of her system.

But Scott didn't feel like the sort of man who went in for flings or one-night stands. He had commitment written all over him. It was stitched into the elbow patches on his blazers and sweaters, and in the crookedness of his smile, and in the way he'd made sure she got home safe when she'd hit her head. She couldn't stop her thoughts from straying to throwing herself at him.

It had been a while since she'd been with a man in bed. In Dina's experience, women were much better at giving orgasms, and not nearly as greedy or competitive about it.

But then again, maybe she'd just picked the wrong kind of men in the past. She found herself picturing Scott again, the tattoos that wound their way up his arms and across his chest. The fresh scent of his cologne. She craved the feeling of him inside her, deep, thrusting, throbbing. This breath of fresh air wasn't clearing her head as much as she'd hoped it would.

"Benti, where did you go?" Her mum stepped through the front door and joined her in the darkness. "They're just clearing away dessert." She paused. "I was worried about you."

"I'm okay, Mama."

Nour huffed.

"I gave birth to you, you can't lie to me." Her mother always had an uncanny way of guessing Dina's thoughts. "What's wrong?"

"Do you ever wonder what our lives might have been like if we weren't witches? Maybe they would have been simpler, in a way. It would be harder for us to hurt people."

Her mother fixed her with a curious look, circling around so that she was standing behind Dina.

"May I?" she asked. Dina nodded. Her mother reached her arms around Dina and placed her palms on Dina's eyes so that the tips of her middle fingers were touching the center of Dina's forehead. Dina closed her eyes and felt the sudden change as her mother's spell came to life around her.

She felt the baking sun on her skin. Her feet sank into the soft earth that she knew instinctively would be a deep orange hue. The distant sound of farm animals carried on the breeze and, closer by, the hum of the wind sifting through the broad bean stalks.

Dina knew where she was. Her mother's family's farm, in rural Khemisset. Morocco. Her mother had grown up there; *this* was where her roots were. Where Dina's were too.

"We've had our magic for as long as we have had our land," her mother said. "It goes beyond spells and charms and evocations. It is an extension of our souls. We cannot imagine ourselves without it, because then we would not be ourselves."

The spell dissolved around her, and Dina inhaled the grassy scent of the English countryside once again as her mother uncovered her eyes.

"I used to think like you did," Nour said, stroking her daughter's face. "Wouldn't it be better for everyone if I couldn't spit out a curse each time I was angry? Or if I didn't scare away men when they saw what I could do? We are strong women, benti, as well as witches. And that will scare some people, sure, but the ones that matter to us, the ones we love most, they will love all facets of us—the magic will not frighten them away."

Dina wanted to tell her mum so badly about the hex just then. She felt her mouth opening, the words ready to spill out, but then the front door swung open. It was Martin.

"I've been asked to let you both know that the party will now be retiring to the Western Parlor," he said shortly, then vanished back inside.

"Are you ready to go in?" her mother asked.

"Yes, I'll be okay."

"I know it's a lot, when you find someone like that it . . . feels scary. Like all your walls are collapsing."

"Mama, this isn't about Scott," Dina replied. She was almost sure she was telling the truth.

"Of course it isn't." Nour threw Dina a wink over her shoulder then strutted back inside.

Dina took a moment more outside in the moonlight until her heart settled back into a calm rhythm. She looked up at the moon. "This weekend isn't about me, or my baggage. It's about Immy and Eric."

Dina knew that this apprehension in her gut would melt away the moment she fell into conversation with her best friends, so she stopped dallying and stepped into the warmth of the house.

She followed the sound of laughter and clinking glasses to what she presumed must be the Western Parlor. The wedding group had thinned significantly. Eric's parents, and Scott's mums—along with a sleepy Juniper who had snored through the entire three-course meal—seemed to have taken their leave for the evening.

Immy's writer friends were curled up beside a tall mahogany bookcase, and Dina heard snippets of their conversation, the words "Lovecraft" and "massive racist" being the more notable ones.

She smiled over at Rosemary but decided to leave them to it. Immy and Eric were sitting beside each other in front of a grand fireplace. Immy had kicked off her high heels and was toasting her feet beside the glowing hearth.

"Dina, come sit here!" Immy squeaked, beckoning her over. Scott, who was sitting on another sofa in conversation with Eric, looked in her direction, his gaze roving up and down. Dina offered him a smile and plonked herself down beside him, kicking off her heels.

"Mulled wine? Or is it too soon?" Scott asked, proffering a steaming jug scented with clove and other delicious spices. He'd taken off his suit jacket and uncuffed his wrists, offering a peek of the tattoos underneath. It was alarmingly sexy.

She flushed with embarrassment, remembering the way she'd fallen asleep in his arms.

"There are soft drinks too, or tea?" Scott offered.

"She's just being difficult. Dina loves mulled wine," Immy remarked.

"Fine, I'll have some. But only because the bride says so."

Chuckling, Scott poured from the jug and handed Dina an extravagant-looking crystal goblet of mulled wine, complete with cinnamon stick and floating star anise.

"You know," Dina began, struck by a sudden flirtatiousness that had absolutely nothing to do with Scott's sexy forearms, "they say that star anise is an aphrodisiac."

Eric tipped his head back and let out a belly laugh.

"That's not a problem for our man Scott. What was the nickname those ladies at the rowing club gave you? The full eight?"

"What does that mean?" Immy asked. Scott was rolling his eyes so far that Dina thought they would fall into the back of his head.

"In rowing, the eight is the biggest boat," Eric explained. "And you have to remember we wore these tiny little Lycra all-in-ones that didn't exactly leave anything to the imagination. So Scott became rather famous—or should I say infamous—for his, um, pronounced package."

Dina squirmed involuntarily in her seat as desire lit her on fire.

"The full eight, huh," she said, surprised at the huskiness in her voice.

Scott angled his face toward hers, and it sent a new ripple of heat over her skin.

"Eric is being hyperbolic."

"No, I am being complimentary," Eric countered, giving his best man a loaded look. There was some strong wingman action going on tonight, Dina thought to herself.

"And did you get to wear this tiny little Lycra thing too?" Immy asked her fiancé.

"I sure did." Dina saw the want in her friend's glance as the pair practically eye-fucked each other.

"Actually," Eric cleared his throat, "I think we're going to try and get an early night. Big day tomorrow, and all that." They both stood up abruptly.

"Don't they say something about the bride and groom being apart for the wedding night?" Scott teased.

"Tradition, schmadition. The wedding isn't even tomorrow." Immy laughed, before Eric practically carried her out of the room. Dina's heart felt light, seeing Immy this happy.

"Are you going to bed too?" Dina asked Scott. She suddenly became aware that they were alone in the parlor. Immy's writer friends must have trailed off to bed while they were chatting.

The fire crackled merrily in the hearth, the scent of burning cedar warming the air.

"I won't if you won't," Scott all but growled, a challenge clear in his voice.

The star anise was clearly getting to her because she was just about ready to jump Scott's bones.

She exhaled slowly. If she met Scott's gaze, she knew she would be defeated by it.

"Let me read your palm," Dina said, her voice hoarse.

Ever so slowly, she shuffled closer to him on the sofa, turning so she faced him. Her body was hot and slick and ready, and it didn't help that she was imagining what Scott's head would look like buried between her thighs, his rough, calloused hands gripping her ass.

Scott's hair was jet black in the firelight. He rested the back of his palm on her thigh, and that touch alone was enough to send another surge of desire through her. Dina felt the heat of his hand through the velvet of her dress. Only a few inches to the right, and a little higher, and she'd be done for. What would that hand feel like caressing her clit, plunging into her now soaked pussy? Dina forced the thought away. If she was actually going to perform an accurate reading, she couldn't let her own desire get in the way.

She delicately pressed the tips of her fingers, still cold from being outside, against Scott's fingertips, opening up his hand.

"Your fingers are cold," he said. He lifted her hand up to his mouth and blew gently on them, his breath warming her. Dina sucked in a trembling breath.

"There, now you can start," he said. This man was going to be her undoing.

"You see this line here?" she said, as she stroked a finger across the center of Scott's palm and down to the sensitive part of his wrist. She felt goosebumps rise on his skin as he shivered imperceptibly at her touch. "This is your life line. See how long it is, going all the way down to your wrist?"

Scott nodded, leaning in closer. "What does that mean?"

"It's a good sign. It means you'll live a long life."

"I guess I'll go ahead and book that skydiving trip then," he joked, making Dina roll her eyes. He tipped his head to the side and laughed, the corners of his eyes creasing, making her stomach tumble. She felt positively giddy.

Dina drew a finger along the line that cut horizontally through the center of Scott's palm. She could feel the thrum of his pulse.

"And that one?" he asked, his head bending closer to Dina's. She couldn't help herself; she inhaled the scent of his cologne again.

"This is your heart line. It's . . . it's deep."

"What does it mean if it's deep, Dina?" He growled her name.

"You'll have one great love in your life. You'll . . . be with them for a long time," she whispered.

Dina felt part of herself deflating as she read Scott's palm and thought of the woman who might be the love of this man's life.

She wondered if she would treat him like he deserved to be treated, with kindness and passion. At the same time, she mourned her own love life, knowing that because of the curse she could never be this person for him.

But then Scott reached his hand up to cup Dina's chin, bringing her face up toward his. His eyes were a bottomless brown flecked with gold, and she could see the bump along his nose where he must have broken it. Their breath mingled.

Scott's gaze flicked to her mouth, and she found herself biting her lip. Half an inch more, and their lips would meet. Maybe it didn't matter that he could never love her.

"Ahem." Someone obnoxiously cleared their throat nearby. Dina looked up, just about ready to throw a hex at whoever had dared to interrupt this moment. Martin, the steward of Honeywell House, stood in the doorway, holding a tray of half-empty glasses. Unfortunately, Immy would be very angry at her if she hexed the butler two nights before the wedding.

"I was just coming in to clear away the glasses," Martin said peevishly. Dina screamed internally as Scott pulled away.

"That's fine, Martin," he said, suddenly composed. Dina did not feel composed. She had nearly kissed him, and what would it have meant to her? It would have been more than a kiss, she knew. She wasn't in the business of lying to herself. But she couldn't go down that road. After all, she'd be the one that got hurt in the end.

"We were just going back to the cottage anyway," Scott said, reaching out for Dina's hand. She wanted to go with him, she wanted to hold his hand. Desperately. But she pulled away, standing, smoothing out the crumples in her dress.

"I think I'm going to go for a quick walk, actually, just to clear my head."

A weight pressed down on her chest. Before Scott could say anything, Dina ducked past Martin and out of the room.

She knew the night air wouldn't make her feel any better. She just needed to get away from Scott, and the feeling in her gut when she was near him. Dina's heart pounded in her chest as she fled into the woods. The weight of the forest settled over her like earth over long-buried bones.

"Please don't let me fall in love with him," she whispered to the woods—half spell, half prayer. But the forest, if it was listening, didn't answer her.

Chapter 13

Scott felt Dina's heart beating against his chest, and the slow rise and fall of her breath. Her mountain of curls spilled over the pillow, tickling him—he didn't care. She had wriggled herself closer until she was essentially on top of him, her thigh and arm thrown over him, her face tucked into the curve of his shoulder. When Scott's alarm rang and he woke to find himself alone in a cold bed, he groaned. Dina was invading his dreams now—how was he ever going to find peace again now this woman was in his life?

He thought about last night. What had happened? They definitely would have kissed if it hadn't been for Martin's interruption. But then Dina had run off into the woods, and he hadn't heard her enter the cottage until an hour or so later, deep into the quiet hours of the night.

What had changed in that split second? The way she had been with him, that look she had given him as she'd read his palm, as if she wanted to climb into his lap. He'd barely been able to keep his hands off her. It would have been so easy to pull her to him, to slip his hand under the folds of her dress, tugging aside whatever lacy thing she had on underneath. She would have felt soft and warm against him, he was sure of it. So what had changed?

Scott dressed with his mind in a haze, running his fingers through the knots in his hair, contemplating tying it up into a bun and then wondering what Dina's opinions on man buns were.

He threw on a white T-shirt and knitted cream jumper, jeans, and boots. Immy and Eric had planned a day full of activities for the wedding party, starting with a scavenger hunt in the main house later that morning and some kind of mysterious outdoor activity that afternoon.

Scott walked out into the main living area of the cottage. It smelled like butter and cinnamon and coffee—sweet, sweet coffee. The hearth wasn't lit, yet the cottage was toasty warm. The pale morning light filtered in through the windows, and outside the trees were alive with birdsong. There was clattering coming from the kitchen.

Scott turned the corner to see Dina muttering to herself, bending over something on the counter that was obscured from his view. He leaned against the wall, arms folded. He could watch her bending over like that all day. He felt himself growing hard in his jeans.

"Oh, you're awake!" Dina squealed as she turned around. She was wearing a frilly apron and her face was smudged with flour. "I thought I had at least five more minutes before you came out."

"Five more minutes for what?"

The sweet frown on her forehead and the way she was obscuring what was behind her made him crack a smile. She was just so damn cute. Dina grinned and patted one of the high chairs by the kitchen counter as she walked over to the stove.

He looked down. A mug of steaming coffee had appeared before him, and he wasn't sure how it had got there. He must be more tired than he thought.

"This is my way of saying sorry for last night. I just . . . wasn't feeling myself. And when I feel like that, I like to bake. It helps clear my head," Dina said, setting down two plates in front of them.

It looked mouth-wateringly good.

"Dina, these look amazing. I've never seen pancakes like this before."

"They're called baghrir. Kind of halfway between a crumpet and a crepe. And I also made some chocolate rye bread and strawberry jam, from scratch, because I was feeling indecisive." That would explain the delicious berry scent in the air then.

"Thank you," he said, reaching out to rub flour off the tip of her nose. She went still as he touched her, his hand moving and cupping her cheek.

"No one has ever made breakfast for me before, Dina," Scott said.

His heart thrummed dangerously in his chest, so loud he was sure she could hear it. Almost imperceptibly, she pressed her cheek into his palm, resting her face in his hand. He could have stayed like that forever.

"You have to add butter and honey to the baghrir, it's the best way to eat it," Dina said, breaking Scott's gaze. The way she smiled at him sent a jolt straight to his heart.

"Aye aye, Captain." Scott winked, reaching out for the butter. "Now I know you bake like this, I'll be in that café every morning."

Dina sat beside Scott, rolling her baghrir and eating it with coffee. Scott tried to focus on his breakfast, but he couldn't. He could barely eat, even though every mouthful was utterly delicious.

"I'minheffen," he muttered with a mouth full of baghrir. "Seriously, this might be the best breakfast I've ever had."

He'd forgotten how it felt, being with someone like this—the giddy feeling in his chest. He couldn't help but imagine what it would be like to spend more mornings with Dina, waking up in their bed, eating breakfast together in a sunny kitchen before he pulled her onto his lap. Imagining a future was a dangerous thing, but for a short time, Scott let himself revel in the idea of it.

"Are you heading to the house this morning?" he asked.

"Eventually. But I need to finish baking the cinnamon rolls for tomorrow. One of my many maid-of-honor duties." She grinned, pointing at the trays of cinnamon rolls that were waiting their turn in the oven.

"Looks like you've done most of the hard work already, but I'm happy to help with whatever's left." Scott pulled off his jumper, revealing his tattooed arms. Dina swallowed audibly.

"You want to help?" She tilted her head to look at him appraisingly.

"If you'll let me."

She didn't need asking twice. She hurried around the kitchen, bossing Scott around for the next twenty minutes. He adored every second of it, seeing Dina in her element.

"No, here, like this," she said, taking hold of his wrist and showing him the correct way to mix the icing so that he didn't whip too much air into it. Her fingertips rested on his forearms and he wished she would trail them higher.

When Dina bent over to take the final tray of baked cinnamon buns out of the oven, he almost groaned aloud. Her top had ridden up, displaying two dimples at the base of her back. He wanted to lick them.

When she placed the tray down on the counter and glanced over at him, he was sure the hunger was written all over his face. At some point in the last hour—really, since he'd woken up and discovered Dina had made him breakfast—his brain had stopped working. All he wanted was Dina.

He watched her in silence as she drizzled the icing glaze over the buns. The sugary, buttery scent wafted through the air, and Scott wondered if Dina would taste like that too. Like sweetness and spice.

"Do you want to try some icing?" she asked softly.

Scott moved closer to her, closer than he needed to be. Instead of taking a spoon, Dina ran her finger through the leftover icing in the bowl and held it up.

Scott took her finger in his mouth, licking firmly with his tongue. She tasted like sweet lemon and vanilla. All the while, Scott held Dina's gaze, saw the same fire he felt stoked in her too.

Ever so slowly, she pulled her finger back from the warmth of his mouth.

"You taste good," he said. He couldn't wait another moment.

Scott ran his hand through Dina's hair, coming to rest at the back of her neck, his other arm moving around her waist. Pulling her closer. They were chest to chest now; he could feel the heat of her breath on his mouth.

Scott bent down, inches away from her mouth. A question.

"We said just friends," Dina whispered.

Just friends. And he'd gone and messed it up by trying to kiss her. Scott pulled away, his arms falling to his sides.

"You're right. I'm sorry. Just friends," he said, trying to keep the disappointment out of his voice.

Dina didn't step away and looked very much like she was fighting some kind of internal battle. *Give in*, he thought, *let me kiss you.* But she had said "just friends," and Scott would respect Dina's wishes. But that didn't mean he wouldn't be thinking about this for a long time.

Chapter 14

"Welcome to the first of today's activities!" Eric cheered. The entire wedding party was standing in the Little Parlor, ironically named for its size. Three ivy-clad windows looked out over the main drive up to Honeywell House, bathing the room in autumn sunshine.

"This morning you'll all be taking part in a scavenger hunt around the house."

Dina couldn't help but grin as she heard the words "scavenger hunt." Immy grinned back at her, knowing just how intense Dina's competitive streak was.

"Immy and I have written a list of strange items that we've spotted around the house. Now, there are more than thirty items on here, and you don't need to find them all. Each person needs to bring only three items from this list to us in order to win a prize. Come and get your lists. You have an hour!" Eric clapped his hands, and started the timer.

Dina glanced over at Scott, who had carefully situated himself on the other side of the room to her. He looked equally gleeful at the prospect of the hunt; somehow it didn't surprise her that he had a competitive streak too.

"Every woman for herself?" Rosemary chuckled beside her.

"I'll see you at the finish," Dina replied, as the two of them split up.

Dina took a moment to go through the list before she made any rash decisions. It was everyone for themselves, though she noticed both her parents and Scott's had gone off in pairs. Cheaters.

The list was a veritable cabinet of curiosities. Among the objects was a taxidermised squirrel, a small still-life painting of an eighteenth-century dildo surrounded by flowers, a lover's eye ring, a preserved blue butterfly, a jar of apricot jam that had gone out of date in 1904, and an edition of *Sense and Sensibility* that apparently had a love letter scrawled on the inside cover.

Dina decided to look for the jam jar first—she knew her way around a kitchen pantry. Taking the servant's staircase down, she strode through the open kitchens of Honeywell House until she found a small closet door labeled "Pantry." The scent of dust and old preserves hit her nose. Whoever was cooking the meals for the wedding guests must have installed a more modern pantry on the premises because this one certainly didn't see a lot of use.

She found the jam jar easily enough, even without needing to use a searching charm. She'd avoid using magic here if she could; Dina believed in winning fair and square.

She wondered which items Scott had gone in search of; would he hunt down the still life with the dildo perhaps? Or the lover's eye ring? Of course her mind went straight to the gutter when thinking about Scott. She needed to get a grip.

She hadn't been thinking this morning, not at all. Not when she'd let him suck icing off her finger, and definitely not when she'd nearly pressed her lips to his.

At this point, it didn't feel like a matter of *if* she was going to give in to her craving for Scott, but *when*.

The hunt for the blue butterfly was a little trickier. Looking at a map of the sprawling estate grounds, Dina guessed that she might find it in the blue room. No luck. And guessing from the other guests she spotted in there, she wasn't the only one after the butterfly. She needed to up her game.

If she was a man of the landed gentry in the 1800s, where would she put a prized butterfly specimen? Somewhere she could look at it. Somewhere like . . . a study. Dina walked as quickly as she could through the hallways, up the main staircase with its twisting oak banisters and gothic paintings, and into the Master's Study. It was a dark room, a room made for smoking cigars and contemplating one's life by firelight.

And there it was, in pride of place above the hearth. She nabbed the frame off the wall and set off for the library, because where else would the copy of *Sense and Sensibility* be?

The library was unexpectedly on the top floor of the house. Clearly, whoever had lived here once had wanted a view of the grounds as they sat in the window and whiled away an afternoon reading. It was the library of Dina's dreams. Floor-to-ceiling mahogany bookshelves lined the walls, with a sliding ladder to help reach the highest shelves. A weathered carpet in the center of the room muffled her footsteps. Cozy-looking armchairs sat under tall reading lamps and there was a display case of yellowing maps of the shire.

She was just browsing the shelves, searching for Austen, when the door creaked open. Scott stood in the hallway, surprise lighting his face.

The two of them, alone again.

"What are you doing here?" he said, stalking into the room.

"Same as you, I expect."

"Found it yet?"

She narrowed her eyes at him. "Not yet."

"Well then." He grinned and raced toward the nearest shelf. Oh, it was *on*.

Dina dashed to the shelf nearest to her, running her fingers along the spines. No Austen. The books weren't even stored alphabetically, nor by color. It's as if they'd been arranged by . . . genre. Scott had clearly got the same idea as her, as they rushed to the same part of the library where she'd noticed a romance novel before.

There it was—a non-descript green leather book with fine gold printing on the spine. *Sense and Sensibility.* Dina was aware that Scott was looming over her as they both reached out at the same time to grab the book. They tugged, but the book didn't move.

Instead, they heard a whirring, followed by a thunk. The entire bookcase creaked open, revealing a hidden door.

"No fucking way," Dina whispered. Immy and Eric had definitely known about this when they'd added it to the list. She looked up at Scott, who looked just as surprised as her. "We have to go in there."

"After you."

Dina stepped cautiously into the passageway, ducking out of the way of some of the more gnarly-looking cobwebs, aware that Scott was close behind her. She reached behind her and took his hand, tugging him onward. She couldn't shake the electric jolt that coursed through her as their hands touched.

"What do you think is down here?" Dina said. The narrow passage twisted ahead of them, lit only by the lights from the library at their back.

"Hopefully something with a high ceiling," Scott muttered behind her.

"You're claustrophobic?"

"A little. But I'm fine with you," he replied, a softness in his voice that struck her straight in the heart. This man was going to ruin her.

They walked on a little further, but with a final corner the passage opened up into a small room. Though perhaps "cupboard" was the better word to describe its size. Cut into the wall was a sliver of window with a stained-glass design depicting two lovers in each other's arms. Dina wondered if Immy had intended for her to find the room all along.

"It's a lovers' nook," Scott said, wonder in his voice. "They were relatively common in the late 1700s, built for unchaperoned lovers to find a moment to themselves. I've never actually been in one though."

"Well, it's certainly not made for more than two people." Dina laughed, swallowing her nerves. Here they were again, in startlingly close proximity. Maybe it was a sign from the universe, as her mother had suggested. Perhaps the time for denial was over.

She was acutely aware that Scott still held her hand and was absentmindedly drawing circles in her palm with his thumb.

"We're just friends," she whispered.

"Yes."

Dina sucked in a breath. "But if we weren't just friends, what would you do?"

Scott stilled and stepped closer so that his chest was flush with Dina's back.

"If we weren't just friends . . ." he said slowly, "I would do this."

He bent down and pressed a single kiss on the curve of her neck, before trailing his lips up to the shell of her ear. A shiver rippled through her.

Scott's hands found Dina's waist and pivoted her around to face him.

"If we weren't friends, I would do this." He tipped her face up to meet his, his lips finding hers, and the kiss devoured her. He tasted like Earl Grey and cinnamon and warmth. Dina's lips parted almost in surprise, her mouth molding to Scott's, her arms winding around his neck. She needed to be closer, closer.

Scott's tongue flicked against her own, his lips pressing down on hers hungrily. She wanted him, all of him. When he ran a hand down her back, grabbing the curve of her ass, she let out a whimper and he groaned into her mouth in response.

"Christ, Dina," Scott hissed, his mouth finding her neck, his arms pulling her up so that she could wrap her legs around his waist, running her fingers through his hair. He pressed her against the delectably cold glass of the window.

It was all heat, all delicious hunger, and she gave in to it. Scott's lips continued downward, his tongue lapping at the softness between her breasts. She'd never been so grateful to her past self for only putting on a camisole under her cardigan.

Scott brushed a finger across her nipple and need jolted through her, arching her back into him.

"Please," she moaned.

He didn't need asking twice. The heat of Scott's mouth found her breast, his tongue flicking at the hardened bud of her nipple. Goddess, this felt good. She pressed her hips into him, relishing his groan as his erection pushed against his jeans. She continued rubbing against him, chasing the hot friction.

Scott kissed her again, and without removing his lips from hers said, "I won't last much longer if you keep doing that."

With her free hand, Dina reached down to his belt, unbuckling it. She was trailing a finger across the V of his waist, when voices sounded nearby. Too near.

"Is it in here?" one of the voices said. Oh fuck, were they about to be found?

Scott and Dina froze. Ever so carefully, Scott lowered Dina to the floor, refastening his belt with one hand. He didn't step away from her though.

"No, it's not here. Let's try the next room," another voice said, and a moment later the door of the library creaked shut.

They both exhaled, before breaking into laughter.

"That was close," Dina said, smoothing down her hair. She didn't want the moment to be over. Scott reached down and pulled up the straps of her camisole his palm resting on her collarbone for a moment before drawing away.

"What now?" he asked.

"I guess we finish the scavenger hunt."

"I've already won my prize." He grinned.

"That was cheesy as hell."

"Sue me."

"I want . . ." Dina began. "I want this to continue. But I'm not really looking to date right now." She had to set this boundary, more for herself than for Scott. She could give in to her desires for the weekend, but then this *had* to end. She couldn't risk the hex noticing him.

Scott's expression tightened for a moment.

"If all you want is this weekend, then that's what we'll have," he replied, brushing a curl behind her ear. "But we should go back, otherwise Immy and Eric might send out a search party."

"Maybe we shouldn't tell the others either. Otherwise they'll—"

"They'll get excited. I understand." Scott bent down, his lips tantalizingly close to hers. "It can be our little secret."

Chapter 15

In the end, neither Scott nor Dina won the scavenger hunt and they were the last ones back to the Little Parlor.

"Where have you been?" Rosemary asked, pulling Dina aside. "And why do you look so smug?"

"I do not look smug."

"You absolutely do. What happened? Anything to do with you and Scott walking in together?"

Dina rolled her eyes but couldn't keep the smile from her face. "Nothing happened."

Rosemary narrowed her eyes. "You're a terrible liar, Dina Whitlock. But I'm going to assume you have a good reason not to tell me, so I'll keep my opinions to myself . . . for now."

Unlike Immy, who was a locked box to which Eric had the key, Rosemary was truly a "secrets to her grave" kind of friend.

"Do you know what the next activity is?" Dina asked her, noticing that a lot of the wedding party appeared to have opted out of this one. She looked around for her parents and was horrified to see them drinking tea around a table with Scott's mums. She flicked him a glance. He had seen it too.

Should we go over? she mouthed at him. He smiled but shook his head.

"Something outside. Immy's keeping it all very hush-hush, but look at her, she's practically bouncing."

It was true, the bride-to-be was clearly ready to make a move. In the end, only eight people from the wedding party went out for this activity, with most of the parents and grandparents choosing to rest before the festivities to come.

As the group walked across the east field of the property, led by Eric and Immy, Dina took a moment to bask in the afternoon sun. She'd always felt a strong connection to the earth through her magic and noticed the change in seasons more than the average person, but being outside of London, surrounded by green hills and woodland, the connection was more alive.

As they walked, she pointed out a variety of herbs and flowers to Rosemary, who was working on a botanical horror and wanted to know how readily available poisonous plants were in the English countryside.

The entire time, Dina was acutely aware that Scott was close behind her, listening to their conversation about flowers. Her mind kept traveling back to the lovers' nook. To the feel of his body pressed against hers.

They reached a gate where the field met the woods. It was one of those country gates that wasn't so much a gate as two crossed planks of wood used as steps over a wooden fence. Dina was perfectly capable of climbing over herself, but as Scott reached out a hand to help her down from the step, she reached out her own in response. His grip was warm and firm, and it steadied her. She couldn't believe this man was literally making her weak in the knees. She was becoming a walking cliché.

"Do you have a favorite flower or plant, Dina?" he asked, his voice low enough that only she could hear.

"Why, are you trying to buy me flowers, Scott Mason?" Dina batted her eyes dramatically. "Lemon verbena, though. That's my favorite. It's a pretty hardy plant, and you can turn it into a tisane. In Morocco we call it louiza."

"Louiza?"

"You add the leaves to boiled water and they let out the most deliciously sweet fragrance. Not exactly lemony—more like a honey balm."

"What does the tea taste like?" he asked.

"Sort of like chamomile maybe, but with more body, and sweeter."

Scott nodded, looking as if he was storing away that information for later use.

"What about you then, since we're on the topic of favorite plants?" Dina stepped over the roots of a nearby oak that had clawed out of the earth, and nearly lost her footing. She leaned one way to counteract the slip, which meant that she ended up falling into Scott. He gripped her waist with both hands, steadying her.

"It's going to sound silly," he said, "because everyone loves them, but roses. A very specific type of rose though. A couple of years ago I went to the M'Goun valley."

"Hold up," said Dina. "This isn't your way of telling me a story about that time you were in Morocco, just because you know I happen to be from there, and you're trying to impress me, is it?"

Scott chuckled, running a hand through his hair.

"Maybe I was trying to impress you a little bit, but it's true either way."

"In that case, please continue."

"I was there to research some of the protective charms the farmers use in that valley, specifically to protect against pests ruining the flowers before they're picked. I was up one morning, really early, and I ended up going with this shopkeeper, Hamid, on a walk past the river. I swear, I could smell them before we even turned into the valley. And then it was just pink, as far as I could see. Even the women picking the roses wore pink, so their heads looked like pink boats bobbing up and down in this sea. And the smell was so . . . thick, you know? Best way I can describe it. Like honey cake, and fresh watermelon and treacle all rolled into one. I could taste it in the air, it was so strong. I bought so many bottles of rosewater on that trip I must have looked like some kind of smuggler at customs."

"It sounds amazing. I've always planned to go for the rose festival but whenever we go to visit, time is always taken up by seeing family. Which is nice and all, but for a country that's half my heritage, I haven't seen much of it." Dina shrugged.

They turned a corner, the treeline beginning to thin as the dense forest petered away into scatterings of trees.

"I want to know more about those protective charms though. What were you studying them for? Was it for the exhibition you mentioned?" she probed. Dina realized she wasn't just making conversation for the sake of it, to pass the time until they reached the secret activity (Immy hadn't told her what it was despite her prodding). She genuinely enjoyed speaking with Scott.

"Yeah, for that. It's all about protective charms from cultures around the world. Looking at symbols—like the eye—which are found everywhere, often used for the same thing."

"Fascinating."

"I think so. The museum wasn't super keen on the idea at first. It involved a couple of other complications I insisted on."

"Oh? Like what?"

Scott offered Dina a sheepish look.

"It might sound a bit silly, but I insisted that if we were going to borrow artifacts from other countries, whether they were family heirlooms in private collections or ones already owned by state-run museums, we were going to craft a smaller exhibition or installation, featuring those artifacts, that would eventually tour the countries they came from. So, any artifacts borrowed from Morocco for the exhibition would mean that at some point on its tour, the exhibition would go to a museum there, probably in Rabat or Casablanca."

"That doesn't sound very controversial to me."

"Well, it was. You'd have thought I'd suggested burning one of the entombed mummies from the ancient Egypt exhibit from the way they looked at me. It was unheard of, apparently."

"But they agreed to it, in the end?"

"They had to. The exhibitions they've been running of late have been too academically focused." Scott fished into his pocket and pulled out a small turquoise bead that had a scarab etched into it. "See this, right? The ancient Egyptians associated scarabs with new beginnings, rebirth, the start of a new day. And they would carry them, as jewelry or charms, as a reminder of that. People will come to the exhibition and they'll see these beads—well, this is a replica, but one like it—and it'll make the history feel real." His eyes lit up as he spoke.

"I get it. You see a charm made hundreds of years ago and it's not all that different from the lucky rock you keep in your glovebox. I guess it reminds us that history is full of people like us, who had their own worries and fears they wanted to be protected from. Is it open now, then, the exhibition?" Dina asked.

"Not yet. A few weeks until it's ready. But I could give you a special tour, if that's something you'd be interested in? It seems like it would be your sort of thing." He smiled down at her, and Dina felt a stirring deep in her belly that felt suspiciously like lust and . . . something else.

No, she was clearly imagining it. It was only lust. She was attracted to his brain just as much as his body, clearly. But he wanted to show her the exhibition in a couple of weeks. Which would mean they would still be seeing each other then. Oh no, this very much went against her "this is only a weekend fling" plan.

Dina didn't have time to answer, as Immy and Eric paused in their walk to get everyone's attention.

"All right, everyone, you're about to see what I've been keeping secret from you all . . ." Immy shouted at them forebodingly. As they turned a corner, Dina saw it. Ahead of them, situated in the center of a grassy field, was Immy's secret activity. A hedge maze.

"Fucking spooky," Rosemary muttered.

The small hill they stood on looked down over it, allowing Dina to see just how complicated it was. This wasn't the kind of maze you could sit by and wait as your children scurried to the center and back. This was a no one-gets-left-behind, don't-break-out-into-smaller-groups kind of maze.

Dina shot a look at Immy, who was practically squealing with delight. Everyone seemed to be excited; there was something about mazes that felt like a playground for grown-ups. Everyone except Scott. Dina tried to catch his eye but his gaze was firmly set on the maze, his jaw clenched and a rigid set to his shoulders.

Eric clapped him on the back and gave his shoulder a squeeze. Dina thought she heard him whisper something about not worrying, but she couldn't be sure. It looked to her like Scott didn't want to go into the maze. He'd said he was a little claustrophobic—would that affect him in the maze too, even if they were outside?

She could always cast a little anti-anxiety charm; they always worked well in situations like this. He wouldn't even know.

Power twitched at her fingertips. It was Samhain after all, and her power swelled within her, aching to be used. The magic that came with Samhain was different from the other dates like Ostara or Beltane. It was wilder, and it came with its own shadow.

And with the old woods at her back, and the rolling fields before her, she was all but breathing the magic in. It seeped from the soil into her body and wound its way like deep green tendrils into her heart.

Rory's face popped into her mind. That was what happened when she used magic on others. There was no use even considering it; she had better forget the idea immediately.

"Let's team up!" Eric called out to the group. They split into two groups of four, and as Dina wandered closer to the hedges she noticed that whoever had pruned them had done so with a ruler, because there was not a leaf out of place.

"First team to get all the way to the center and back wins," Eric proclaimed.

"I want Dina on my team!" said Immy.

"Immy, we're doing bride versus groom. You can't have all the good picks, and we both know Dina has the sense of direction of a bloodhound." Eric laughed.

Immy rolled her eyes at Dina.

"Fine, you go with Eric. But if you win I will fire you as my maid of honor."

"Someone's feeling competitive I see," Dina responded. The rest of Eric's team quickly assembled, claiming Rosemary and one of Immy's cousins, Tom, who seemed uninterested in the whole affair.

Scott was on Immy's team and was staring at the entrance to the maze like it was a monster that was going to swallow him whole.

"We don't all need to go in. People can stay out here if they want," Dina said aloud, hoping that would make it clear that Scott had no reason to go in if he didn't want to.

"Dina, don't be silly, we have to go in as teams," Immy replied, completely oblivious.

"Who takes left, who takes right?" Rosemary asked, inclining her head toward the two diverging paths just inside the maze's entrance. The hedges had to be at least eight feet tall.

"We go left and you go right, Immy?" Eric suggested.

"What do we win?" Tom chipped in, apparently suddenly interested.

"Everlasting glory, obviously," Immy cackled.

Dina sidled up to Scott.

"Are you okay?" she asked under her breath. He looked a little pale and was biting his lip—and not in a sexy way. "You don't seem keen on going in."

"No, no. It's fine. I'm fine," Scott replied, wiping his clearly clammy hands on his trousers. "It'll be fun," he said, probably in an attempt to convince himself. She reached out and gave his shoulder a squeeze.

"Dina, no cheating! Get back over here," Eric called. Once they had conferred in their teams over possible strategies—not that it was possible to have much of a pre-planned strategy for navigating a maze—Immy counted down from three and the game began.

Scott offered Dina a half-smile as he reluctantly followed Immy into the maze. Dina and Eric took the left path, followed closely by Tom and Rosemary.

The maze swallowed them up. It had been a warm morning, at least by late October standards, but a damp coolness settled over them once they stepped into the shade of the hedges.

Unlike the woods, Dina didn't feel any kind of magic in the bones of the maze. It wasn't particularly old, nor menacing. Which was a good sign. The last thing they needed was a maze with an attitude. Dina had been in one of those in Vienna before, and she'd had to cast her way out, leaving scorch marks in the brush.

They stopped once they got to a fork.

"I say we go right. Dina?" Eric asked.

"Why would Dina know?" said Tom.

"Ah. Well. Dina tends to be good at these kinds of things. Bloodhound instincts, like I said," Eric replied carefully. Behind Tom, Rosemary was wiggling her fingers around, pretending she was performing witchcraft and cackling silently—she looked unhinged, and Dina loved her for it.

"I say we go right," Dina said. She couldn't be sure; she didn't have any kind of prescience. But, like most witches, she possessed a gut instinct—though some might call it a sixth sense. When it told her which way to go, she normally followed, no questions asked.

Occasionally, they heard Immy's group through the hedges, and saw a flurry of color on the other side as they walked past. Once, Dina thought she smelled Scott's cologne and felt a sudden need to reach through the hedge for him. Though she had to admit that a pair of bodiless arms poking out through a hedge wouldn't exactly be comforting to anyone, let alone someone who clearly didn't love mazes.

"This is perfect writing fodder," Rosemary remarked, as they took a path to the left. Silence hung heavily in the maze, and a low mist collected at their feet. It had grown quite cold, and the sunlight had petered away into that half-brightness of a fully gray sky.

"How so?" Dina asked.

"The gothic maze, the creepy woods, and the manor with rooms full of antlers and taxidermy? It's deliciously spooky. The house isn't haunted though. I checked."

"What about the maze?" Dina asked, looking around her as fogged rolled in.

"No ghosts here. Some in the woods though," Rosemary responded matter-of-factly.

Dina smiled at her. "One day we're going to create a TV show called *England's Most Haunted* and it's just you and me wandering around old estates where I get all freaked out and you tell me that it's just a regular building."

Haunted or not, Dina couldn't deny the spookiness of the maze; it was also proving surprisingly difficult to complete. They took turn after turn, several times ending up where they'd been a moment before, not that it was easy to tell. Every wall of green leafage looked identical. Finally, when everyone's legs were starting to get tired and Tom had complained about being thirsty at least four times, they found the center, complete with a tarnished bronze sundial. There was no sign that Immy and her team had beaten them to it, but they couldn't be sure.

"Does that mean we win?" Tom asked. He'd been intermittently checking his phone and seemed miffed that there was no signal here.

"Not yet," said Eric cheerily. "We need to get back to the exit first."

They followed the route back as best they could, with a couple of wrong turns here and there.

Dina felt her chest expand and let out a deep exhale as they saw the maze's exit.

Maybe it was just knowing that Scott wasn't having a good time, but it was definitely not as fun as she'd hoped it would be.

"Looks like we won!" said Eric, high-fiving each of them. "Immy is never going to forgive me," he said to Dina.

"Bet you she brings it up in her vows tomorrow," she laughed.

"Wouldn't surprise me one bit."

"Aww, you beat us! Damn!" Immy cried as her team slunk out of the maze from a different path. "I really thought we had you there." She slumped.

Eric picked up his fiancée and swung her around. "I can share some of my everlasting glory with you if you want."

"Mmm, okay then." Immy leaned in to kiss her fiancé.

Dina looked away to give the couple a moment of privacy and searched for Scott. But he wasn't anywhere to be seen.

"Hey, Immy, where's Scott?"

"He's right—" Immy turned around and looked at her smaller team. "Huh. I swear he was right with us. Wasn't he?"

The others shrugged. Dina stared back at the maze, standing ominously tall and in shadow.

"Oh shit, he's still in the maze."

Chapter 16

"*O*h, this is not good, this is not good," Eric muttered, pacing back and forth. "Scott hates closed-off spaces. I thought he'd be fine but . . . shit, I shouldn't have let him go in there. Okay, you all wait here, I'll go get him," he said, about to march in.

Dina put out a hand to stop him.

"Eric, I've got this."

"No, Dina, it's on me, I—"

"*You* can stay out here and think of something that will take Scott's mind off this when I get him out. All right? As you said, I have the sense of direction of a bloodhound. I'll be in and out in no time."

"Are you sure?" Eric frowned.

"Babe, it's *Dina* we're talking about. She's got this," Immy reassured him. Dina didn't want to waste another second. Without hesitation, she plunged back into the maze.

Dina thought about how long it had taken them the first time. If Scott was freaking out in there, then she needed to get to him quickly.

The tall hedges of the maze huddled around her, giving away none of their secrets. She took a few right turns, and stopped, now firmly out of sight of the others. She needed to cast a spell.

It would need to be a little more powerful than the average spell to help her locate Scott, so she pulled out the amethyst pendant she wore around her neck. It would act as a conduit of sorts.

Dina reached into her pocket and pulled out a few stems of chamomile she had foraged earlier. They were such delicate, beautiful little things, with their sweet honey scent, and they would work perfectly.

"Sorry," she whispered to the flowers, before crushing them in her palm. Dina didn't often use this kind of magic, because truthfully she rarely needed it, and because it involved destroying life. A little devastation here, a pinch of ruin there; it gave the magic that extra bit of oomph. Given that it was Samhain, there should have been enough magic in the air to tap in to that this kind of spell wouldn't be necessary. But the maze dulled it somehow. Perhaps it was all these neatly manicured hedges—there was something distinctly clinical about them that felt at odds with her magic.

She felt the spell take effect. *Scott, where are you?*

Dina took a deep breath, closing her eyes and focusing her mind. She thought only of Scott. And how much she wanted to find him. The amethyst pendant tugged her forward, her eyes flying open. She held the chain of the necklace, but the stone itself was pulling her forward, and now to the right, as if it were being pulled toward a magnet.

She powered on, following as the amethyst led her around twists and turns. She didn't bother to keep track of the path. She could use the same spell to get them out if she needed to.

Dina heard Scott before she saw him.

Panicked, shallow breaths came toward her from across a hedge, and when Dina turned a corner she found Scott sitting on the ground, his back against the hedge, head buried between his legs.

Dina fought the urge to smother him with a hug. If he was

panicking, too much physical contact could make it worse. She'd seen that before.

"Scott?" she said. His gaze shot up, his eyes reddened with tears. When he realized it was her, he quickly wiped his cheeks.

"I'm fine," he said, clearing his throat.

"I don't think you are," she said, kneeling down beside him. "The claustrophobia?"

Scott sucked in a breath and nodded. "I lost the group and I just—"

"I get it."

Scott raked his fingers through his hair and turned to Dina.

"Not very manly to be caught crying by the woman you're trying to impress, is it?"

"According to who?" Dina laughed. "You're still trying to impress me then?"

He stood, brushing dirt off his trousers.

"Is it working?"

"Hmm, you'll have to wait and see. Let's start by getting you out of here, shall we?"

"You're my knight in shining armor, Dina. I'd follow you anywhere."

There was a seriousness in his tone as he spoke those last words, and Dina found herself reaching out toward him. Cupping his face between her hands, she brushed away the last remnants of tears from his cheeks. God, his eyes were maddening. She could look into them forever.

"For the record," Dina said, "I do think it's manly to cry. It shows that you're not afraid of expressing emotion, and that's fucking hot."

"Is it now?" Scott grinned fiendishly.

"Did someone tell you it wasn't?" she asked out of curiosity. Scott frowned, as if he was remembering something painful, and she felt a sudden distance between them. Someone had made him feel that way, and he didn't want to talk to her about it.

"I'd like to get out of here," Scott said, changing the subject. "But honestly I might have another panic attack if I get lost again."

"That's okay, I have a way of getting us out quickly."

"Oh yeah?"

"I memorized the route." He looked at her with an edge of suspicion, but was clearly too stressed to really give it much thought. The way he was looking at her was too raw; Dina could barely meet his eyes and at the same time she couldn't look away. Before she did anything stupid she blinked her gaze away and pulled a silk scarf from her pocket.

"Do you want me to cover your eyes?"

"You want to blindfold me? I would have thought a common first date was more like dinner, maybe some drinks—"

"He had a panic attack two minutes ago and now the man is attempting banter," Dina deadpanned, pinching the bridge of her nose.

"What is the purpose of said blindfold?"

"I figure if you can't see the maze, then maybe you aren't as likely to have a panic attack. But granted, I don't know what triggers them for you," she hastened to say.

Scott looked down at the silk scarf in Dina's hands.

"Let's try it. I think we should try it. Keep distracting me until we're nearly out and then you can watch as I leg it for the exit."

"Done. Bend down." Scott did as he was told, and Dina wrapped the silk scarf around his eyes, tying a knot at the back of his head, not too tight. She felt Scott's warm exhale against her cheek, and her body ached to close the space between them. It helped that he couldn't see her, couldn't see how dilated her pupils were, how the blush had stained her lips and cheeks. How easy it would be to kiss him again. "All done," she whispered, pulling away.

Dina pulled out another chamomile flower from her pocket, redoing the spell to take them out of the maze. She pictured the exit and the sweeping fields that rippled out from it, and a moment later the pendant was pulling them down a path.

"Take my hand," Dina instructed. She felt Scott's warm grip in hers.

"I thought you were a curator—why do you have so many calluses?" She thought that perhaps chatting would keep his mind off being in the maze. They twisted this way and that, but Scott's footing didn't falter.

"Ah, that'd be the rowing. I have to keep them on my palms otherwise the blisters get very painful."

"I forgot about the rowing. What was your nickname, the one Eric mentioned?"

"I was hoping you might have forgotten about that. The full eight." Scott sighed.

"Ah yes, that was it." Dina suppressed a giggle. Goddess, she was *giggling* now. If they hadn't decided this was a weekend fling *only*, Dina might have suspected she was growing feelings.

"I love it out on the river," Scott said, a calm note coming into his voice. "There's so much space out there. No matter what the weather's like, you can always be sure of two things: that going with the current makes you feel like the most powerful person in the world, and that no matter what you do, you'll always get wet feet."

"I've never actually been on the river—like, that close to it, I mean," Dina said. It wasn't as though she didn't want to, but unless you took up rowing, got on one of those tourist barges, or had two hours to waste on a commuter boat up the river, there weren't many options to see the Thames up close and personal.

"There's nothing like it. You see London in a whole other way. There's a moment, when you're rowing out west, past Kew, when one second there are houses, and pretty little cottages and people cycling and walking their dogs. And then the next second, they disappear. The river bends, narrows, and suddenly it's just brush, river reeds, and fields opening out on either side of you."

"I'd like to see that," Dina said earnestly.

"I'd like to take you there," he replied, sending her insides tumbling.

And just like that, they turned a corner and the maze's exit lay before them.

Dina held Scott's hand until they were a few steps away. The sun had already rolled over for the afternoon, the mist that had gathered around them dissipating in the cold sunshine.

I don't want to let go of his hand, Dina realized. Scott probably didn't even realize that they were almost out of the maze. She could keep walking beside him for a bit. But then maybe he'd be weirded out when he saw how far she had walked him blindfolded.

"We're almost out," Dina said reluctantly.

Scott pulled off the blindfold and squinted in the light, looking down at Dina. He breathed a sigh of relief, his eyes dropping to her lips.

He smiled. "You didn't have to come back for me, but you did anyway."

"We're not in bloody World War Two, Scott." Dina whacked his elbow. All of a sudden she was off the ground, and in Scott's arms. He held her close, the after-effects of his panic attack still apparent in the way his arms shook slightly.

"Thank you. I mean it."

"You'd have done the same for me," she replied, suddenly sure that it was the truth. If she'd been in trouble, Scott would have come for her. The witchy gut instinct did not lie.

She felt Scott's hands firmly gripping her, and she wanted to be closer to him. Perhaps he sensed the way her eyes traveled up his body hungrily, because he didn't put her down immediately, but drew her closer. Dina placed her hands on his chest, feeling the heat of him. He smelled warm.

"Dina, I—" Scott's voice was rough. He was looking at her like he wanted to devour her. She wanted him to. Dina licked her lips, tipping her face toward his.

"Shh, I think they're having a moment!" came Immy's high-pitched whisper from nearby.

Scott lowered her back to the ground, but his hands remained around her waist. She spotted the rest of the group just outside the entrance to the maze.

"I see you made it out in one piece," Eric said, clapping Scott on the shoulder. "Sorry, mate, I didn't realize it would be so bad in there," he said sincerely.

"Hey, it's fine, I survived," Scott replied. "Dina's the one who needs the medal though: She had to deal with me in a less-than-ideal state."

"The hero of the hour." Eric smiled at Dina, nodding his head in thanks.

So much for keeping their weekend fling a secret. It was abundantly clear to all her friends that something was going on between them. Ah well, in for a penny, in for a pound.

Scott clearly had the same idea as they wandered back to the house. He bent down and planted a kiss, barely a brush of his lips, on Dina's temple.

A soft shiver rippled over her skin. The kiss was a promise. Tonight, after her Samhain ritual, Dina knew exactly what she was going to do to Scott Mason.

Chapter 17

*D*ina stood in her bedroom in the cottage, looking out at the moonlit forest. So much was happening so fast. They had kissed, and it had been better than she'd imagined. Goddess knows that she'd been imagining it.

She had dressed in a daze, throwing on a silky purple dress that corseted her, making her tits look about as voluptuous as they could be. The whole time, she thought about Scott. It might have been a blessing in disguise that they'd been interrupted in the lovers' nook, because otherwise she wouldn't have stopped. Being around him unleashed something inside of her; she found herself craving things she hadn't wanted before.

But there was still a part of her she was holding back: her magic. Maybe it was the wedding, seeing most of her friends and family coupled up and in love, but Dina felt a growing urge to reveal her witchcraft to Scott. She felt more at home around him than she'd ever felt with anyone else. Even Rory.

How would he react if she showed him her magic? Would he become angry and jealous as Rory had? She hadn't felt the need to share her magic with other romantic partners before sleeping with them, but with Scott it felt like a bridge she had to cross. She felt a need for him to understand her entirely—body and mind and soul. To see this facet of her and accept it.

A reminder of the hex scratched at the back of Dina's mind, but she chose not to pay attention to it. When she was around Scott, the hex and her problems all felt far away. Like they belonged to another Dina—not her, not right now.

There was a knock at her bedroom door.

"Dina, are you ready?" Scott asked.

They had one final dinner before the wedding tomorrow, and Dina didn't want to waste another minute alone in a room when she could be with Scott. If all she could have was this one perfect weekend with him, she would take it. Even if the feelings stirring inside her told her she wanted more.

Heart in her throat, Dina opened the door to Scott.

He filled the doorway, dressed sharply in a maroon two-piece suit that brought out the darkness of his beard. She saw the way he took her in, his eyes darkening as they trailed down her body, leaving scorch marks in their wake.

"Fuck, Dina. You're gorgeous," he growled. "Would you like me to escort you there?"

Her mouth felt dry. "Escort me? That's very gentlemanly of you."

"I have been known to occasionally act like a gentleman."

"Is that so?" Dina took Scott's proffered arm and they headed out of the cottage, locking the door with the giant wrought-iron key.

The forest stilled around them, waiting. Night had settled in, bringing slivers of moonlight with it that pierced through the canopy of great oaks and spruces. The path was barely visible in the blue-black night. Dina shuddered in a breath, suddenly nervous now that the moment had arrived. The moonlight had made the decision for her. She would show Scott her magic, here and now.

"There's something I think I want to show you," she said abruptly, her words almost sounding like a question.

"What is it?"

"You won't freak out?"

Scott tilted his head and brushed his lips against hers.

"You can tell me anything. It might surprise me, but I won't run away," he promised.

"I must be going crazy, doing this so soon," she muttered. "Wait here."

She dashed back to the cottage. She hadn't performed this spell before, but the way to do it had already formed in her mind, easy as breathing. Dina re-emerged with an empty teacup, mischief alive in her expression.

"You ready?"

He swallowed, nodding.

Dina raised her arms, palms facing upward, the teacup held high. The forest grew dark around them. Like any sliver of moonlight was vanishing, leaving them in absolute black.

Only it wasn't for long, as a pool of silvery substance—not liquid but not air either—began to swarm around her, like it was raining moonlight. She turned her face to the sky and was bathed in a milky glow. Sometimes she forgot how much joy raw magic brought her.

The rivers of moonlight twisted in rivulets across her body, until they all collected into the teacup in a shimmering liquid. For a moment, the air around them was scented like fresh coffee and spices.

Dina met Scott's eyes, testing him. He couldn't speak, but he wasn't running away.

With an ecstatic smile, Dina flicked the teacup, flinging moonlight outward, splashing it against the trunks of trees, coating ferns and shrubs near the path like silver luminescent paint. As it landed, it began to fade, until—within seconds—full night had returned. Dina set the teacup down on the front step of the cottage.

As if nothing peculiar had happened, Dina looped her arm back through Scott's. As if she hadn't just upended his world. Her arm was warm in his, and he held her as close to him as politeness would permit.

"Was that moonlight?" Scott said, his voice raw. "In a teacup?"

"It was," she whispered back.

They walked on in silence toward the candlelight emanating from Honeywell House.

$\mathcal{S}$cott splashed his face with cool water. He was in a small bathroom just outside the North Parlor, where the braver among the wedding party had decided to forgo a night of beauty sleep and were instead playing a highly competitive game of Scrabble.

What had he witnessed?

She had looked like a wild and beautiful creature, a goddess, something ethereal and undecipherable. Dina had filled his vision, the pale light dancing around her, as she'd broken his world, and everything he thought he knew, apart.

He was ninety percent sure that Dina was a witch. The other ten percent . . . well. He was flirting with the idea that she might be some kind of djinn, or succubus, but neither of those terms felt quite right. And "magician" made him think of rabbits in hats and coins collected from behind ears. No, if there was ever a word to describe Dina Whitlock, it was "witch."

Scott didn't think he'd forget this night for the rest of his life, and there was absolutely no way that had been an illusion or a trick of the light.

But if Dina was a witch, what did that make him? Was he under her spell? From the way his cock had gone rock-hard the moment she'd returned his kiss in the lovers' nook, he was certainly under some primal influence.

After the maze it had taken all his willpower not to carry her straight to the cottage, throw her down onto the kitchen counter and make her come over and over again. He bet her face looked lovely when she came.

There was no doubt in his mind now that she wanted him back. He splashed his face again, trying to regain some semblance of composure. The cool water was helping. Alcohol had been free-flowing at dinner earlier, though Scott had stayed away from drinking too much. He wanted to remember every second of tonight and getting drunk reminded him of Alice.

He wasn't proud of what he'd become in the weeks after he'd found out that she'd cheated on him. He'd wanted to forget all about it and drink himself into painless oblivion. Everywhere he looked, there she was. The sofa that they'd picked out together when she'd first moved in. The mugs she'd bought him as gifts in the cupboards.

He was haunted by the pictures of them on the wall. He'd looked so happy back then, so unaware. And she'd looked happy too. How could she have lied to him that entire time? In all those years, how did he never see the truth in her eyes?

Scott splashed more cold water onto his face, washing away the memories.

That part of his life was over now, he reminded himself. He had a new apartment, and he was more himself than he'd felt in a long time. He was making London his home again. He would be there for his mums, for his friends, and for Dina—if she'd have him.

Scott made his way back into the parlor, just as Dina screeched at the top of her lungs, "I win! Pay up, fuckers!" To which he heard simultaneously shouted replies from Rosemary of "'Qi' is not a word" and "You don't win money in Scrabble."

Dina caught Scott's eye as he made his way back to the group.

"Scott, can you please mediate for us? These halfwits are saying I made up 'qi'!" Dina rolled her eyes dramatically. "It's the vital force that is inherent in all things."

"Sorry to break it to you all, but Dina is right. 'Qi' is a Scrabble word. Also spelled 'K-I' or 'C-H-I.' Let's see . . ." Scott bent over the board and caught a whiff of Dina's perfume—vanilla and cinnamon.

"Q is worth ten, but you have it on a triple letter so that's thirty-one points total. She beat you all!"

Immy huffed loudly and looked like she was ready to upend the board.

"Oh, come on, Immy, you know you can never beat me at Scrabble, especially not tonight." Dina sidled over to her friend and threw an arm around her.

"My job is literally words, Dina. I do the words!"

"I know you do, honey."

They whiled away the rest of the evening with party games: charades, pin the veil on the bride, and for those willing to contort themselves in all manner of positions, Twister. Scott found it particularly hard to concentrate on that game when Dina reached her arm over him to touch a red circle. Her breasts, delectably pushed up in that sin of a dress, brushed against his chest, and shortly after he had to excuse himself from the game, lest the wedding party see his erection.

And then again, when they played a round of Pictionary, Dina became particularly frustrated with her team's inability to guess what she'd scrawled on the board, and she pulled her hair free of its updo. Dark brown curls cascaded around her face as she locked eyes with Scott, and he wanted nothing more than to wrap that hair around his fist and have her paint his cock with her lipstick. She had unleashed something in him.

As it grew closer to midnight, Scott noticed that Dina, Immy, and Rosemary had begun exchanging furtive glances with complicated facial expressions—the secret language women had with their friends that he had no hope of understanding. There was something in the air tonight though, even he could feel it.

He looked over at Dina, currently playing darts in a corner of the parlor, her skin glowing a burnished gold by the firelight.

Was it her magic that he felt? His brain was still trying to define what he'd seen her do with the moonlight. Mostly, he felt relieved. He'd always wanted to believe in magic, to believe that the world was bigger than what he saw around him. He'd tried so hard to believe. In a way, he'd dedicated his work to it. But Scott didn't have to try anymore. Dina was the manifestation of everything he'd so desperately wanted to believe in.

Being alive meant being vulnerable, and she'd trusted him with the most vulnerable side of her. He wanted to be worthy of that trust. He wanted to earn it, and continue earning it, for as long as she'd have him.

"I recognize that look," his mum said, coming to sit beside him on the window seat. Juniper jumped into the space between them, wriggling around on her little legs until she found the perfect spot to nap, her head nuzzling into Scott's side.

"What look?"

"The way you're looking at her," Alex said, tipping her head in Dina's direction. "Why didn't you tell us you had a girlfriend?"

"I don't."

"I see."

"It's all very new."

"Pssh," his mum said, waving her hand dismissively. "New doesn't matter. When you know you know. I told Helene I loved her on our second date."

"Not everyone can be that lucky. What if . . . what if she doesn't want what I want?"

"Did she say that?"

"In so many words."

His mum reached out and squeezed his hand. "Well, maybe

I'm biased, but seeing you two together, it doesn't look like just a weekend thing. I worry about you getting hurt. I just . . . I don't want to lose you again because a relationship went south and you need to escape."

Scott glanced at his mum. She wore a sorrowful expression.

"If it doesn't work out, I won't leave again. I promise." He tickled Juniper's head and she wriggled further onto his lap, her belly splayed upward for more scratches.

"I should never have left in the first place," he admitted. "I didn't know what I was doing, I just had to get out."

Alex smiled. "I get it. You don't need to justify yourself to me. You know we both love you, whether you're here or on the other side of the world." She pulled him close and pressed a kiss to his temple.

"I love you too," he said. They sat together for a moment more, until Juniper began dreaming, letting out small yips in her sleep.

"Better get this one to bed," his mum said, scooping Juniper into her arms. "She gets cranky in the mornings, just like Helene." She smiled, love written all over her face. "Goodnight," she said, "and whatever you get up to tonight, I don't want to hear about it." Then she winked and left the room.

Scott sat for a little longer by the window, enjoying the crisp air and view of the full moon, until something moved in the corner of his eye. Outside, walking through the fields, was Dina. He watched her, paying particular attention to the sway of her hips as she walked, until she disappeared into the treeline. Where was she going this late on Halloween? Shortly after, he spotted Immy and Rosemary heading the same way.

"Ah, spotted them did you?" Eric said, walking over and handing a beer to Scott. They clinked the bottles together then moved back to the worn leather sofa by the fire.

"Where did they go?" Scott asked.

"Ah, um, it's a secret bachelorette thing." Eric was slurring his words a little.

"I see. A secret you can't even tell your best man?" Scott laughed.

"Don't pull that card. Look"—Eric took a small sip of his drink—"I am under oath not to tell anyone about the field."

"What field?"

"Ah shit. The north field. Look, just . . . don't go there, okay. It's a private thing they do every year. Something, I dunno, magical."

"Hmm. My lips are sealed."

Eric brushed his hair back out of his face and grinned over at Scott.

"I get married tomorrow."

"I know."

"Isn't that insane?" Eric's eyes gleamed with excitement. "Do you remember when we were at that bar in Iceland and we made that pact to only ever get married at the same time?"

"Yeah," Scott laughed, "I remember."

"Well, I think I might need to back out of that deal, unless you have something to tell me?"

"No weddings on the horizon for me." Scott smiled, though it didn't quite reach his eyes.

Eric leaned closer. "Is it going to be hard for you tomorrow?"

"Because of Alice? Maybe. But I'll be too happy seeing you tie the knot to care."

Eric nodded. He took another swig of his beer.

"She never deserved you, you know. I always thought that."

"Hindsight is twenty-twenty."

"What about Dina then?"

Scott arched an eyebrow. "What about her?"

"I don't know, just thought there might be something going on between you two."

He wasn't wrong, but whatever was going on between Scott and Dina right now felt too *big* to try to describe. His heart thrummed even thinking about her.

"I plead the fifth," Scott said.

Eric chuckled. "I see how it is."

They sat for a while in peaceful silence. The fire burned low and the room slowly emptied out as the remaining wedding party trickled off to bed.

"I've missed this," Eric began. "Maybe it's the full moon. But . . . I don't know, man, I just . . . it's not easy for me to . . . I missed you. I missed having a best friend."

Maybe it *was* the moon, because he'd never had so many heart-to-hearts in such a short space of time. Or maybe that was just what weddings did—they brought out feelings that had lain dormant for too long.

"I don't know how much it's worth, but I am sorry that I just upped and left. I should have told you, should have trusted that you'd be there for me."

"I know you are. And you're here now, that's all that matters."

They drank in silence for a little longer, until Scott realized that Eric had fallen asleep, and he woke him and told him to go to bed.

Scott sat there for a while longer, until the fire had burned down to glowing embers.

Chapter 18

It was a fairy moon. Pearlescent, glowing, and hanging low in the sky—it was the kind of moon that spelled mischief and delight. Dina stood at the edge of the north field, where the fire was already burning. It had all been arranged by Nour, a kind of witchy wedding gift. Dina inhaled the midnight air, sweet and smoky. Her mother was silhouetted by the fire, loosening her hair from the updo she'd styled it in for the evening. Dina would be like her mother tonight: untameable, wild.

Dina longed for this night every year.

Honeywell House was a shadow in the distance, the lit windows nothing more than fireflies floating in the night.

Normally she would travel up to Little Hathering, where she and her mother performed their ritual in the courtyard of the house. That's how they had always done it, ever since she was a child. The house would, of course, dress itself like some kind of opulent glade, and she would feel the heat of the fire, even if it was all a glamour conjured up for their amusement.

Since Dina had met Immy and Rosemary, they'd joined the ritual too. All women were witches on Halloween night.

If the woods had felt thick with magic before, tonight they were practically pounding with it. The pulse of magic ran through Dina's body like a second heartbeat.

She strode through the long grass, relishing the feel of the cold earth against her bare feet. This is what Samhain was all about. Connection. Chance. The veil was at its thinnest—anything was possible tonight. Dina had never felt so acutely like she was in the exact right place at the right time.

"Aywa, are you going to stand around all night?" her mother shouted at her as she approached. Dina had changed out of her evening dress into something lighter and more billowy. In this case, she'd opted for a light blue gondora. The kind that she only wore in the height of summer when she was pottering around and cleaning the house. It billowed against her skin, barely there. She should have been cold, but there was too much magic burning through her, and the blaze of the fire was strong.

Immy had gone for some kind of Victorian nightdress, while Rosemary had opted for a loose black T-shirt and jogging bottoms.

"It's different tonight, can you feel it?" Dina asked.

"Mmm. It's this place. It has a weight to it. I wouldn't be surprised if there's some kind of holy site, or some saint's bones buried around here somewhere," her mother replied. Nour stood before the bonfire that towered over them both. Dina noticed her mother wipe a single tear from her eye.

"Mama, what is it?"

"I'm okay." She sniffed. "Just remembering doing this with my sisters. We always went out to the broad bean field for nights like this. There was just something about being on our own land, all together. I'd never felt so powerful."

Her parents had taken her to Morocco lots of times since then, and her mother's spirit always seemed to quieten when they were there. Dina couldn't imagine how hard it must be, to feel homesick but not want to go home, for fear of the pain the memories would bring. She pulled her mum into a hug, smelling the rose-scented shampoo she used.

"I can feel them tonight though. They're here with us, celebrating. I think it's this place—it's full of ghosts."

Dina nodded.

"I felt something in the woods too, but I couldn't place it."

"Did you say full of ghosts?" Rosemary asked. "Because you're absolutely right. I've seen so many around tonight. I don't know if it's this place, or if it's Halloween, but they're . . . brighter than usual."

Sometimes Dina forgot how normal it was for her friend to see the other side—she imagined this was a little like how others felt when she showed them her magic. Thankfully, Scott hadn't freaked out after her stunt with the moonlight. In fact, she recalled the way his gaze had softened, the way he had exhaled slowly when she'd shown him her magic. Almost as if he'd been relieved.

She still wasn't entirely sure what had come over her earlier. Deep pulses of magic had thrummed from the forest floor to the full moon above, pushing for freedom against the fibers of reality, and Dina had needed to set them free just as much as she needed to breathe. Her intuition told her she was safe with Scott, and if she was honest, she wouldn't have been able to stop herself. A big part of her wanted Scott to see her for who she truly was, magic and all. She wanted to be her true self around him, no more hiding. The idea that this was a weekend fling felt more and more fleeting. It was all too easy, surrounded by magic and moonlight, to forget about the hex. It was so much easier to pretend.

"I hope we haven't missed any of the witchy stuff." Immy traipsed toward them, the hem of her nightgown soaked in mud.

"Did you buy that from an antique shop or something?" Dina asked.

Immy swished in her dress. "Yeah, I'm pretty sure it's a burial dress. So someone must have died in it and then a gravedigger robbed them of it. Isn't that cool?"

"I don't understand you children," Nour sighed.

Dina chuckled. "I hope you know you're insane, Immy."

"I hope it's all right that I didn't wear anything flowy," Rosemary said, looking at the billowing dresses they had all chosen.

Dina grinned. "As long as you can dance in it, it doesn't matter what you wear. Or you could go naked."

Nour cleared her throat and locked eyes with each of them, the weight of her magic settling over them like a warm blanket.

"Summer is gone, soon winter will be here." Nour handed each of them a black Babylon candle. "Tonight we will celebrate the last of the light, and we will remember those who have left us, and those we still hold dear. Tonight, we will hold a light in their memory, so that as we dance, they will dance beside us."

"Dina, did you bring the music?" Nour asked.

Dina put her portable speaker and phone down on the ground. "This bad boy is fully charged, so we don't need to worry about the music cutting out this time."

"Has that happened before?" Rosemary asked.

"Yeah, just once." Dina winced. "Do we have any requests?"

"Ooh, what about some Whitney Houston? My grandma loved Whitney," Immy said.

"Me and my sisters used to sing 'I Have Nothing' in the car at the top of our lungs," Nour agreed.

"Whitney it is." Dina selected a couple of her greatest hits.

Somewhere in the distance, a church bell chimed midnight.

Nour looked up at her daughter and smiled a witch's smile. "It's time."

Sparks from the bonfire caught on the wind and spun ceremoniously into the air. One by one, they approached the fire with their candles.

Babylon candles weren't your regular black spell candle. They could only be used once a year—Samhain at midnight—and they lasted only a few minutes. Rosemary might have been able to see the ghosts of people who hadn't crossed over, but a Babylon candle allowed anyone to spend a few fleeting moments with their loved one on the other side.

"For Khadija," Dina's mum said as the bonfire lent its fire to the candle. The flame flickered an incandescent blue. Immy sucked in a breath.

"For Naima," Dina said as her candle was lit. A peal of laughter echoed in her ears, and for a moment she smelled honeysuckle on the air. A flicker of her aunt's spirit, ready to dance beside them.

"For Grandma," Immy whispered as she lit her candle over the fire. Her grandma had died six months ago, and Immy was still grieving that she wasn't there for the wedding.

Immy gasped, her eyes flying open wide as the candle flamed blue. "I think . . . I think I can feel her." She smiled. Nour squeezed Immy's hand.

"For my mother," Rosemary said, her face still. Blue light flickered from her candle, and she said nothing, her eyes locked on something in front of her. Even witches couldn't see spirits that had crossed over, but with Rosemary's gift, Dina wouldn't be surprised if she could see her mother's spirit before her. Dina saw the tears flowing freely down Rosemary's cheeks, saw the way her friend reached out a hand and whispered "Hi, Mama" to the open air.

They placed their candles, the flames dancing wild and blue, around the bonfire. Babylon candles were thin and fragile, just like the visiting spirits that they helped tether to the mortal plane for a short while. They wouldn't last more than three minutes.

Dina pressed play, sending "I Wanna Dance With Somebody" blasting out of the speaker. Dina shrugged out of her clothes until she stood totally naked in the field. Immy looked a bit abashed but did the same. Nour was already naked and bopping along to the beat, her wild hair swaying about her, as was Rosemary.

Nour sang at the top of her lungs. As the chorus came, Dina lost herself to the song. Her feet skipped and danced around the bonfire, throwing out moves she would never in a million years have been seen doing in public.

When she looked over at Immy, her friend's head was tipped back in laughter, and she looked like she was spinning someone around in a dance. *She's dancing with her grandma.* Dina's heart lifted.

Over on the other side of the fire, Dina could just about glimpse Rosemary twirling around, her red hair blazing in the firelight, her face lit up with an incandescent happiness.

Dina threw up her hands and sang, and she thought she heard a woman's voice, a little raspy and slightly accented, singing just behind her. The wind lifted up around her, and she was spinning, kicking her feet up in the air. Dina imagined how her aunt would be dancing right now, if she could see her—probably throwing around some questionable dance moves from the eighties.

Dina glanced over at her mum, who seemed to be hovering slightly above the ground, doing what looked like a mish-mash of several different disco moves. She hadn't seen her mother this happy for ages.

The song reached its climax, and Dina tipped her head back and howled with joy. Tonight, they were all shedding the versions of themselves that had to be neat, tidy women.

Tonight, they were wild things.

The music died down until all she could hear was the crackling of the bonfire and her breath heaving in and out. The Babylon candles had burned out, and were now a seep of black wax coating the grass. The spirits were gone.

"That was amazing," Immy said, wiping the remains of tears

from her cheeks. "I never really got to say goodbye. But . . . but that felt like a proper goodbye."

"I'm so glad, habiba," Nour said. Dina pulled Immy into a hug and pressed a kiss to her cheek.

Rosemary walked over, muddied and glowing.

"Thank you," she said, wiping the remnants of tears from her cheeks. "I didn't know how much I missed her until now." She pulled Dina into a ferocious hug.

"I hope you don't feel too upset?" Dina asked them both.

"Only the good kind of upset." Immy smiled sleepily. "But I do think I'll head back to the house. After all, I should probably try and get some semblance of beauty sleep before tomorrow."

"Wait, what's happening tomorrow? Something important?"

Immy elbowed Dina, then threw her burial dress back on and headed back across the field.

"I'll go too, though I'm not sure if I'll be able to sleep." Rosemary grinned and followed after Immy.

Nour was sitting by the bonfire, her muddy feet stretched toward it.

"Mama, do you want me to stay with you for a bit?" Dina asked.

"No, no. You don't need to worry about me. I told your father that if I wasn't back by one he could come and get me."

"Baba's still awake?"

"He can never sleep on Halloween. He might not be a witch, but he can certainly sense something." Nour saw Dina's worried look. "Honestly, habiba, I'm fine. I just want to spend a bit more time out here before I go back. Besides, I have the sense that there's someone else you need to see tonight."

Dina flushed. There was no use lying to her mother; she had the sixth sense of a predator.

"Mama, it's late. It's been a long day. He'll probably be asleep."

"Hmm, somehow I doubt that."

Dina stared into the crackling fire.

"What . . . what if it's a bad idea?" she asked. *What if I like him too much and I get him hurt?* she wanted to say, but didn't.

Her mother stood and brushed one of Dina's curls behind her ear.

"I am not going to give you a lecture about how all of life is a risk. You know that already. But I am going to tell you that there is a man waiting for you in that cottage who cares about you very deeply and I think you care for him too. You would be a complete idiot to not give something like that a chance. And I did not raise an idiot."

The hex was on the tip of her tongue. Dina hesitated. She could tell her now, get the truth out in the open. Her mum could help her break it, help her find a way to be with Scott without getting him hurt.

But what if she took it the wrong way? Dina would have to tell her she was bisexual; how would Nour look at her after that? What if she became angry? Would it ruin the wedding? The risk was too high.

For tonight, at least, Dina could pretend. She could pretend that there was nothing stopping her and Scott from being together.

Dina kissed her mother and picked up her phone and speaker. She was halfway across the field to the woods when she realized she had forgotten to put her clothes back on.

Chapter 19

That's one hell of a spooky moon. Scott pulled the door of the cottage closed behind him. Round and crystal white, like a big, unblinking eye. Or like someone had taken a hole punch to the night sky. At least it would make it easier to see his way through the woods. He wasn't even sure what he was doing out here, at this time.

He'd lain in bed, tossing and turning. Sleep wasn't having anything to do with him tonight. Where was Dina? What was she doing out there in the north field?

When Scott closed his eyes, all he could picture was Dina. Dina by the firelight, Dina arching against him with his mouth on her breasts. He could still smell the scent of her skin against his: vanilla and cinnamon. Scott ached for more. He just had to touch her, be near her. Christ, he was already hard just thinking about it.

He'd slipped on the first pair of jogging bottoms and trainers he could find and headed outside. He could breathe easier in the night air.

Was it normal to feel like this with someone you'd just met? He'd heard stories of people who just *knew* the moment they'd met that they'd found their person. As his mum had reminded him, his parents had been two of them. A voice deep in his head told him that it shouldn't be this easy, not after Alice.

Scott began making his way down the path away from the cottage, vaguely aware that his feet were taking him in the direction of the north field.

He couldn't even begin to compare Alice and Dina. With Dina everything felt so . . . easy. Liking her was easy, and he suspected that loving her would be even easier. It would feel as natural as breathing. Perhaps it already did.

Scott tripped, a branch nabbing his ankle out of nowhere, sending him flying into a nearby thorn bush. *Fucking great*, he thought as he stood back up. His arms had a few scratches and his jogging bottoms were dusted with soil. He was suddenly thankful no one had seen him fall over. But where had that branch come from? Clearly he was so busy mooning over Dina he was unable to watch his footing.

Adrenaline-shaken from the fall, Scott continued onward down the toadstool-lined path that meandered through the woods. He couldn't shake images of Dina from his mind. She'd bewitched him, and she hadn't even needed her magic to do it.

Scott tried to think of something else, but it was difficult with all the blood rushing straight to his cock. He just needed the air, needed the walk. Anything was better than tossing about in bed.

Scott heard a shuffling sound in the forest to his left. In the same moment, the air around him stilled. There was no sound, not even a whistle of the breeze through the canopy.

"Hello?" he called. It was probably just a rabbit. Or a deer.

The forest stood dark and imposing on all sides of him, and he became suddenly aware that he was far from the cottage. There were no signs in these woods, and if there were they had long ago been swallowed by moss and tangled vines.

Another crunch in the shadow of the trees. Was there a dark shape moving there or was it his imagination? A horrifying thought came to Scott unbidden. If Dina had magic, and witches existed, what else might exist? What other things from myth and fairy tale might call these woods home?

And why did he inexplicably feel that whatever this was, it wanted to hurt him?

Scott felt a warm hand touch his back, sending a shiver across his body.

"What are you doing out here?" Dina spoke from behind him. She traced a finger along the muscles of his arm, trailing it into his hand, placing her palm against his. Warmth spread through him.

Scott glanced back at the trees, but whatever he'd seen had vanished when Dina had touched him. He was probably just sleep-deprived and insatiably horny and it was messing with his head.

"Just out for a walk. Needed to clear my head," he rasped, turning to face her.

Scott knew, somehow, that if he looked down at Dina, it would be the end for him.

"Was your head feeling particularly full of something?" she asked innocently.

He couldn't help himself any longer. He looked down at Dina and, fuck, she was there, stark naked. His brain short-circuited; it was too much. Moonlight bounced off her deep honeyed skin.

"Fuck, Dina. Look at you." Scott's voice was hoarse. She stared up at him with molten eyes. She was perfect, fuck, she was perfect. Just as he'd imagined—no, better than he'd imagined.

The curve of her hips, the softness of her belly and the swell of her breasts, her nipples stiff. For him. His eyes feasted their way down her body, to her inner thighs. If he kissed her there, would she be wet for him?

Her face was only hunger, only lust. He needed to have her.

Scott pulled her closer, running his fingers through her hair, down the curve of her shoulders and back. She fell into him with a moan, twining her arms around his neck, and it was all heat.

Scott cupped her chin, tipping his face down to meet her. The first touch of her lips sent a jolt straight through him. If he didn't stop himself he would devour her. His hands found her ass and it was so round, and there was so much of it.

"Christ, Dina," he growled against her lips, "you smell like fire." Those lips parted for him and she was all sweetness and warmth and delicious hunger. His tongue flicked against hers and she murmured into his mouth, pressing her breasts against his chest, running her nails across his back.

"I need you," she whispered, and Scott had never heard anything better in his life. His lips found her neck and trailed down to the softness between her breasts. No thoughts, just need. His mouth found her breast, and as Scott's tongue flicked the stiff bud of her nipple Dina moaned, her back arching and her head tipping back.

"You like that?" he said, refusing to remove her breast from his mouth as he spoke.

"Mmm." Dina ran her hands down his chest, knotting her fingers through his chest hair. Claiming him. And fuck, he wanted to be hers. Those same fingers tracing the deep V of his belly, dipping beneath his jogging bottoms. He was so hard he was close to bursting. If she touched his cock, he'd probably come right then and there.

"I need to hear you say it, Dina. Tell me."

"I need you, please. *Scott*." The way she said his name—he

was lost. Scott lifted her up as she wrapped her legs around him. He wanted to slip his fingers inside her. To kneel before her and worship that pretty pussy with his mouth. If she tasted anything like how she smelled, Scott would lose his mind.

"I need you, but not here." She looked up at him, a mischievous glint in her eye. And then Dina took off at a run, rushing back through the trees toward the cottage.

Christ, the way her ass bounced up and down as she ran; he was ruined. He was going to make her scream his name, again and again.

She was making him chase her, and he was more than happy to. With a growl, Scott began to run, chasing Dina through the winding trees and onto the path to their cottage.

Dina fell against the door, her chest heaving.

Without words, Scott pulled her up into his arms, his lips crashing into hers, and he kicked the door of the cottage closed behind them. She was his.

Chapter 20

*W*hat Dina needed more than anything was to have Scott inside her. All around her. It surpassed want. She needed him, his body . . . his everything.

From the moment she'd seen him in the woods, the moonlight casting shadows on the muscular ridges of his back, the tattoos that snaked up his arms, the geometrical patterns and lines that curved around his chest and back, she'd been done for.

When he'd turned to look at her and noticed that she was naked, his eyes were suddenly all darkness and desire. Wetness had immediately slicked her inner thighs. Her pussy had throbbed for him. Ached for him to touch her. And then he had, and she was moaning against him and it was like they fit together.

Now, here they were. He kicked the cottage door closed and turned to look at her. His expression lit up greedily as he drank her in, his erection pushing hard against the cotton of his jogging bottoms.

Dina had no control. She wriggled herself into Scott's embrace, their mouths pressed roughly together. They sank onto the sofa, all twisting limbs and moans.

Scott's mouth traveled down her body, his mouth sucking roughly at her breasts. His hands gripped her hips and pushed her further into the sofa, prying open her legs. His mouth moved hungrily up her inner thigh, pressing rough, short kisses into her skin that didn't quite reach her center. He was teasing her, making her wait. Making her beg. She needed more.

"Touch me, please." She'd never begged for anything in her life. Not for touch, not for sex. And definitely never for oral. But if Scott didn't attach his sexy fucking mouth to her clit right this second she was going to expire.

"I'm not just going to touch you, sweetheart," Scott said, looking up at her, his voice growing even deeper. "You're going to come all over my mouth until I tell you to stop. You say 'red' and I'll stop, understood?"

She nodded. He was possessive. She hadn't known she wanted that, but fuck, she did now.

The roughness of his beard as he settled his face between her legs was excruciatingly delicious.

Scott's tongue flicked her clit, sending a shudder through her. Before Dina could catch her breath, his tongue parted the wet folds of her pussy, pushing inside. His lips were everywhere, sucking against her wetness as if he wanted to taste all of her. Dina hooked her legs around his shoulders.

"You taste so good," he groaned. Damn, this man knew exactly what he was doing. She opened for him, and Scott slid a finger into her smooth heat.

She moaned, bucking her hips into him. He only fucked her harder with his fingers, curving his hand so that she could rock against him.

"Good girl, just like that," he whispered, the heat of his breath on her cunt.

Between the pressure of his tongue and his lips and the slight scratch of his beard, and now his fingers, Dina felt the edges of an orgasm beginning to curl through her.

"Can I touch you here?" he asked, meeting her gaze across

the rise of her stomach. She felt the barest touch, further back, skimming the edge of her ass. How did he know? Dina had never told anyone that—what she wanted, where she wanted to be touched. How did he know?

"*Please,*" she begged. Scott didn't need to ask twice. This time, three fingers plunged into her, two at the front and one teasing her at the back. His tongue lapped her up, circling her clit. Building, building.

"You're so perfect . . . fuck, Scott, there, right there, right—" The orgasm shattered through Dina, an ecstatic ripple from deep inside that rove all over her body. Just as she came, Scott thrust his tongue deep into her and drank her all in.

Her body was jelly, her limbs heavy and sensitive and deliciously warm all at the same time. She knew he would make her come again tonight. Scott's beard was all wet—*with her.* It shouldn't have turned her on so much to see herself all over him, but it did.

Scott groaned, palming his own cock, as if he couldn't stand another second. That wouldn't do.

"Dina," he moaned as she crawled off the sofa, pushing him back and slotting herself between his legs so she could see his full erection up close. There was just . . . so much of it. Veined thick ridges, and dark hair at the base. She felt slick again just looking at it. It had been a while since Dina had taken a cock in her mouth, but she was desperate for it now.

She had never really wanted to before and had done it more out of a sense of duty to reciprocate. But now Dina wanted to. No, she *needed* to—to please Scott. She wanted to be on her knees for him. To make him feel good, like he'd made her feel good.

"Dina, *fuck,*" Scott moaned as she took him into her mouth. She looked up at him as she teased the tip of his cock, salty and hot and throbbing. She liked knowing he was watching her.

Dina pressed her tongue against the flatness of his shaft and pumped up and down at the base with her hand. She alternated, moving down and sucking on his sac, which had Scott growling and reaching out to hold her hair back.

"I want to see you. Can you take all of me?" he said, his voice low and rough.

Dina didn't answer, just took his hard flesh into her mouth, sucking it deeper and deeper, feeling him pulse and thicken each time.

"Good girl, take it all," he hissed, driving his hips forward.

Scott gripped all of her hair in one fist as she tugged at him, her tongue stroking the tip.

"Where do you want me to come, baby?" Scott gritted out. "Tell me."

Dina looked up at him, desire flaming through her.

"Let me taste you."

She wrapped both of her hands around Scott's cock as her lips pressed down, the veins of his cock bulging beneath his skin.

"Dina, Dina, fuck—" With a hard thrust that sent sparks to Dina's eyes, Scott came. His warmth spread through her mouth. But she didn't stop. She gripped and tugged at him, suckling with her tongue and drinking him in, until there was nothing left.

Scott pulled her up onto his lap, and although he had come he was still hard for her.

Scott wet a finger in his own mouth and cleaned up the corners of Dina's with a softness she hadn't expected. Something deep in her chest swelled.

"I messed up your hair," he said, in a way that wasn't quite an apology.

"I messed up your beard," she replied, delighting at his smirk.

How was she ever going to get enough of this man?

Scott trailed the rough pads of his palms down her shoulders, raising goosebumps over her skin. She was acutely aware that she was naked, her thighs splayed on either side of Scott's, her pussy only inches away from his cock. All it would take was for her to lift up her hips and tip forward, and she could feel him deep inside her.

She'd always known she fell into a more submissive role, but she'd never been able to give in to it as much as she had tonight. It was like Scott had seen into every one of her fantasies and brought them to life. She could trust him to take charge and to keep her safe.

And she wanted nothing else than to be pounded into oblivion.

"Oh no, I know that look." Scott pulled her down for a kiss, nipping her bottom lip with his teeth. "You want me to slam inside your pretty pussy, don't you."

"I do."

"Well, I'm not going to tonight. I'm going to take my time with you, Dina Whitlock. I'm going to fuck you so hard you won't know how to say anything but my name."

Anticipation pulsed through her.

"But . . . I want—"

He caressed her hardened nipples with his thumbs, making her hiss.

"I know. Me too. But not tonight. We have a wedding to go to tomorrow, remember?" Scott smiled cheekily as he lifted her into his arms and stood up, his hands kneading at her ass as he carried her. She felt her limbs go loose. Now she thought about it, it had been a long day, and she was exhausted.

His chest was so warm, and she felt like she could tuck her chin into the crook of his neck and smell Scott's scent forever. He carried her across the cottage and toward his room.

"My bed is over there," Dina whispered sleepily as Scott kicked open the door to his room and tossed back the duvet.

"Not anymore. You're sleeping with me, okay?"

"Yes, okay."

Scott placed her down into his bed, and she shivered against the chilled sheets. But only for a moment, because then Scott was behind her, his warmth against her back. His chest hair brushed up against her skin. She felt safe, she was home. A single kiss was pressed to her neck. Dina snuggled back into Scott and let sleep claim her.

Chapter 21

Dina woke up in a bed with sheets that smelled like cedar and fresh soap. Scott's smell. A sunny haze of light lit the trees outside, turning the evergreen leaves different shades of emerald. The things he'd said to her last night. Wanting to take his time with her. Oh goddess, it was enough to make her tingle with anticipation.

Only she wasn't in his arms, and his side of the bed was cold. Dina rolled over. A sinking feeling grew in the pit of her belly. This had happened before. She would spend the night with someone, her feelings would get the better of her, and then in the morning they'd be gone.

When was the last time she'd been so gooey over someone like this, over a *man* especially? She wished she could lie in this bed all day, smelling Scott's scent and not thinking about why he wasn't here with her.

It was so peaceful, the bed sheets so soft and warm, maybe she could just close her eyes for a bit longer . . .

FUCK.

The wedding. The fucking wedding. Immy was going to murder her. Worse, Immy was going to have her hung, drawn, and quartered and served up on a platter labeled "Worst Maid of

Honor in Existence, One of a Kind." Dina hurled herself out of bed and out the door. And nearly careened into Scott who was walking back—deliciously shirtless—with a cup of steaming coffee in each hand.

"Whoa there," he chuckled. "Where are you racing off to?"

"What time is it?" she squeaked. "We're so screwed."

"Dina, we're fine. It's seven-thirty. You just slept through the alarm. We have like two hours to get ready."

"It's seven-thirty . . . I slept through the alarm? I've never done that before." Dina stopped in her tracks. What magic had this man performed on her last night to transform her into a heavy sleeper?

"Well, you did have quite a late night," Scott said, barely able to keep the smugness off his face.

It was a good thing he had such a handsome face, otherwise pre-coffee Dina might have been tempted to wipe that smile right off. How had she never noticed the small scar above his right eyebrow before? Oh crap, she was mooning over him.

"Please say one of those is for me." She eyed the steaming mugs in his hands.

"Short answer, yes. But I wasn't sure what kind of coffee you drank, and you looked so cute sleeping—and snoring, by the way—"

"I do not snore."

"Sure. Well, you were asleep so I didn't want to wake you to ask, so I made, uh, a few different options." Scott shrugged, handing Dina a mug. "This one's just black, and there's a latte and a cappuccino waiting for you in the kitchen." She could get used to being treated like a princess. Wordlessly, Dina put down the cup of black coffee—her preferred form of coffee for first thing in the morning—and wrapped her arms around Scott's neck, leaning in to meet his mouth with hers.

Scott let out a surprised groan of delight as she kissed him, and hastily placed his own cup of coffee down so he could fold Dina into his arms. Like she belonged there.

This kiss was different to any of last night's. It was slower, deeper. Both of them taking their time, getting to know the touch of each other's lips, breath mingling.

Scott broke away, placing a flurry of kisses along Dina's cheek and jawline and neck, sending shivers through her that rolled right down to her toes. This kiss was sweet, and caring, and it was making her heart beat at a pace it only tended to reach during a heavy gym session.

"You smell like chocolate," Scott murmured against the hollow of her collarbone. "Is it magic?"

Dina let out a laugh of delight. This man . . . this man was going to end her, he was so fucking cute.

"Not magic. Just cocoa butter. But we should probably talk about the magic." She leaned back, but Scott's arms remained wrapped around her, one hand slowly caressing the small of her back.

"Okay, we can talk about it." His hands moved to grab her ass and scooped her up. Without thinking, Dina wrapped her legs around him.

"Scott, I said we need to talk about the magic!" She laughed as he carried her into the living room.

"We are, I just wanted to make you more comfortable," Scott replied as he plonked Dina down onto a pile of cushions on the sofa.

"And you needed to carry me?" she called after him as he went to fetch their mugs of coffee.

Scott handed her the coffee, and she noticed that his hands were so large that his fingers enveloped the whole circumference of the mug. And she knew what those hands could do . . .

He looked at Dina, his eyes darkening as he sat beside her on the sofa.

"Yes," he said responding to her question. "I—I can't stop touching you, Dina. I don't want to. I've wanted to touch you since, well, since we met."

"Since we met? I wasn't exactly at my best when we met at the café," she said.

"Well, I wasn't on my best form that day either, but that didn't stop me noticing how beautiful you were."

God help her, she was blushing. Dina tucked one of her curls behind her ear.

"The magic," she said matter-of-factly.

"Right. Are you going to make me guess what you are in some kind of convoluted *Twilight*-style reveal? I can do the whole spider-monkey thing if you're into it." Scott grinned.

"I'm sorry, but are you insinuating that you've seen *Twilight*?"

"I have two mums, of course I've seen *Twilight*."

"Consider me impressed. But no, I wasn't going to make you guess. I think it's fairly obvious—I'm a witch." Dina exhaled. Just saying the word in front of Scott felt like a weight being lifted.

He knew now; he knew the secret she only shared with a select few. Maybe this was self-sabotage, and he was about to run a mile. But then again she'd already shown him her moonlight spell, and he hadn't run away from her then.

"I know you're a witch, Dina," Scott said, his voice low and soft. She looked up and met his eyes. Warm, inviting. He wasn't pushing her away. "And I hope you know this, but your secret is safe with me. I love that you have magic, and I love that you trust me enough to share that part of yourself with me."

She squeezed his hand and he let out a hiss. Dina looked down, noticing an angry burn on the back of Scott's hand.

"What happened?" she asked.

"It's nothing, I just burned myself with the kettle this morning by accident."

"Well, it doesn't look like nothing. Here, let me . . ." She placed both hands over the burn and muttered a small spell in Darija. A warm light glowed against Scott's skin for a moment, and she heard him sigh. When she lifted her hands the burn was healed to a silver scar.

It was just a burn, she told herself. It couldn't be the hex. Not yet. It was too soon.

"You beautiful witch," Scott growled, and pulled her onto his lap. Dina's legs straddled his waist, and she became acutely aware of the fact that she was wearing nothing but a cotton camisole and a pair of knickers.

Scott's palms trailed down her arms, sending shivers across her back—and lower. Her nipples hardened to points, arousal flaring inside her.

"*How* am I supposed to go and get ready when you're over here looking like this?" he said roughly, his eyes dark. His thumb stroked her nipple over her top and she let out a soft moan.

Scott tugged down her camisole and his lips found her breast, his warm tongue caressing her nipple, before he bit her ever so gently with his teeth. Shockwaves of desire rippled through Dina, her back arching.

He ran his hand over her knickers.

"So wet for me already," he hissed.

The prospect of getting ready for the wedding felt far away as she pressed herself close to Scott's chest, feeling the fast thrum of his heart. He was as wild for her as she was for him.

Her fingers teased their way down his chest and the line of dark hair that disappeared into his jogging bottoms.

His cock was already hard, and the feel of it pushing against his trousers, solid and thick, left her panting.

"Dina, let me taste you again," Scott rumbled, his face buried between her breasts, his fingers tugging at her underwear.

"Yes," she whispered back. She couldn't get her knickers off fast enough.

And then, at the worst possible moment, just as Scott's fingers teased the entrance of her swollen pussy, there were three knocks at the door. A shadow was visible through the small convex window that was set into it, but Dina couldn't tell who it was.

Scott groaned and pressed a kiss to her shoulder, his fingers reluctantly sliding away from her pussy to rest on her thigh. Oh, she was aching for him.

"Who is it?" Scott called out with gritted teeth.

"It's Martin. I've been sent to, er, deliver a message. From the bride and groom." For a moment, panic flushed through Dina and she looked over at the clock that hung above the fireplace. But no, it was only seven forty-five—she still had ages to get ready before she needed to go and help Immy with her dress.

"What's the message?" Dina asked. She was glad that Martin hadn't asked to be let inside; she didn't feel like getting off Scott's lap just yet. From the way his arms grasped her ass cheeks, she was sure he didn't want that either.

"They wanted me to say, and these were their words exactly: 'Just a reminder that you can't spend all day bonking, because you have a wedding to attend.'"

Dina barely stifled a laugh.

"Was that it?"

Martin cleared his throat awkwardly. "Yes, that's all."

"Well, thanks for checking in, Martin. You can tell the bride and groom not to worry, we'll save our bonking for later," Scott said.

"Right. Good." And then Martin's shadow was gone, and they heard his shuffling footsteps heading back along the path.

Scott turned back to Dina.

"Who says 'bonking'?" He exhaled a laugh.

"That would be Immy."

"Ah, I should have known. It seems like we have our orders." He stared at her breasts mournfully.

"Did you mean what you said?" Dina asked.

"About what?"

"About saving our, um, bonking for later."

Scott smiled, and moved his head toward Dina's, meeting her lips with his own. She savored the warmth of his mouth, the taste of him. Scott tipped her face to the side, his mouth meeting her ear.

"Oh, believe me, I meant it."

Chapter 22

"Put it down, Immy—don't make me use a stun spell."

"You wouldn't dare."

"Don't try me. Put the eyeliner down."

With a dramatic sigh of reluctance, Immy put down the black liquid eyeliner she'd been threatening to use on herself. Dina scrambled to get it out of the bride's reach, throwing it to Rosemary, who cleverly tucked it away somewhere Immy wouldn't be able to locate it for the next twenty minutes.

Dina looked at her friend, who was currently staring mournfully at herself in one of those illuminated Hollywood mirrors.

"This isn't cold feet, is it?" Dina asked.

"No, nothing like that. I just don't—this doesn't feel like me," Immy replied, gesturing at the full face of contour makeup featuring a bronze smoky eye and dark nude lip that a makeup artist, one that Eric's parents had booked, had just finished.

"You look beautiful," Rosemary chimed in, and Immy smiled weakly.

"She's not wrong," Dina added, "but if you don't feel like yourself then we need to fix that, don't we."

"I can just feel how heavy it is on my skin, and these eyelashes are seriously weighing me down." Immy looked pointedly at Dina. "Is there anything *you* can do to fix it?"

Spells to alter things like paint and makeup weren't Dina's strong suit; she fared much better with baking spells. Thankfully, there *was* someone nearby who could fix this.

Dina tapped one of the pendants around her neck three times. *Mama, can you come up to the bridal suite, please: We need your help.*

Dina felt her thought travel into the pendant, which felt warm to the touch. A moment later, the shadow of a voice echoed in her mind. *I'm coming.*

Nour swayed into the bridal suite in a teksheta of midnight blue and gold, complete with billowing silk sleeves embroidered with golden crescent moons.

"Wow, Nour, I don't think you've ever looked more like a witch," Immy exclaimed.

Nour laughed. "It's a good thing I'm here to work my magic then." She strode purposefully across the suite to Immy's chair.

"Oh, habiba, what did they do to you!" she tutted, squishing Immy's face between her hands.

"Can you fix it, Mama?" Dina asked.

"Mmm. I came prepared." Nour reached into a pocket deep in the folds of her teksheta. She removed a small paper pouch that smelled strongly of saffron and nutmeg. And magic—a scent that Dina couldn't truly describe. Like the air before a summer storm, the shivers you get when you listen to a beautiful piece of music, mixed with that feeling of waking up and seeing the first snow of winter.

"What's that?" Immy inquired.

"This is a little concoction I use myself, but it's not to be trifled with. I need you to focus, Immy. I'm going to count to three, then I'm going to blow this powder onto your face."

". . . Okay," Immy said, sounding unsure.

"And when I do, I want you to imagine how you've always wanted to look on your wedding day. How you imagined your makeup, but more importantly how you wanted to feel inside. All that joy, all that excitement. Keep your eyes closed. Understand?"

"I think so," Immy replied. She looked to Dina for reassurance, so Dina smiled back.

"Okay, count of three. Dina, take a step back so it doesn't go all over you."

Dina did as she was told. The spell wasn't for her; she didn't want to accidentally affect the magic by standing too close.

On the count of three, Nour opened the small parcel and blew the golden powder onto Immy's face. She was enveloped in a cloud of sparkling gold and deep amber, until the powder dissipated into the air as if it had never been there at all.

Not even a stain on the furniture.

"Immy, you look stunning!" Dina squeaked, as Immy turned to behold herself in the mirror. The slickest cat eyeliner and bold red lips stared back at her, and Immy couldn't help but beam. She got up and threw her arms around Nour, pulling Dina into the hug too.

"What would I do without you both!"

Nour stood back and looked over the makeup appraisingly. "Very good. Very good. Now don't party too late, because that's going to disappear from your face at three-thirty A.M. sharp."

"Why three-thirty?"

"Rules are rules." Nour took Immy's hand in her own. "Immy, I'm so proud of you. You look beautiful."

"Thank you, Nour," Immy replied. "Don't make me start crying now you've fixed my makeup!" she cried, patting her eyes with a tissue.

"Okay, okay, I'm just being an emotional old lady. You can cry all you like though, it's waterproof."

As she stood in the doorway, she looked back at them.

"My girls," Nour smiled. "All grown-up and getting married."

Dina let out a laugh. "Only Immy's getting married, Mama."

Nour gave her daughter a sly, knowing smile. "Don't question a witch's intuition, Dina. It never lies."

And with that, Nour sauntered out.

"A whole family of witches," Rosemary said. "Do you think you'd ever let me write about it?" She looked over at Dina hopefully.

"Sorry, I already sold my life story to Immy," she said.

"Yeah, and I've got exclusive rights!" the bride cackled. "Right, you two, help me into my dress."

Immy's dress was a thing of beauty. Dina remembered her description of her dream dress: a deep-plunge neckline, and long sleeves that widened at the forearm. It looked like it could have been Morticia Addams's wedding dress, if she'd ever worn white.

"I think I'm going to cry," Dina sighed as she draped the veil across Immy's face.

"You better bloody not or I'll start crying. And then I'll start sweaty crying and I'll be a wreck before we even get downstairs," Immy sniffed. Dina handed her friend the bouquet of sunflowers.

"Eric's one lucky bastard," Rosemary said.

Immy looked at herself in the full-length mirror, her blonde hair cascading down her back in an elaborate plait, fresh flowers woven into the braid.

"Yeah, actually, he is."

Dina's heart lifted as she heard the confidence in Immy's voice. It hadn't always been like this; she remembered late-night phone calls filled with tears when other boys had broken her heart.

And with each broken heart Dina had performed just a tiny little hex, so the next day they would step on dog shit. If they treated her friend like shit, then they would have to step in it. Dina was a firm believer in poetic—and petty—justice.

"I think they're ready for us," Rosemary called from the doorway.

Dina arched an eyebrow. "You ready to get married?"

"Hell yeah!" Immy laughed and took Dina's outstretched arm. Dina wasn't just going to play the role of maid of honor today. She was going to walk Immy down the aisle.

Chapter 23

The morning had gone by in a flash. Dina had regretfully placed a spell on her door that wouldn't let her open it until she was ready—and in her words, "not super horny." Scott had a million and one questions about the functionality of a spell somehow measuring her horny levels and interpreting them for the logical operation of the door like some kind of magical chastity belt, but mostly he was secretly chuffed that Dina wanted him enough that she had to bespell herself in order to get ready on time. His growing ego worried she might get stuck in there perpetually.

He didn't have the same magic at his disposal, and it had taken quite a few deep breaths and distracting thoughts to get his semi to go down. Dina had called to him when she was leaving the cottage to go and help Immy prepare—and, as pre-agreed, he'd reluctantly remained in his room until she was gone. That lock spell hadn't seemed so stupid anymore.

It had taken an obscene amount of willpower not to open up his bedroom door and scoop Dina into his arms. He would tip her onto the kitchen counter and bury his face in the heat of her thighs, just to hear that sweet little sound she made in the back of her throat as she came, and then he'd fuck her on every single surface and against every wall of the cottage. He would have her screaming his name on her knees tonight.

But he'd remained firm. Christ, had he remained firm.

This was Eric and Immy's wedding day. He had to be there for his best friend, just as much as Dina needed to be there for Immy.

Scott found Eric doing stress push-ups in his suite.

"I hope those aren't cold-feet push-ups," Scott laughed as he closed the door behind him.

"Not in a million years—have you *seen* Immy? I'd be a madman," Eric huffed, sitting back on his knees. There had always been this ease between them. If Scott had had a brother, he imagined it would feel a lot like what he had with Eric.

"I got you a little wedding gift," Scott said, pulling out his phone. Eric arched an eyebrow, as he re-centered his tie.

"Oh?"

"Here. Take a look." Scott handed over his phone and watched in delight as Eric's eyes widened at the picture.

"Is this what I think it is? Mate, are you serious?" Eric clapped an arm around Scott, pulling him into a hug. "A boat? A fucking boat?"

"You deserve it. How many years have we spent rowing in that shitty little rented pair."

"Ah, I see. Really this is a present for you."

"For you and me both. But there's something else. Zoom in there." Scott pointed at the left corner of the photo.

"Fuck off!" Eric exclaimed as he noticed it. Scott had named the new boat the *Immy*. "This is some seriously cheesy shit, but I love it. Seriously. Scott, thank you," he said sincerely.

"What do you think Immy will make of it?"

"She'll probably call us backward for deigning to do something so medieval as naming a boat after a woman, but I'm sure she'll secretly love it."

"Maybe you could even take her out in the boat once or twice," Scott suggested.

"Ha. We tried that once. She counted the number of times I splashed her and then she wouldn't speak to me for the corresponding amount of hours. My lovely wife-to-be does not enjoy the wet or the cold."

"Not long until it's just 'wife.'" Scott smiled. "You ready?"

*T*he double doors to the grand ballroom of Honeywell House swung open to usher them inside. It was the kind of room that people dreamed about for their wedding, with white wood paneling on the walls, tasteful chandeliers, and floor-to-ceiling windows that looked out over the rolling hills and autumn-tinged trees of the estate.

In the corner of the room, a woman was playing a harp, the soft melody of "At Last" echoing through the space. Their cue to begin walking down the aisle.

From the ceiling, lanterns in sage green and robin's egg blue hung like jewels, glowing gently. Flowers were gathered and tied to the seats that flanked the aisle: irises, bluebells, peonies. All of Immy's favorite blooms, some of which weren't even in season at this time of year. That had been a maid-of-honor task for Dina's magical expertise. Immy had asked for multicolored sunflowers and Dina had made them for her.

"This is really happening," Immy whispered through her veil, her arm linked with Dina's. She was so glad her friend had asked her to walk her down the aisle.

Dina glanced over at Immy, but her eyes were focused on Eric, standing at the end of the aisle, his red hair ablaze in the sunlight cascading in through the window.

All the guests' eyes were on Immy, their smiles wide, handkerchiefs dabbing away tears as they took in the beautiful bride.

Everyone except Scott. He met Dina's gaze with a ferocity that took her breath away. The room fell away. The whole world fell away. It was just the two of them. His gaze held hers and she felt a tug, deep within her chest. A tug that was pulling her to him. It wasn't just a desire to be near him, but to know him, his every oddity and penchant and habit. She wanted to see him first thing in the morning and last thing at night. She wanted to know exactly what he would order at every restaurant, what his comfort movies were, what songs he listened to when he needed to drown out the world.

Dina tried to stifle the feeling of dread biting at the heels of her joy. She should have known he'd be trouble for her, and she desperately didn't want anything to happen to him. She thought of Alex, the chef she'd dated and the burns he'd received, and Eliza and her head injury. What would the hex do to Scott if she didn't push him away now?

There was still no denying how she felt around him. Scott made her feel more whole, more complete. He made her want to be a better version of herself.

Tears pricked at her eyes, and she wanted Scott to come and kiss them away and tell her it would be all right. Maybe she could find a way to break the hex this time? Maybe Scott would reveal himself to be some kind of womanizing asshole, making it easier to walk away, but Dina knew that wasn't the case.

She pushed back against the feeling that wanted to name itself, held the door closed as it prodded every chamber of her heart.

Anyone looking would just think that Dina's tears were from happiness for her friend.

She caught a glimpse of her mum in the corner of her eye, and the knowing smile on her face as she took in Dina's expression. Her mother knew she barely ever cried, and Dina bet that sly witch knew exactly what she was crying about now.

They reached the end of the aisle and Eric was smiling at Dina as he took Immy's arm from hers and helped his bride onto the dais.

Dina moved numbly to stand at the side, her fingers gripping the bouquet. She wished there was more air in this room. And she wished for a future with Scott where they could be together and the hex would never hurt him.

Dina took her hope and pressed it down into a kernel in her heart. A small but heavy weight that sank into her stomach, viscous and bitter.

The ballroom was cavernous yet stuffy, and she trained her attention on a patch of dust motes visible in the rays of sunlight streaming in through the window. Dina quietly forced one deep breath and then another, as the harpist plucked the last few notes of the song.

At least now all she had to do was stand here, and smile. She could do that. Dina pasted a smile onto her face and kept her eyes firmly on Immy's tear-streaked cheeks.

God, how selfish do you have to be to be crying about your own love life at your best friend's wedding?

The beginning of the ceremony went by in a blur. Eric had the whole room laughing during his vows, although Immy's reaction was more like laughter intermixed with sobs. Then Immy almost whispered her vows to Eric, as if her words were for him and him alone.

The officiant then led them through the more formal parts of the ceremony, and the exchange of rings. Now Dina was up. She snapped out of her haze.

Striding over to stand between the bride and groom, Dina began her handfasting.

She held in her hand three ribbons plaited together, all of them different colors. Red for passion, yellow for joy, and green for loyalty. Dina couldn't imagine a couple better suited to each other and had beamed when they'd suggested she do a handfasting.

"If you could place your hands together, palm to palm," she announced, her voice trembling a little. She didn't usually mind speaking in front of people, but the emotions of the day were clearly taking their toll. She risked a glance at Scott, and as his warm smile enveloped her, she found it a little easier to breathe. Her voice steadied.

Dina took the plaited ribbons and began to wrap them ceremonially around Immy and Eric's joined hands.

"These are the hands of your best friend, your lover, your partner, through all the trials and tribulations of your life, who on this day you have promised to love and support forever. These are the hands that will wipe tears from your eyes, and give you strength when you need it. These are the hands that will still be reaching for yours, even when you are old and gray and dreaming of sleep."

Someone sniffed away tears in the audience, and Dina relaxed slightly. Crying aunt, check.

As she spoke, Dina let a small flurry of magic escape her fingertips, delicate and silk-like.

The magic wouldn't change anything about Eric and Immy's relationship; it would just help strengthen the bonds they'd already made. Dina liked to think of it this way: If Immy and Eric ever got into an argument over some trifling, unimportant thing, they would find themselves remembering this day, this moment. They would feel a tug on their wrist, urging them closer to each other, toward the familiar comfort of each other's arms. Passion, joy, loyalty.

To Dina's eyes, the magical bond glowed a deep gold. No one else would be able to see her magic, apart from her mum. Immy smiled up at Dina.

She stepped back and watched as the officiant pronounced

them husband and wife. Eric folded Immy into his arms and Dina couldn't help but feel the surge of joy in her heart.

After that, the ceremony was over. The harpist began playing again, this time a more upbeat romantic tune. Immy pulled Dina in for a bear hug with surprising strength given her smaller stature.

"It was perfect, thank you," Immy cried into her hair.

"You don't need to thank me for that, Imms, that's all on you two." Dina leaned back and took her friend's cheeks in her hands. Immy was incandescent with joy, and it had rubbed off on Dina. Today wasn't a day to wallow; there were plenty more days for that if she needed them.

As Dina stepped back, Immy and Eric were swarmed at the edge of the altar by their friends and family. She glanced around the room, her eyes instinctively searching for Scott. God, one night of hot, heavy nearly-sex and already she was lost to this man.

Suddenly, there was a large warm hand around hers. A growling, low voice in her ear. Warm breath sending tingles down the nape of her neck.

"Come with me," Scott said, and he pulled Dina out of the crowded room. His hand enveloped hers entirely, tugging her gently down the hallway. He didn't speak, didn't even glance at her, but a small smile quirked the corners of his lips upward. Where was he taking her?

With a flash of a grin, Scott opened a door to a room off to the side. Some kind of antechamber, or maid's room.

Honestly, Dina wasn't paying it an iota of attention. Because Scott was there, and his arms were around her, and when she looked up at him his hair was doing that amazing, curly thing that it did. Scott tilted his face down to meet hers, smiling all the while.

The kiss was breathless, desperate. She needed to be closer to him—more than this. She needed his skin on her skin. His lips on her ear, his tongue trailing down her neck, between her breasts. He let out a muffled groan as he pried Dina's breasts free from the constraints of her dress, taking one of them into his mouth. Scott's hands grabbed hungrily at her thighs, and it was possessive—and Dina fucking loved it. She thanked the goddesses that she'd decided not to wear tights beneath her dress, giving Scott easy access to slip his hand beneath her already-soaked underwear.

A voice just outside the door. Fuck, someone was outside. The door handle began to twist, Dina's heart flaring in alarm.

"Fuck. Not again," Scott muttered, but he seemed to have more of his wits about him than Dina did.

He scooped her up and rushed into the nearby closet, which happily appeared to be mostly empty, save for a few coats (maybe they were in a cloakroom then?), and he managed to pull the door closed just as someone walked into the room.

It was pitch black inside the closet, and Dina was acutely aware that her breasts were still out, pressed against Scott's heaving chest. She couldn't see him, but she felt him lean down to whisper in her ear. "That was close." His breath sent shivers across her collarbone.

"Yeah," was all she managed to whisper back, her voice shaky. There were two voices in the room, and not ones she knew well. Wait, that was definitely the registrar. And the other voice . . . Martin, the steward. What was it with this man and interrupting her and Scott?

Even so, Dina didn't mind being in an enclosed space with Scott. She could feel the thick bulge of his erection pressing against her hip. She bet if she took him in her mouth now, the tip of his cock would already be wet.

Scott seemed to have similar ideas, because his hands had moved to cup Dina's butt cheeks, massaging them. He let out a sound that was partway between a moan and a vibration, as he slipped a finger, and then two, into Dina's soaking pussy. Dina bit her lip, but a small squeak came out. They were going to need to be a lot quieter if they were going to do this.

"Such a pretty cunt," Scott growled, moving lower. And then his face was buried between her legs. He lapped at her wetness with his tongue, first soft and then harder, flicking her clit in such a way that it sent shudders through Dina.

She never came this easily, this quickly. Yet now she could feel it building with each motion. Scott's fingers plunged in and out of her, while his mouth sucked, kissed and did all sorts of wondrous things. He was everywhere at once. Dina ran her fingers through his hair, relishing the feeling of having him between her thighs. Like he was meant to be there. The voices still spoke on the other side of the door, but they were a whole world away. Nothing else mattered now.

"Come for me, good girl," Scott whispered, his mouth still moving against her. Scott knew what Dina wanted; he would give it to her. Dina wrapped her legs around Scott's upper back, resting them there. From the way Scott shifted himself, she knew he liked it. And—oh fuck—she couldn't hold on anymore, not when he did that thing. The orgasm swept over her in delectable waves, bright spots of light dancing before her eyes.

Only she wasn't blacking out, there really was light in the closet, and it was coming from her. Small thimbles of light bubbled up and out of her skin, floating around them like dandelion seeds. Or fireflies. Scott looked up from between her legs, his face smeared and shining with her orgasm. His eyes widened as he took in the sight.

"Well, that's definitely never happened to me before."

How many times in Dina's life had she orgasmed? Not once had actual sparks of magical light burst from her body. Immy and Rosemary were going to flip a lid when Dina told them about this. Maybe it was this place, its magic. Or maybe it was Scott.

Scott looked at her in the faint, golden glow. His face was full of wonder, and something else, something that made Dina's heart soar. Her pulse thrummed in her ears.

"Amazing, you're amazing," he said. Not an ounce of fear or apprehension.

"I don't know how it happened," Dina whispered back, but she couldn't wipe the smile from her face. A devilish grin appeared on Scott's face.

"I know how." He smiled, before burying his head between her legs again, and shattering Dina's world into a million glowing pieces.

Chapter 24

*S*cott had thought he was in trouble before, but that was barely scratching the surface. Now, though, he was in deep mires of shit. A real quicksand situation.

Scott had told himself that he was trying very hard not to fall in love with Dina. No way should he feel this happy; it was unnatural.

Throughout the wedding afternoon he'd found himself attuned to her. The way her face had crinkled in delight as she'd presented Immy and Eric with the tower of cinnamon buns. When he'd given his speech, reading out a passage from Eric's teenage diary, it was her laughter he heard the loudest.

Dina's insistent joy was wearing down the guards he'd placed around himself after Alice. It had taken every single ounce of his strength not to tell Dina about his growing feelings when those sparkles had popped out from her. She'd been literally glowing for him; and from the elated post-orgasm surprise that had been written all over her face, he'd known this was special for her too. From somewhere deep in the back of his mind, the logical part of his brain cried out that it shouldn't have been possible. But that was Dina for you. Everything about her defied expectations.

Christ, he wanted to lavish this woman for the rest of their lives. He couldn't get enough of her taste, her smell. The way her eyes widened as she took him all in. The way he'd woken up to a mouthful of her giant octopus hair in the morning and wouldn't have had it any other way. Her kindness, her intelligence; every newly discovered facet of her personality made him care for her more deeply.

Was he kidding himself? After this weekend was over, and the glitz of the wedding faded into memory, would she still want to be with him? An ache grew in his chest at the thought of not seeing Dina every day for the rest of his life.

But it started off the same with Alice, didn't it? that evil little intrusive voice piped up. He'd been smitten then too, not that that had ever changed on his part during their time together. But perhaps that was his problem.

He fell in love too easily, trusted too quickly. He hadn't noticed the signs with Alice; the sex had been good, and he'd known his way around her body, but there were times he'd sensed her heart wasn't in it.

That he was just a body there to fuck her and be fucked. With Dina though, she'd been all there. She'd wanted him—Scott—the whole time they'd been together. Fuck, he was hard again just thinking about the way she'd taken him in her mouth last night—eager, so eager.

She didn't mind the way he became possessive in the bedroom, the way he took charge. In fact, she liked it. Like she was made to be pleasured by him.

He wanted her pretty mouth around his cock again, and the red lipstick she was wearing now was definitely not helping. It made her lips look plump, edible. He wanted to see it staining his body.

He had to at least try to simmer down a little or he was never going to get through the evening. They'd made a pact earlier in the closet, after all the floating lights had faded (he couldn't wait to make *that* happen again), that they wouldn't escape to any more closets, or back to the cottage, before the night was over. They were best man and maid of honor after all; they had duties to fulfill.

Duties which had mostly involved force-feeding water and espressos to drunken uncles who seemed to have started on the prosecco too early. One of whom was now snoring away on a loveseat in the corner of the ballroom.

The stewards of Honeywell House had really outdone themselves with the decoration. As with the rehearsal dinner, everything was lit by candlelight. Delicate crystal chandeliers hung from the ceiling, light danced from the brass sconces on the walls, and there were pillars holding bowls of water with small tealight candles floating on the top in the shape of water lilies. It was like a set from one of those Nancy Meyers movies his mums had made him watch growing up.

Earlier, during the reception, Scott had seriously considered taking Immy aside and asking her to throw the bouquet to Dina. And then he'd thought better of it because he'd realized that would make him look like a crazy person.

Was he really thinking of marriage already? Of course. It was impossible not to when he looked across the dance floor and saw Dina busting out some seriously dorky moves with Immy. Somehow she made even silly air punches look graceful. And the way the candlelight set her warm brown skin aglow, she was perfect to him.

"You're not being very subtle you know," a voice said from beside Scott. Dina's father stood there, a wise smile on his face. He could see how Robert Whitlock could have used his height and build to seem imposing—for someone who he'd been told was an accountant, the man was built like a competitive weight-lifter.

"What do you mean?" Scott replied, though his innocent tone was fooling no one.

"Anyone with eyes can see that you have it bad for my daughter." Uh-oh, was he about to have the "stay away from my daughter" talk with Robert?

"Sir, I—"

"Dina is a big girl, she can make her own mind up about who she wants to be with. I'm not going to stand in the way of that."

Phew, thank fuck for that. He'd been ready to fight for Dina if need be.

"But, my Dina is very special." Robert trained a quizzical look on Scott. "I wonder if she's told you just how *special* she is?"

It took Scott a second to register what he meant. The magic, he was talking about the magic.

"She has. I can't say I fully understand it all yet, and it's a lot to take in. But it doesn't faze me, not one bit."

Robert Whitlock's shoulders sagged with relief ever so slightly, and he gave Scott a hefty pat on the back. "Good man. Good man," he said, smiling.

For a brief second it made Scott wonder if Dina had shown anyone else her magic before, someone she'd been in a relationship with. He wondered how they'd taken the discovery.

"If you don't mind me asking, how did you find out about Dina's mother?"

"Oh, Nour was terrible at hiding it really. On our second date, we had a picnic, and she'd made these amazing puff pastry triangles called briouats. They're filled with almonds and honey and some such. Well, it was the best damn thing I'd ever eaten. That evening, when I went to my fridge, there were three briouats wrapped in foil. I definitely hadn't put them there. What was even stranger was that they kept reappearing in my fridge each day if I'd eaten them the day before. Just like, well, *magic*.

Of course, she never owned up to it. But I had a pretty good idea of what I was dealing with from that day on." Robert laughed as his wife swayed out from the growing crowd on the dance floor and came toward them.

"Did you find out if he's her boyfriend?" Nour asked her husband, her eyes narrowing suspiciously as she looked at Scott.

Robert pressed a kiss to his wife's head and laughed good-naturedly. "Between the two of us I think we might scare him off, cariad."

"So you're not dating our Dina?"

"I—not yet. I would like to be, but I think that's up to Dina," Scott replied. Having this chat with both of Dina's parents was only slightly mortifying. He'd be lying if he said he wasn't a little afraid of Nour though.

"Hmmph, that girl," she said, rolling her eyes. Then she reached out and took Scott's hand in a firm grip.

"What is—"

"Shh. I need to concentrate." Nour held up a finger, silencing him.

"Are you reading my palm?" he asked tentatively.

"No. I am reading your aura. It is very different, now stop asking questions."

Scott stood there in silence while Dina's mum read his aura, feeling strangely vulnerable. He had a feeling that the aura Nour was reading was not the same as the one that his mum Helene used to complain about seeing hours before a migraine kicked in.

She squeezed his hand and let it go.

"Did that work?" Scott asked, unsure.

Nour looked up at him appraisingly and smiled.

"I knew it. You two are good for each other," she said matter-of-factly. "But don't tell her I said that."

Scott smiled. "I won't."

Before Nour could attempt any other kind of "readings" on Scott, Robert dragged her back to the dance floor, where they disappeared among the throngs of dancers.

Scott chuckled as he watched Eric throw Immy into the air, twirling her around. He scanned the room. There Dina was, dancing in the candlelight, her brown and purple curls flicking back and forth, looking like a fucking goddess. And there was . . . what was his name? One of Eric's extended family, some cousin who worked in finance, who appeared to be eyeing up Dina as he stalked toward her.

Not just eyeing her up, he was eye-fucking her. Unpleasant shivers crawled up Scott's arms. Hell no, this was not happening.

Before he knew it, he was walking through the mass of tipsy dancers, making a beeline for Dina. Even with his long strides, he didn't reach her until Kyle—what kind of a name was Kyle?—had already started chatting away, salivating all over her. From the way Dina looked back at him, she didn't seem overly impressed.

". . . Anyway, can I buy you a drink? You look like a cosmo kind of girl," schmoozed Kyle, the walking ick, patting his overly gelled slicked-back hair. The smell of aftershave on him was overwhelmingly sour.

Dina's mouth was about to open in reply, but Scott couldn't help himself.

"There you are," he said, and he reached an arm around Dina's waist, tugging her close to him. She fit him perfectly, her ass brushing against his thighs.

Dina looked up at him, fully aware that Scott was acting like a possessive asshole, the twinges of a smile tugging at the corners of her full mouth.

"Hey, you," she replied, and pressed her body closer to his.

Fuck, this woman.

"Oh, hey dude," Kyle slurred to Scott, "didn't see you there." His eyes flitted sheepishly between the two of them. "So you hitting that then?"

Scott felt the vibration of anger coursing through Dina. If it was up to him, he'd get Kyle kicked out of the party right now, the leery piece of shit.

"He most certainly is hitting that, Kyle," Dina said, her voice silky soft, like she was a predator about to pounce. "You, however, won't be hitting anything for quite some time."

She framed it as an insult, but Scott noticed the spark of magic that jumped from her finger to Kyle's drink.

Before he could respond, Scott gripped Dina's hips and whirled her away into the center of the dance floor.

"What did you do?" he asked, smiling at Dina's cat-that-got-the-cream expression.

"Let's just say that Kyle will struggle to get it up for the next few days." She giggled.

"You were nicer than I would have been. He looked like the kind of guy who would spike your drink if he ever managed to wrangle you into letting him buy you one," he said, realizing now that Kyle had managed to rile him up.

"Well, it's a good job that you were here to save me then." Dina chuckled, winding her arms around his neck, her fingers playing with the curls at his nape. "That was very caveman of you. Me Scott. Dina my woman. Kyle no touch," she grunted out, but she leaned into his touch just the same.

"I didn't like the way he was looking at you," Scott said, leaning in to inhale the sultry scent of her skin. He wanted very badly to plant a row of kisses on her neck, to send delicate shivers up her spine.

"And how was he looking at me?" One of Dina's eyebrows curved upward.

"Like you were . . . well, not how a man should look at a woman."

"I didn't realize I'd stepped into the Regency era tonight. What's next, pistols at dawn?"

"Ha-ha. Though you don't seem to mind that he's turned his attentions elsewhere?" Scott mused, bending closer to Dina, brushing his lips against her ear.

"No, there's no one else I'd rather be dancing with," she said, looking up at him with those fathomless dark eyes.

She shifted closer, her breasts pressing against his chest, the stiff peaks of her nipples visible through the velvet slip. All for him. He was already hard, his bulge pressing against the material of his trousers.

"Let me kiss you," Scott whispered. And she did, their lips meeting, melting against each other. There was no universe in which he would tire of having her in his arms.

When they broke apart, Scott kissed the freckle above her eyebrow, and she didn't move away. They stayed like that for a while, Dina's cheek tucked beneath Scott's chin, swaying in the candlelight.

Others moved around them, the songs changed, but they carried on dancing. Never moving an inch farther apart. Scott could have stayed there forever, feeling the gentle swell of Dina's chest against his.

A peacefulness of the kind he hadn't felt in a long time spread out through his body. Home; he felt at home with Dina. Had he ever felt like this with Alice? Scott racked his brains but couldn't summon any memory with such clarity.

In fact, all of his memories of Alice seemed to be graying at the edges. Like they had happened in a past life, to another version of himself. A different man to the one who was slow-dancing with this magical goddess of a woman.

Dina shifted, tilting her face upward to look at him.

"Do you want to go back to the cottage?" she asked softly, the question carrying a weight to it. His body immediately reacted to her words, his senses tripping into a higher gear. He was aware of her breath against his neck, the supple curve of her belly and hips, the thickness of her ass. He wanted, he needed.

"Yes," Scott all but growled, delighting in the unsuppressed passion which flared in Dina's eyes in response.

"We should say goodnight to Immy and Eric."

"We could do it together?"

Dina smiled. "I'd like that."

Chapter 25

*D*ina's heart was just about ready to beat out of her chest. Any minute Scott would be here.

She'd wanted to walk back to the cottage—their cottage—with him, but as they'd been about to leave, Eric's rather tipsy father had cornered Scott into a conversation about his travels. Scott had tried multiple times to disengage himself, but once her own parents had walked over and got involved, there was no chance they'd get to leave together.

Dina had feigned tiredness and bid them all goodnight. Scott had glanced at her over the heads of the others, watching her leave with a hunger in his eyes.

I'll be waiting, she had mouthed at him. But how long could she stand to wait? She was already slick between her thighs, her folds swollen, aching to be touched by him.

Dina stood in her bedroom in the cottage, the room lit only by moonlight. *Of course* the moon was full tonight. She was so full of magic she was ready to burst. After earlier, in the closet, she was a little worried about how it might come out. Those twinkling lights that had emerged when Scott had made her orgasm . . . that had been new.

But more importantly, it hadn't fazed Scott. He hadn't run away, or even looked afraid. If anything, Dina thought he liked seeing what he did to her, how far she lost herself when she was around him.

She couldn't stand the feeling of this dress on her any longer. The only thing Dina wanted touching her was Scott's hands. She unclasped the dress at the back, and began tugging the straps down from her shoulders.

"Undressing you is my job," growled a low voice from behind her. Her body reacted to Scott's presence. If possible, even the sound of his voice was making her wet.

"Come and do it then," she whispered, her voice trembling. She heard him step toward her, acutely aware of his presence. The room thrummed with an invisible energy, like a thunderstorm waiting for release. His breath against the back of her neck; rippling shivers of anticipation.

Scott raked his fingers down the curve of her waist, roughly cupping her ass. She let out a whimper as he touched her, the heat of his hands on her sending her reeling.

"I need you out of this dress," he said, his breathing jagged. His fingers undid the rest of the clasps, and the wisp of a dress fell to the floor.

"Fuck," he groaned. "You weren't wearing a bra this whole time?" His mouth found the curve of her neck. "Why didn't you tell me?"

"You'd never have made it through the evening," Dina replied, much more coolly than she felt.

Scott huffed a laugh into her neck.

"You're right about that." One hand curved around to cup her breast, the other slipping around to her front, fingers grazing the seam between her thighs, pulling aside her knickers. He didn't touch her just yet, his fingers straying perilously close to her heat but at the last minute teasing away. Dina let out a moan of frustration at the almost-touches, arching her back, pressing her ass into Scott's firm erection.

"Please," she whispered. Scott had unlocked something in her. She knew in her gut that she could relinquish control to him. Dina spent her days being in charge, working hard. But here, with Scott, she could let it all go. He could be in charge. And damn if that wasn't the hottest thing in the world.

"I need you," she whispered.

Scott brushed her hardened nipple with his thumb until a shock of lust ran through Dina's entire nervous system. It was like he knew all the ways to drive her insane for him.

"Will you beg if I don't give it to you, Dina?" he whispered in her ear, sending a tremble right to her core. She would, she'd beg. With one rough tug he pulled her underwear off.

"Yes," she hissed as he caressed the seam of her pussy, his fingers rubbing against her clit with just the right amount of friction. She wasn't sure how long she could last.

When he plunged his fingers inside of her, Dina cried out. How could it feel so good? Had it ever felt this good with anyone else?

"Tell me, Dina. Is this all for me?" Scott growled against her throat.

"Yes, take it. Take me." She shuddered as his fingers pressed deeper, as she rode the palm of his hand.

"So fucking wet," he groaned. The hard press of his cock against her ass cheeks nearly sent her into a frenzy as he continued to fuck her with his fingers.

"Bend over for me so I can see you," he said, and Dina bent forward, resting her arms on the bed.

Scott was gone for a split second, and as his fingers left her she already felt bereft.

"Please, please," she moaned again, now on all fours.

"Such a pretty cunt," Scott said, his voice breaking apart behind her.

Then suddenly the emptiness ended, and Scott's mouth was

there, licking, sucking at her pussy. Drinking her in. Dina let out a cry of pleasure as the tickle of Scott's beard brushed against her folds.

He buried his face in her pussy, his tongue pushing inside her, flicking back and forth. And then his fingers were there as his mouth found her clit and sucked and kissed and then the orgasm broke through Dina, arching her back in pleasure, and she grabbed fistfuls of the bedsheets. Scott didn't let up; he continued to hold her there, burying his face deeper into her seam.

"Good girl," he said, lifting Dina back up as if she weighed nothing. She was glad to have his hands on her. She wasn't sure she'd be able to use her legs at that moment.

She faced Scott, looking up at him through half-closed eyes. The aftermath of the orgasm still rippled through her in electric shockwaves. But she still wanted more, needed more.

She needed to be filled by him.

"Fuck me, please," she begged, slick from seeing the way his beard shone with her. Scott craned his neck, his mouth closing over hers. She could taste herself on his tongue. This kiss wasn't soft.

It was lust, firm and wanting and crazed with desire. Their bodies wrapped around each other, fingers teasing, holding each other like they were the last people in the world.

"Why are you still dressed?" Dina said, her breath mingling with Scott's. An urge overcame Dina, and she sank down to her knees in front of him.

"Take off your shirt," she demanded. Scott stared down at her, his eyes dark. He pulled the shirt off over his head, not even bothering to undo the buttons.

Christ, from this angle he looked like he'd been carved by the gods. Thick, packed muscle. Black hair that sprawled out from his chest, down to the waistband of his trousers.

Dina couldn't drag her eyes away from him, as she unzipped

his fly. His cock practically sprang out, the thick, pink tip pushing out of his boxers. She tugged those down too.

And there he was. Heavy, muscled, thick dark hair. The tip already wet. A groan emitted from the back of Scott's throat as she took him in her mouth.

Dina wanted to be tantalizing. She wanted to tease him. But the moment she took him in her mouth, all of her plans broke down. She was desperate for him, she wanted to please him. Make him feel as good as he'd made her feel. Scott's hand caught in her hair, pulling back her curls from her face.

"You look like a goddess. On your knees for me." The way he spoke, that low, gravelly voice, it drove her insane. She sucked, moving her hand back and forth, taking him as deep into her throat as she could stand.

"Dina, *fuck*, Dina," Scott said. She could feel his inhibitions falling away as he thrust into her mouth. She hadn't known she liked that, Scott fucking her face, but she loved it.

And then suddenly Scott's arms were around her waist, lifting her up. Placing her on the bed, but not gently. He kicked off his trousers and boxers and then bent down, feeling for something in his pockets.

"I need you now," he growled. "Can I have you, Dina?"

"Yes, yes," she said, leaning back on the bed, shifting her hips so she was open for him.

"I need to get protection. It's in my room," Scott said, beginning to turn around.

"Are you clear?" Dina asked.

"I am, I can show you—I have a text on my phone," he replied.

Dina shook her head. "I trust you. Scott." She beckoned him to her. "I have the coil. We don't need to use a condom."

Scott reached for her, his strong arms tugging her onto his lap, the muscles of his thighs splayed out beneath her.

"Fuck, Dina," he groaned as she took his cock in her hands again. Fuck, how was this thing going to fit inside her? "If you keep doing that I'm not sure how long I'm going to last," he hissed.

"I need you inside me," she said, and with those words, Scott lost all semblance of control.

He tipped Dina backward, her back flat on the bed, her legs raised against the front of his chest.

The tip of his cock teased her opening.

"You want to feel me, sweetheart? All of me?" Scott asked roughly, rubbing her clit with the velvet tip of his cock.

"*Scott, yes,*" Dina hissed as he plunged into her, and the shock of his size was electrifying. She nearly came then and there just from the sheer force of it. He took up all the space inside her, and more. Scott wrapped his body around hers, the hot, firm parts of him pressed against her, turning her limbs to jelly.

Each thrust sent her spiraling, and her thoughts dissolved. It was only Scott's body and hers. Their mouths met, and as he thrust deep, Dina felt that this was it, this was as close as she could be to him. And still it wasn't enough. She needed him, closer, closer. More. When Scott's hand found her clit as he continued to drive inside her, each movement deeper, harder than the last, she lost herself again.

Dina couldn't tell where she ended and where Scott began; it was hot and messy and every millisecond of it felt excruciatingly good.

"I want to see you," he said, scooping her up and swinging her on top of him, so her thighs straddled his. "Ride this cock," he ordered.

The command shivered through her deliciously. Dina was on top of him, and as he lay back she planted her palms on his chest, feeling the rollicking beats of his heart, knotting her fingers around the black curls of his chest hair.

This was all new; she'd never been on top with a man before.

It had never really felt like there had been time for it, like the guy had always been chasing his orgasm, and having Dina on top would have been seen as a waste of time.

But not for Scott. He hissed with pleasure as Dina ground down on his cock, her hips thrusting back and forth, each movement sending a surge of delicious pulsing through her.

It was almost too much for her, taking him all like this. Scott gripped her ass, keeping her moving with him as the wave of pleasure rocketed over her, the jagged, raw orgasm rushing through her.

"Scott, Scott," she whispered, and he was there. His huge arms wrapped around her, his chest pressed against her, rocking gently as pleasure throbbed through her.

"I can feel you coming. Come for me, sweetheart, come on this cock," he hissed into her neck, licking up the sweat that beaded there.

Dina's body felt like jelly—had she ever come this many times during sex? She had a mind to wonder if this was even possible, but then again, she hadn't expected her magic to show itself in unexpected ways tonight.

She wasn't just being held in Scott's arms; she was safe there.

"I'm not done with you, Dina, not yet," Scott growled, rolling Dina over to her hands and knees. Scott's rough, calloused palms ran down her back, rubbing and massaging her ass cheeks.

"God, you're so beautiful, how are you so beautiful," he whispered, wonder in his voice. And then he pushed himself inside her, a perfect fit, and Dina melted away into a frenzy.

Each thrust seemed to push Dina deeper and deeper into a place that was warm and fuzzy and glowing with light. She didn't have the words to name it. It didn't have a name. Scott wrapped a hand around her, grounding her, his other hand slipping around her front and between her legs, teasing her swollen clit.

Dina let out a groan of pleasure; she'd thought her body was done but it showed no signs of stopping yet.

"Christ, Dina, I'm not sure how much longer I can hold on," he panted, his thrusts quickening. "Can I fill you up? I want to fill your pretty pussy." He bent over her so he could whisper in her ear, nipping at her earlobe with his teeth.

"Yes," she begged, "inside me," and that was all Scott needed to hear.

He let out a loud hiss of pleasure, his fingers rubbing Dina's clit just right at the same time, and the orgasm broke apart, shattering over them. Like a rumble of thunder. A bolt of lightning.

The cottage went dark. They lay there, panting and holding each other as heavy drops of rain began to fall.

Chapter 26

*S*cott had sometimes wondered how it would feel to have no bones. This was probably as close as he was going to get. Contentment didn't even begin to cover it. Dina's scent was all over him, and after they'd finished, they'd lain on the bed in a tangle of sweaty limbs. At some point, Dina had fallen asleep, and Scott had woken her up by kissing along her collarbone. Then he'd continued trailing that line of kisses all the way down her body, past her navel, to the warm seam of heat between her thighs. They'd lost themselves to each other for a while again after that.

Dina had left the room to clean herself up, and while she was gone Scott had smoothed the crinkled bedsheets. He'd lain on the bed, staring at the ceiling, enjoying the cool air of the autumn night and the sound of rain on the roof of the cottage. He wasn't sure how the next part would play out; would she come back into his arms? That was what he wanted, no doubt about it.

Or would she put her guard back up? The façade that said: *I'm not ready for this, stay back.* He wasn't sure what to make of it. Sometimes it was like she was two different people. She was clearly stopping herself from fully relaxing around him, safety-belting her emotions.

He couldn't fathom why, but if it was something that was in his power to fix, then he'd bloody fix it.

There was no doubt in his mind now that he was perilously close to falling in love with Dina. If it was possible, the sex had only made him fall further. The way her body had taken him in, safe and warm and secure, as if she'd been made for him.

Scott wondered if he should offer to go back to his own bed, in case that's what Dina wanted. He leaned over to flick on the side lamp, but the bulb was blown. It wasn't just that lamp; he tried all the light switches in the room. All of them were out.

"Promise you won't laugh at what I'm about to tell you," Dina said, standing in the doorway of the room, her skin still glistening from the shower.

"Hand on my heart," he said. He was glad she'd come back, but how was he supposed to think straight now he knew that's what she looked like wet? His cock was already swelling just at the sight of her luscious curves and soft belly.

"I think I might have caused a power cut."

"What? How?"

"When we, um, came together. I think my magic just—*pfff.*" Dina blew out a raspberry from between her lips. "And then there was some lightning, and boom."

"Oh, sorry, I think I'm going down. Oh no." Scott collapsed backward onto the bed. "I can't take it, it's too heavy," he moaned.

"What's heavy?" Dina asked, coming up to him.

"My ego, it's just too huge. How am I supposed to carry this around now I know I can turn you into a walking, orgasming EMP bomb?" He let out a huff of laughter as Dina fell on top of him, and he cradled her in his arms.

"I knew you'd be insufferable about it," she said, but she was grinning from ear to ear.

"Can I stay with you tonight?" Scott asked, tucking a stray curl behind her ear. The smile slipped from her face, and an unsure expression remained. "Only if you want," he added. The last thing he wanted was to make Dina feel like this was going too quickly.

"I do, it's just . . ." She frowned.

"Just what?"

"I think we might get hurt," she said, her voice ever so quiet.

His heart stuttered. "I won't hurt you, Dina. I could never hurt you."

"People around me. People I care about, they get hurt." She breathed against his skin. Scott reached out and tipped Dina's chin up so their eyes met.

"Dina, I know there's stuff you're not ready to tell me. I know that. And I'll never push you. But I'm not going anywhere. You're not going to wake up one morning and find that I've disappeared, nothing like that. I know it's a lot to ask of you this early, but you can trust me."

Dina looked searchingly into his eyes, like she might find her answer there, though Scott wasn't sure what she was looking for. All he could do was hold her and be there. And love her, if she let him.

Eventually, Dina closed her eyes, tucking her head onto his chest.

"Is that what happened to you? She just left?" Dina whispered, her hand absentmindedly stroking the dark hair that trailed down Scott's stomach.

"I wish. I think it might have been easier if that's what happened. Cleaner, maybe. No, I was away looking at artifacts in Scotland. I finished early, so I caught a train home to surprise her."

Scott felt himself falling into the memory of it, the bitter taste of that day sticking to the roof of his mouth. The excitement he had felt on that train journey home, thinking about how he could surprise Alice and take her out for a fancy dinner.

"When I got back to the flat, the first thing I heard was the creaking of the floor. It really is such a cliché. I walked in on her and one of her friends, a guy named Marc."

"Marc with a 'c'?" Dina asked

"Yeah."

"Oh, so he was definitely a lame-ass then."

"Ha-ha. Sure was." Somehow, talking about it with Dina, the bitter taste faded. He'd spoken about it all in therapy of course, but there was something different about getting it all off his chest with Dina here. He was laying himself bare before her, and she wasn't running for the hills or calling him damaged goods.

"What did it feel like, when you saw them?" Dina asked.

"I was angry, but not as much as I thought I would be. There was just this deep hurt, and that feeling of *Oh yeah, this all makes sense now.* And then instead of dealing with my feelings I just went abroad for two years."

"You were purging yourself of it."

"Yeah, I guess so. But I wish I'd never left. I missed out on so much. Seeing my best friend fall in love, being there for my mums. It doesn't weird you out to hear all about my baggage?" he asked, running his fingers through her hair. He wasn't sure when it had happened, but they had both slipped under the duvet, Dina's icicle feet wrapped around his calves.

"Not weird," she replied sleepily. "I want to know you." She yawned, her head growing heavy against his chest. Before long, Scott heard her breathing fall into a slower rhythm, with the cutest little snores.

He stayed running his fingers through her hair until sleep claimed him too.

Chapter 27

*D*ina couldn't stay in bed, even with Scott breathing deeply beside her. During the night, he had curled his body around hers, enveloping her in his warm, masculine scent. The hair of his chest tickled her back, his hand splayed out against the softness of her belly. It had been one of the best sleeps of her life, at first. The woods had whispered around them; it was cold outside but the duvet was deliciously cozy with them bundled underneath. She'd slept heavily for a few hours at least.

Until the nightmare came. Images of Scott covered in burns, or Scott lying in a hospital bed unable to remember her name. Scott with his arm and leg bandaged up; Scott with bruises, moaning in pain. Worry infiltrated her dream and pinned her down, making her watch the horror as it unraveled. All of the hurt she would cause him. Scott looking at her, resentment in his piercing gaze, knowing that she was the one causing his pain, she was the only one to blame. *Everyone who loves you will be hurt.*

It was too much to bear. So as the dawn light began to trickle through the curtains, Dina slipped out of bed, making sure that Scott still slept.

Carefully, she went about the house, putting on clothes, tucking her feet into boots. With a quick spell to muffle the sound of her unlocking the old wooden door, Dina left the cottage.

Thrushes sang in the trees all around her, and even though it was almost the start of winter, the woods were as alive as the first day of spring. Sunlight glinted gold on the trees, and she heard rabbits scrabbling about in the brush. Dina wandered through the trees, not heading anywhere in particular, just trying to clear her head. In the distance she saw the bonfire from two nights before. She would walk as long as she needed to for this feeling to fade.

The hex knew how she felt about Scott. But how did he feel about her? The things he said, the way he held her . . . it made her wonder. And then there were the signs: the burn from the kettle, the incident in the maze. Were they just bad luck, or was it the hex?

Fear suckled at her like a hungry leech.

If she was smart, she would pack up and go. She would tell Immy that she didn't want to see Scott again, and she would craft some kind of spell so he never set foot in her café again. He wouldn't understand why, and maybe that was for the best.

Dina meandered down a path that hadn't been trodden on for a long time, vaguely aware that she was being led somewhere by the magic of this woodland. It was a shy kind of magic—the kind that might vanish if you paid too much attention to it. So she didn't, she just continued to put one foot in front of another and see where it led her.

Dina knew that she'd lied to herself when she'd decided that sleeping with Scott would get him out of her system. Clearly, it had had the opposite effect. She couldn't stop thinking about him, dreaming about what it might be like if they could return to the real world, the world outside of this cottage and the wedding, and still be . . . together. Would he pop by the café every morning on his way to the museum? No, he'd walk there with her from her apartment (or his), and he'd sit and drink his coffee as she put the first batch of cakes in the oven. In the afternoons she'd go and visit him in his office and he'd show her all the amazing things he was working on.

Dina didn't even realize she was crying until the tears began to drip down her chin. She shouldn't be imagining this future for them; it was too dangerous. But perhaps—perhaps there was a way. If the universe could only give her a sign that she was making the right decision.

Dina looked up and found herself in a quiet glade, though that was the only thing her eyes could make sense of. Sunlight, much brighter than the tepid dawn, beat down through a circle of sky above her, a deep summer blue. Her skin prickled with an awareness that magic was at work here, though she wasn't sure if it was a witch's or the woodland itself. The entire glade was impossibly carpeted with bluebells. It was November, they shouldn't have been in bloom. But there they were, a dense meadow of bluish-purple flowers swaying in the breeze before her eyes. Impossible. Magical.

Dina felt a smile tickling the corners of her mouth. Perhaps this was the universe's way of telling her what to do. Perhaps, if bluebells could grow in a woodland glade in November, she and Scott could do the impossible too. If it wasn't in her power to break the hex, then she would do the next best thing. She would find a way to keep him safe.

"*W*as I that bad in bed that you're already trying to murder me?" Scott asked, grunting as he sat up against the pillows, sipping from a coffee Dina had made him.

"Don't move, I'm making sure it fits. I'll get you a longer chain when we're back in London," she said. She'd spent the entire walk back to the cottage considering her options. Sage and rosemary were the easiest protective herbs she could get her hands on quickly, and if she could get Scott drinking a tea made from them that would certainly help. But the best protection she could offer him would be her evil eye—her nazar amulet. The chain was a little short for him, but she still clasped it around his neck.

Dina wished there was a way she could tell if it was working, but if nothing bad happened to Scott then that would show her. And if she read his tea leaves carefully every evening then perhaps she could stop him from doing anything that might cause him harm. It would be laborious, keeping Scott safe and protected from the hex, but she was willing to put in the work. For the first time in a long while, Dina felt like she could fight back. The walk in the woods, and probably the multiple orgasms she'd had last night, had reinvigorated her spirit.

Scott pulled her onto his lap, and she wrapped her legs around him.

"Why am I wearing your necklace?" he asked.

"I want to keep you safe."

"Why wouldn't I be safe?" As he spoke, Scott planted kisses along her collarbone, almost absentmindedly. His mouth was warm against her skin.

For a split second, Dina considered telling Scott the truth about the hex, about everything that had happened to the people she'd cared about romantically. But the happiness in Scott's eyes stopped her. This was still new, their relationship blossoming but still in those fragile, early stages. She didn't want to do anything to push him away, not now that she'd realized how much she cared for him. Was it a selfish decision? Undoubtedly. But she was determined that with enough protection charms, she could keep him safe.

"No reason. Just keep it on please, for me?"

Scott frowned, then nodded, patting the evil eye around his neck.

"It feels strange to ask this, but when can I see you again?" he said.

Dina agreed, it was odd. It felt like they'd gone from not knowing each other at all, to . . . well, to something that was feeling awfully like love. All Dina knew was that she felt at home around Scott, and that he made her giddily, incandescently happy.

"I'm going to be staying in Little Hathering until tomorrow."

"So am I," he grinned. "Is it totally weird if I introduce you to my parents? After all, I've already met yours. And they . . ." He paused.

Dina frowned. "They what?"

"Let's just say they've given me their seal of approval."

She groaned, rubbing her face. This was mortifying.

Scott kissed her until the embarrassment faded.

"I'd like to meet your parents," she said. "I probably owe them for stealing you all weekend."

*I*t was bittersweet to leave the cottage. So much had happened since they'd arrived here only a few days before. Dina whispered a silent thanks to the woods around her as she walked back to the main house hand-in-hand with Scott.

The first thing she noticed in the breakfast room was her mother surreptitiously pouring an anti-hangover charm into the freshly squeezed orange juice. From one glance at the table where Immy, Eric, and Rosemary sat, she understood this to be a necessity.

"Why do you look so fresh?" Rosemary groaned, both hands wrapped around a giant mug of coffee. Her eyes flicked down to where Scott and Dina's fingers were intertwined.

"Oh, I see," she said, raising an eyebrow and smiling knowingly.

Immy and Eric must have caught on, because they both let out a whoop.

"Fucking finally, mate," Eric said, clapping Scott on the back as they sat down.

Immy leaned across Rosemary, and whispered, "Was it as good as you imagined?"

"Even better," Dina said smugly.

"You're a couple then?" Rosemary asked.

Dina glanced over at Scott, who was doing a very good job of pretending he wasn't waiting to hear her response.

"He's my boyfriend," she said, loud enough so that he could hear. "What about you guys? How was the rest of the night?"

"We were so tired I nearly fell asleep in my wedding dress," Immy said. "Thankfully Eric made it up to me this morning."

They both looked at Rosemary.

"Nothing to report here," she said. "Although I did get an email from my agent telling me they've cast the role of Alfred in the movie they're making from my book."

"Who is it?"

Rosemary pulled out her phone.

"This guy." She showed them a picture of an objectively stunning man. Black hair, piercing blue-gray eyes. He had a classic old Hollywood vibe that reminded Dina of Gregory Peck and Gene Kelly.

"Um, is that fucking Ellis Finch? He's smoking hot," Immy said.

"Only one day married and she's already looking elsewhere. What can a man do?" Eric chuckled, kissing his wife's knuckles.

"He's not the right choice," Rosemary said. "He's too—"

"Muscular? Charismatic?" Immy interjected.

"Yeah. All of those things." Rosemary looked at the photo of the actor on her phone, and Dina noticed her cheeks were pink. That was an interesting development.

After breakfast, guests began to trickle back home. Scott and Dina stayed for a while to help Eric and Immy bundle all the wedding presents into the boot of their car.

"You're so in love," Immy said, watching Dina watch Scott as he threw a stick for Juniper across the field.

"Head over heels," Dina replied. She prayed the charms would do the trick.

Chapter 28

Scott was both the luckiest and unluckiest man in the world. Unluckiest because that morning on the way to the museum, he'd stepped into an open grate on the pavement and could have seriously hurt himself. Then he'd only narrowly avoided being bludgeoned to death by a falling roof tile by Russell Square tube station. Luckiest, because he had just spotted Dina, walking up the steps of the museum toward him. And she was wearing a tight pair of black leggings.

Scott cast his mind back. Had he told her about that particular fantasy in the week since they'd returned to London? He didn't think so. But then again, post-sex Scott was liable to tell Dina all sort of truths. Most nights, they stayed up late, intermittently talking and making love. Because there was no denying now that that's what they were doing.

He felt for the spare key to his flat in his pocket. He was planning on giving it to Dina later.

He couldn't drag his eyes away from her plump thighs as she walked up to him. He shifted his already lengthening cock in a way that hopefully wouldn't be too obvious in his slim-cut suit.

Dina must have noticed him shifting because her face broke into a mischievous grin.

"Hello there," she said, leaning into his embrace. "I see you've missed me."

It had been only half a day since he'd been to the café to pick up a pastry, along with a kiss or two, but she wasn't wrong. She ran a finger along his neck, seemingly to check that the hamsa necklace she'd given him was still there. He hadn't taken it off.

Scott kissed her by way of hello, and whispered roughly in her ear: "Are these leggings expensive?"

"They're replaceable."

Scott grabbed a handful of her ass, not caring that there were hundreds of tourists milling around them on the steps. Thankfully, they wouldn't have to deal with them for long, as the museum was closing for the day.

"Good," he growled. "Because I'm going to rip them open later."

He delighted in the shiver that rippled through her.

Scott had been excited for this day all week. The exhibition was almost ready for its launch next Tuesday, and enough of the final touches had been made that Dr. MacDougall had signed off on Scott showing Dina around.

They strolled through the main atrium, Scott's hand resting on Dina's lower back, perhaps a little lower than strictly necessary to guide her through the throngs of people exiting the gift shop.

"I thought you should know I'm not wearing anything under these leggings."

Scott groaned, and seriously contemplated just dragging her back to his office and locking the door.

"Christ, Dina," he choked out. "How am I supposed to string two sentences together now I know that there's only one slip of fabric between my mouth and your pussy?"

Now it was Dina's turn to moan.

Scott pulled her through an unassuming glass door. Next week, there would be a crowd queueing to enter Symbols of Protection here. But for now, they could enjoy the exhibition space unencumbered by swathes of visitors. Even the exhibition hall would be empty of people at this time, all the finishing touches to the sound and lighting to be made tomorrow afternoon.

"Here we are," he announced. The main exhibition poster hung above them, showing a golden acorn that had been crafted in the sixteenth century, likely worn by a merchant's wife while her husband was away traveling.

"Wow!" Dina exhaled beside him. It struck Scott how badly he wanted to impress her. How much he wanted Dina to be proud of him.

The first piece of the exhibition was a brass statue of a dog, placed on a podium at waist height. The dog was curled up, its carved eyes closed, as if it was sound asleep. Most of the statue was a mottled brown color, apart from the dog's snout, which was a shining brassy gold.

"How come that sign says you can touch the statue?" Dina asked. "I thought touching was strictly not permitted in museums."

"Normally, yes, and this is the only piece you're allowed to touch. This"—Scott reached out to pet the cold nose of the dog—"is Frank. Since 1874 he's been sitting on the grave of his owner, James Smythe, who lived up in Inverness. James's family had this statue of Frank created after the dog passed away, because after James died, Frank kept running away and they'd find him sleeping on his master's grave."

"That's so sad, and so sweet."

"Isn't it? But then people visiting the cemetery would pet Frank's nose as they visited their loved ones' graves, and all too soon Frank's snout became an urban legend. It's said that rubbing his snout brings you good luck."

Dina reached out and stroked the brass dog's nose.

"Thanks for the luck, Frank," she said quietly.

They continued the tour of the exhibition. Scott let Dina lead the way mostly; when she showed interest in a specific object they'd pause and he'd tell her a little about how it came to be here.

"You know, I've been wondering something," he said, as they looked through the glass at a carving of a jade dragon. "Can you tell if any of these artifacts are actually magical? Since I was a kid I've always wondered . . . always hoped that perhaps some lucky charms might really work."

Dina scrunched up her face in a frown and looked at the jade dragon.

"It's hard to know. There are so many different types of magic, and there's a lot about them I don't know. Take Frank, for example. Perhaps he didn't start off as a magical object. But over the years, with every hopeful person rubbing his snout and wishing for good luck, who's to say that all that wishing and all that hope didn't turn into something real? But with some objects, like that one there"—Dina said, pointing to a Native American Zuni bear fetish (which some colonial settlers had "sold" to the British Museum back in the 1800s, in a dubious affair)—"that one holds strong magic. I can feel it even through the glass."

They stood before the spotlit stand, looking down at the blue stone bear.

"What does it feel like?"

"Like someone found a way to contain all this wildness and power in stone. And I can smell pine and snow-tinged air, somehow."

Scott sniffed the air, but whatever magic Dina was sensing wasn't open to him.

"We think one of their spiritual practitioners would have carved this bear. The Zuni people believed that the spirit of the animal remains alive in the stone, and will help whoever possesses it. If the exhibition travels to the U.S., we would return the stone to its rightful home with the Museum of Indian Arts and Culture in Santa Fe."

Dina looked up at him, her hand finding his.

"It's incredible, what you're doing. This whole exhibition is incredible."

His heart swelled. But there was one more item he wanted to show her.

"Come this way," he said. Tucked into a corner of the gallery was a nondescript exhibition cabinet. In it was a silver Amazigh amulet, taken from a village in the Atlas mountains.

"Is that—?"

"Yes. It's Amazigh. Do you recognize the symbols?"

Dina leaned closer. She shook her head. "I wish I did."

"The one on the top is the net-and-fish symbol. It's a protective charm. The symbol below it is the weaving comb. It's meant to represent fertility and creativity, but also balance. We think—though many of the details have been lost—that this was likely given as a part of a dowry, or as a proposal gift."

"It's beautiful," she said, but Scott could see the sadness in her face reflected in the cabinet glass. He pulled her back so she was leaning against his chest.

"What's wrong?" he murmured into her hair.

"It's just that you know more about my own heritage than I do. I don't even know the name of the Amazigh tribe we come from, though I'm not sure my mum does either. Sometimes I wonder what it would be like, if I knew more about my past. Are there other forms of magic tied to my history? Were their witches in my bloodline generations ago? Were they venerated as healers, or were they outcast? I just . . . It makes me sad to think about it."

"I'm sorry, Dina. You know, I wonder . . ."

"What?"

"Well, there's this map in the archives that shows all the Amazigh tribes in Morocco and where they were located. It's from the 1800s so it may be outdated, but we could use it to find out what tribe you come from."

"Could we?" She turned around in his arms, excited. "I would love that so much."

"We'll do it then. I'll put in a request to the archives for a scan of the map and we can show it to your mum next time we're there."

It was so easy planning a future with Dina. She made it so easy.

Scott caressed her cheek with his hand, kissing her deeply.

They headed back to the exhibition entrance, the prospect of getting Dina behind the locked door of his office proving so appealing that Scott didn't even notice the falling poster. It collapsed onto the marble floor with a loud crash. A few centimeters closer and it would have hit him.

"Fuck," he said, jumping back, instinctively pushing Dina behind him. "That was close."

Surprisingly, she looked more shaken than he felt.

"Too close," she muttered, frowning down at the collapsed poster. "I have a bag of herbs I'd like you to start carrying with you in your pocket, if that's okay?"

Whatever would make her happy, his little witch.

"Of course," Scott said, sending a message to the construction team to fix the poster before he all but carried Dina to his office.

* * *

"*I*t's so cozy in here," Dina said, running a hand across Scott's mahogany desk. He watched the trail of her finger hungrily.

"What were you expecting, some kind of man cave?" he said, teasing. He turned to lock the door behind them and thanked the heavens that his office only had the one small window. The place was empty now, but still, he'd need Dina to be quiet.

When he turned back around, she was sitting on the edge of his desk.

"Thank you for showing me your exhibition," she said, pulling off her fluffy red jumper. Underneath it, she was only wearing a thin T-shirt, and he could see the stiff peaks of her nipples through the material. She knew exactly what she was doing to him, sitting on his desk like that, her legs just open enough that he could see the seam between her inner thighs. No underwear.

When she reached down and caressed her breasts with her own hands, all his restraint vanished. He strode over, capturing her lips in a long deep kiss. Scott wasted no time removing her top, his mouth finding the heat of her breasts. The small sigh Dina made was enough to have his cock pressing against his trousers again.

"Been dreaming about having you on this desk," he hissed, as Dina used her hands to unbuckle his belt, pulling his cock free. She palmed him, rubbing a thumb over the sensitive tip. Christ, she unmade him.

"I hope you haven't forgotten what you promised you'd do to these leggings," she whispered, nipping his ear with her teeth.

Oh no, he hadn't forgotten.

Scott spun Dina around so she was facing away from him, pressed against the desk. He started by planting gentle kisses to the nape of her neck, the soft curve of her shoulder, relishing the goosebumps he left in his wake.

His calloused hands felt rough compared to the soft suppleness of Dina's breasts, but she arched her back as he stroked her there, feeling the stiff points of her nipples.

"Down on the desk," he instructed. "Good girl."

Dina did as she was told, and Scott licked down the warm skin of her spine until he reached the waistband of her leggings.

Going down on his knees, Scott ran his hands over Dina's plump buttocks. He'd always considered himself more of a boob man until he'd met Dina. Her ass was going to haunt him for the rest of his days if he didn't have it right now. Even just holding it through the leggings was making his hard-on ache.

"You sure?" Scott asked. "I'll buy you a new pair."

"I'll hold you to that," she whispered, hissing out a breath of pleasure as Scott ripped open the seam of the leggings in one swift motion.

She looked like heaven, lying bare for him.

"Are you trying to kill me, sweetheart?"

The last of Scott's words were muffled as he pressed his face into the delicious seam of Dina's ass, trailing his tongue along the slick heat of her. And there she was. Dripping and plump, ready for him.

"Look at you, so fucking wet already." He licked her sweet cunt again with firm pressure, and Dina let out a broken moan that sounded like his name.

He drank her in, savoring each lick, sucking and kissing. Teasing her clit with his tongue as he plunged his fingers into her warm depths, again and again, until she clenched around him and let out a cry.

"Tell me what you want, Dina."

"I need your cock, need your come," Dina whispered, looking back at Scott with an expression of pure lust. He didn't need asking twice.

Opening the rip in her leggings further, Scott pulled down his trousers. There was something about having Dina mostly naked, splayed out across his desk, while he was fully dressed, that almost sent him into a frenzy.

"Fuck, you're perfect, Dina, you're perfect," Scott hissed as he settled his cock between her ass cheeks, relishing the view. She was so wet for him, so ready.

He teased the tip of his cock right at her entrance, desperate to feel her smooth heat around him. Dina hissed, shifting herself so she could take more than just the tip.

"Should I make you beg for it, Dina?" He reached around her, caressing her clit with his thumb.

"*Please*," she moaned, and that was all it took. Scott thrust in, pleasure cascading from the tip of his cock all around his trembling body.

Everything about Dina was perfect, and she was his, she was his.

Scott fisted his hand in Dina's curls; every inch of him sank into her warmth as she writhed in pleasure.

"Come for me again, sweetheart, come all over this cock."

It wasn't long before she shuddered against him, letting out a delicious moan.

Scott rolled her over and scooped her into his arms, resting her ass on the desk. Down on his knees he tasted her again, sweetness and salt and something indescribably Dina.

"My turn," she whimpered, and pulled him up so that he was leaning against the desk and she was on her knees, taking his cock in her mouth. She was every one of his fantasies come to life.

Scott groaned, holding her curls back as she licked from his sac to his tip. She looked up at him, complete trust in her eyes.

"I want you to fuck my mouth."

Scott was lost to oblivion. The way Dina looked up at him, her pretty mouth closed around his cock—it was enough. His entire body shook, thrusting again and again into the heat of her throat until he was inches away from orgasming.

"Can I?" he hissed, and Dina nodded. He let himself go and Dina swallowed his hot come, drinking him in, licking away the mess. Her shredded leggings lay in a pile at their feet. She would need to mend them with magic. Scott pulled her up into his arms, wiping her mouth clean with his thumb. Both of them were sweaty, tired, and perfectly happy.

Chapter 29

*T*his wasn't the first time Dina had been to visit Scott's apartment, but it felt like the most important. Because she was going there on her own, with her *own key*. When Scott had presented it to her, complete with a little keyring that said "Talk to the hamsa" on it, she had squealed with glee and wrapped her arms around him.

Now here she was, unlocking his front door. Scott wouldn't be home for another hour—he had a meeting with the head curator to finish up—but he'd told her to make herself at home.

Scott's apartment, sans Scott, wasn't particularly homey. Everything was so sparkling and new, and the floor-to-ceiling windows, although offering a beautiful view of the river, did make Dina feel a little like she was on show. She hadn't minded that time Scott had fucked her with her breasts pressed up against the cold glass though.

He'd done what he could to make the space cozy, with cushions and rugs and a few potted plants. Still, they spent most of their time at her flat, because Heebie was just about as obsessed with Scott as Dina was.

Today she'd brought some orange and persimmon loaf cake from the café, and she set about brewing herself a cup of tea with the leaves she'd brought over last time. She would have to make sure to read Scott's leaves tonight when he wasn't looking, so she could see any hints of the hex at work. So far, it seemed like the hamsa, the tea leaves, and the midnight blessing rituals she'd done on his behalf were working.

He had narrowly escaped that falling poster at the museum the other day though. It had been a little too close for comfort; she needed to up her game.

Dina kicked off her shoes and changed into some cozy clothes while she waited for the kettle to boil. After the leggings incident the other day, she'd taken to wearing them around Scott in the evenings. They never stayed on for long.

She made her tea and stood looking out at the river, lights twinkling from the restaurants that dotted the bankside.

The door clicked open behind her. Scott stood there, his cheek grazed above the beard, his entire side splashed with mud.

"Don't freak out," he said, offering her a smile. "I'm not hurt."

Dina ran to him as he put down his bag, running her hands over him to check for any injuries.

"What happened?"

"A cyclist ran into me as I was crossing the road. I don't think they saw the stop sign. The bike knocked me over, hence the mud, but I'm fine, Dina, I promise. It looks way worse than it is."

Her hands were shaking as she peeled him out of his coat. No, this wasn't happening. Not yet, please not yet. Her eyes welled with tears and she couldn't stop them from overflowing.

"Hey, hey, I'm okay. I'm okay, sweetheart," Scott said, pulling her into his arms.

"I just—I don't want anything to happen to you," she cried, her face falling into the crook of his neck.

"It's just a shock. I know, I'm sorry," Scott said, smoothing his hands over Dina's back. "Come on, I have an idea," he said, and scooped up her legs so she was wrapped around his torso.

He carried her through his bedroom into the en-suite shower, only detaching Dina from him to tug her clothes over her head.

"We won't be needing these," he said.

She stared at him blearily through her tears. What if she'd lost him, this man who she'd come to care about so deeply? This man who made her happier than anyone ever had, who knew every inch of her body and loved it so well.

The hiss of the shower turning on broke her out of her anxious spiraling, and she watched with a growing hunger as Scott stripped off his own clothing. Would she ever get tired of seeing the dense muscles of his chest, or the dark trail of hair that led down to his, quite frankly, magnificent cock? That seemed unlikely.

"Get in with me," Scott said, and she stepped into the shower. Scott leaned back under the stream of water, running a hand through his hair until it was slicked back to the nape of his neck. Something blipped in Dina's chest. All of this was feeling too real.

She buried her face against the wet hair on his chest, not caring about her hair or her makeup; she was at home in his arms.

Nothing could ruin this moment.

"Dina." Scott kissed her head, his voice muffled by the running water.

"Mmm?"

"Look at me." There was something so raw in his voice that she couldn't help but look up. Scott brushed the hair out of her face, and Dina blinked away the water. He was here, and he was everything.

"I need to tell you something," he began, then closed his mouth.

"Should I be worried?"

Scott cracked a smile. "No, you shouldn't. I just don't know how to say this without scaring you, because it scares me too. I know it's only been a couple of weeks, but *god*, it's been the best weeks of my life."

Dina wanted to respond with something light-hearted like *I'm flattered*, or *That's sweet of you*, but those words felt too empty. Her heart thundered in her ears; she couldn't speak.

"And I want this to continue, I want us to continue. Because I'm falling in love with you, Dina. Sometimes it doesn't even feel real, like I've conjured you from my dreams."

She thought her head would be swimming, but everything was quiet. Only the same thought on repeat: *He loves me, he loves me, he loves me.*

Tears spilled down her cheeks. Scott wiped them away.

He couldn't love her. He shouldn't. She suddenly felt disheveled, makeup running down her face, hair a total mess. She was too loud, too clumsy, her magic too strange. She didn't deserve his love. The intrusive thoughts were infectious, attacking her mind with ferocity.

But that small, quiet voice inside her piped up: *You love him too. You love Scott, and you can make this work. You can make sure the hex doesn't hurt him. You'll fight for him. He's worth it.*

"I love you, Scott. I'm scared, I'm really fucking scared, but I love you." The words tumbled out of her lips but felt right, felt truthful. They held each other, and each kiss said *I love you*, each pull of their lips said *You're mine*.

They had each other again in the shower, their bodies steaming—the need to be closer, closer. Dina's arms wound around Scott, never leaving him for a second. He held her to him, like he would never let go.

"I love you, I love you," he whispered as the world crumbled around her.

Chapter 30

The text came in from Eric just as Scott entered the Reading Room, and even though his phone was on vibrate, the librarian still sent a glare his way.

Someone at work has a litter of kittens, do you want one? Immy is making me take two. Can't bear to split the siblings apart. The text was accompanied with a photo of six adorable-looking tabby kittens.

Let me ask Dina, not sure how HRHH would react. HRHH standing for Her Royal Highness Heebie, of course.

Smart man, came the response.

Scott spent the next ten minutes daydreaming about presenting Dina with a new kitten, and seeing the way her face would light up as she held the small wriggling thing. A few nights ago they'd found themselves talking about children. He could still feel the palpable relief at Dina telling him she knew she didn't want to be a mother. That she was happy being the fun aunt to the kids Eric and Immy would likely have. He would have done it, if that's what she wanted, but he harbored the same feelings. Whenever he pictured his life, kids were never part of that dream. But a house full of pets and Dina and traveling the world with her hand in his—that was Scott's dream. And by some lucky chance, he was getting to live it.

He tried to shake himself back to reality and focus on the task at hand. He only had around ten minutes before the Reading Room closed for lunch. Cold winter light shone in through the windows, the outside air scented with the oncoming snowstorm, and the room was silent apart from the shuffling footsteps of librarians and archivists returning books to their shelves.

He'd promised Dina he'd find out more about her Amazigh heritage. While they still weren't certain which tribe she was from, he'd found a book of Moroccan folk tales from the area east of Rabat that her family was from. And as museum staff, Scott could take the book out on temporary loan.

If the location was correct, then all he needed to do was climb this wooden ladder, and the book would be on a shelf halfway up. It looked a little flimsy, and he hoped it could carry his weight. Scott checked to make sure that the wheels that allowed the ladder to circle the shelf were locked in place. The ladder creaked ominously as he stepped onto the first rung.

He climbed higher until he spotted the book. He only needed to lean out a little to catch a hold of it. Then Scott heard a snap, and the ground rose up to meet him as it all went dark.

Chapter 31

*H*eebie let out a high-pitched yowl that could only mean one thing: Dina was a cruel, cruel mother who deserved to go to jail for never feeding her poor, precious cat.

"Yes, I know, I know. Jail for mother. Jail for a thousand years," Dina muttered in her best Heebie voice, resemblant of a rich old lady of the landed gentry.

Heebie was being particularly antsy this morning as Dina got ready for work, slipping on a cream turtleneck jumper that would keep her warm. She slid open her window a touch, the chilly November breeze sending Heebie bounding for the still-warm duvet. There was nothing better than that first breath of fresh air in the morning.

She slept better when Scott was with her, but they'd spent last night apart since she'd stayed late at Serendipity to bake today's pastries. Dina had been working on a recipe for madeleines that reminded you of the feeling of your first kiss, but Scott kept popping into her head and before she knew it she'd made Scott-infused madeleines that were far too horny and carnally minded for her to serve to any customers.

How quickly her life had adapted to having Scott in it, and how natural it all felt. Dina had found that as the days ticked past, Scott's life intertwining with her own in more and more ways, she thought less about the hex. She still checked his tea leaves, and Scott still wore the evil eye necklace, and it all seemed to be working. Maybe it wasn't as powerful a hex as she'd thought. Maybe it had weakened over time.

Dina sniffed the cold air and felt her magic twinge in anticipation. Perhaps that was why Heebie was meowing and seemed restless. There was a snowstorm in the air. The crisp sting of ice on her nose and the scent of ozone gave it away.

As a familiar, Heebie had an uncanny way of noticing things even before Dina's witchy senses did. Dina turned around to see the cat sitting by her food bowl, scowling in her owner's direction, entirely unimpressed. Or perhaps it was just hunger after all.

She ate a quick breakfast of porridge with caramelized bananas and apples, adding enough cinnamon to warm her cheeks and get her circulation moving. Her phone buzzed from the bedside table.

"Hi, Mama, what's up?" Dina answered.

"Dina, it's your mother."

"Yes, I know, Mama. Is everything okay?" There was a skittish energy in her mother's tone that did not bode well.

"No, habiba. I had a dream last night, about you." Nour's voice was grave. Dina didn't blame her—her mother's dreams had always tended to act more like visions, with even the strangest, surrealist dreams coming true in some respect.

"What happened in the dream?"

"You were building this wall, and it was huge. And I was on the other side, with your father, and Scott was there, and we kept shouting at you to stop building. But you didn't listen. The wall grew and grew and all I could hear was you crying on the other side and I couldn't come and comfort you. And then I woke up." Nour let out a long sigh on the other end of the line. "Does that mean anything to you?" she asked.

Dina stared off in silence, her eyes fixed unblinking on her kitchen counter.

A numbness seeped into her body. It did mean something to her. It meant that her worst fears were coming true. Her mother's magic never lied. There was a very real wall between them, in the shape of the hex. But if Scott was on the other side of that wall—well, that meant he wasn't safe. Her mouth opened to speak, to tell her mother about the hex. But shame gripped her throat, suffocating her.

So Dina said, "No, Mama. I don't know what it could be about. I guess I should expect some bad news?" She probably sounded far too cavalier and wondered if the falseness in her voice was that obvious.

"You sure you don't know what it's about? Could it be about Scott?" her mum prodded.

"Of course not!" Dina replied, with a little too much enthusiasm. Thank god her mum hadn't video-called. She doubted she'd have been able to hide the way the blood had drained out of her cheeks, or the heavy feeling in her limbs.

"Well, all right then. But keep your eyes open, all three of them!" Nour said, a muffled sound coming from her end.

"I will—what is that sound?" Dina heard a faint crackling.

"I'm just burning some sage by the phone. Maybe it'll do something," her mother said gravely.

"I'll be careful, Mama. You don't need to worry about me."

"Oh, Dina, all I do is worry. That's my job as your mother."

*A*s Dina arrived at Serendipity Café that morning there were already a few of her regulars waiting for the shop to open. As well as catering to the harried commuter, Dina had a select few retired regulars who liked to sit with the paper or do their crosswords with a muffin.

"You're early today, George!" Dina winked at one of her regulars as she undid the shutters and flicked open the magical wards that kept the café safe from burglaries and general vandalism.

"It's the cold, I can feel it in my bones today, Dina. I need some of that turmeric drink you made me last week."

"Let's get you inside where it's warm then, shall we?"

Dina spoke a silent spell as she entered the café, and the lights blinked on and the boiler sparked to life, sending heat rattling into the old iron radiators behind the sofas. In ten minutes the whole café would be toasty and warm, smelling like freshly ground coffee. There was nowhere else Dina would rather be.

George settled himself at his usual table overlooking the curved windowpane.

"Make yourself comfortable, I'll be right with you!" she called, as she slipped out of her coat and donned her quite frankly adorable Serendipity Café apron. She didn't need to wear an apron, and certainly the frills weren't necessary, but she felt damned cute in it, and on the colder days it kept her warmer.

Dina spent the next thirty minutes serving a slew of early-morning customers before the shop had even technically opened for the day. She busied herself trying to dust chocolate powder onto cappuccinos in various shapes.

When Robin waltzed in ten minutes early for their shift, at a reasonable seven forty-five, they looked at the filled seats with alarm.

"Did we change our opening hours?" they asked, slipping their own apron on and pushing their hair out of their eyes.

"Nope, but there's a snowstorm coming," Dina replied absently, her mind concentrating on the extravagant and entirely unnecessary latte art she was attempting. It was meant to look like a snowflake but it was more like a misshapen spider web. She frowned, flicking her wrist, and the frothed milk moved around until it looked like a perfect symmetrical snowflake.

"A snowstorm? Oh, well, that explains it then," Robin said dryly.

"People sense these things, even if they don't always realize it. Also, it's bloody cold," Dina replied.

Together, they knuckled down as the rush-hour crowd entered the café.

Dina prided herself on the fact that even the most harried-looking commuters seemed to breathe a little slower as they entered Serendipity, the creases of their frowns flattening out, their shoulders sagging in relief.

Sure, a cup of coffee couldn't make your whole day better, but a good coffee, a really great one, could make all the difference to how a person approached the rest of their day. And in Dina's experience, state of mind always mattered more than actual events.

The rush began to slow down just after nine. Most morning coffee drinkers would be sitting at their desks by now, sipping their drinks and eating one of Dina's delicious cinnamon buns, feeling a little lighter as they scanned through their morning emails. Exhilarated yet cozy. As if they'd just slipped into a pair of warm socks.

Dina tidied the tables, lighting an amber candle on each one with a twirl of her finger as she went past. There were only a couple of people sitting in the café now and they were too enthralled by their books and papers to notice her performing a quick sweep of cleaning magic on their tables as she passed by.

The hum of the coffee grinder normally soothed Dina's inner monologue, but not today. The call with her mum had left her rattled. Dina didn't like the way the image of the dream wall had settled into her bones, nor the way it felt simultaneously surreal and yet familiar. Like she might have dreamed it herself but forgotten it upon waking.

She tried to shake herself out of it by scrubbing the dishes extra clean, but that didn't work. She wished Scott were here already, so she could talk about it with him. Maybe he'd understand. He'd certainly been opening up more to the way her magic worked the past few weeks. An idea popped into her head then: She'd make him a blend of tea. That felt like an acceptable "I need to vent about my feelings but also I think I love you a whole load and my love language is gift-giving" kind of present.

"Robin, can you take over from me out here?" Dina called. A few minutes later the coffee grinder slowed to a quiet hum and Robin emerged from the kitchen with two full bags of deliciously scented ground coffee, which they would sell over the counter.

"You know, I don't even need to wear perfume anymore. People always tell me I smell amazing." They laughed, setting the bags down on the counter. "Are you heading back to bake?"

"No, I think I'll make some tea blends." Dina smiled and headed into the kitchen.

There was some bread baking in the oven, and a row of cupcakes cooling on the counter, which she'd frost in an hour or so. The whole room smelled like a hug.

Sensing a buzz from her phone, Dina pulled it out and opened her group chat with Immy and Rosemary that they'd named "The Weird Sisters." It was a flurry of photos from Rosemary that she'd taken at her local haunted house and Christmas tree fair.

Immy had responded with: **Did they have a chainsaw room with a murderous Santa like last year?**

Dina replied, **Cute, let me send you my mulled wine recipe,** to which Rosemary responded: **Yes please! And no creepy Santa but they did have axe-wielding elves, had so much fun.**

Her friends were insane—and she adored them.

Dina hummed to herself as she pulled out an empty jam jar from a busy cupboard. It was still labeled "Apricot Jam" from the batch her mum had made for her last year—jam that tasted like bottled sunshine.

There wasn't an exact science to the magic, but Dina often found that the best tea blends were ones she put into second-hand jars, ones that had been full of delicious, wonderful things.

She clipped her curls out of her face and headed into the pantry. The walls were lined floor-to-ceiling with all manner of jars and boxes, all individually labeled in Dina's messy hand-writing. She kept her spices together, along with other baking essentials like fresh vanilla, cake flour, and a tin that was labeled "Eye of Newt" but actually contained nutmeg.

Her tea selection had several shelves dedicated to it. Aside from the specialty blends she made for the shop, Dina kept a collection of tea and tisane ingredients, which she could mix into more personal blends at a moment's notice. Dina never felt more in her element as a kitchen witch than when she was look-ing through her pantry.

Scott's tea blend needed to be something that encapsulated his energies yet also helped him in some way. A tea to drink in the middle of a long work day, Dina decided.

She twirled a curl around her finger as she focused. She hadn't met any of his fellow curators yet, but from what Scott had told her they could be a bit of a handful. So the kind of tea that would help him get through a long meeting. Something to sharpen a tired mind. Dina knew just the thing for it.

She scooped up several jars and laid them out on the counter before her. Black tea—a full-bodied assam, cacao nibs, dried gin-ger and . . . it was missing something. Dina stepped back into the pantry and surveyed her shelves with her hands on her hips.

She knew that this would need one more ingredient to be perfect for Scott. Lion's mane mushroom? Perhaps a little too earthy. Clove? Too heavy: It would overpower the other flavors.

As her eyes skirted over the rows of jars, she spotted it. A small glass jar with a dark red powder in it. Dried beetroot! Perfect! Energizing yet slightly sweet and smooth, and it would make Scott look like he was drinking some kind of red-velvet-themed drink. Which was also his favorite cake flavor. Dina smiled as it all came together.

She didn't want to rush this. It wasn't every day you made your first magical tea blend for the man you were in love with.

Dina made two jars full of Scott's blend—one for his office and one to keep at home. She scrawled his name on the two labels and stuck them onto the jars. She even added a love heart; she couldn't help herself. She lifted one of the jars to her face and took a deep inhale. Warm, spiced, and sharp—just like Scott.

Suddenly, her phone vibrated in her pocket.

"Hello, is this Dina Whitlock?" A woman's voice she didn't recognize.

"It is."

"My name is Claire, I'm a paramedic and Scott has you down as his emergency contact. I don't want you to worry, but we have Scott in our ambulance at the moment, and we're taking him to hospital."

Her blood froze.

"What happened?"

"He had a fall at the British Museum. A ladder broke underneath him, we think, and he hit his head."

Oh god, no.

"Can I talk to him?" she said. Her body felt numb; her voice belonged to someone else.

"Not right now, I'm afraid: We're still waiting for him to regain consciousness. Because it's a head injury, we'll need to take him for some scans once we arrive at the hospital, just to make sure there's no internal bleeding."

Dina heard the beeps in the background, pictured Scott lying unconscious in the ambulance, blood seeping into his hair.

This is all your fault. You did this.

"I'm coming. Tell me where to go," she heard herself say, and she bundled on her coat and left the café.

Wake up—please, Scott. Wake up.

Chapter 32

The first thing Dina did on her way to the hospital was call Scott's mums. And then Eric. They were all on their way, but it would take them another hour at least. She paced around the waiting room, casting every kind of spell and charm she could think of from a distance.

Guilt rotted its way through her body. This was her fault. She'd known the hex was still in effect; she'd seen the signs and chosen to ignore them. If anything happened to Scott, she was the one to blame.

He had to wake up. He had to be okay.

"Dina?" A nurse had popped her head into the waiting room. "He's awake."

She rushed to him.

"Hi, sweetheart," Scott said, lying in the hospital bed, his cheeks pale, a bandage on the right side of his forehead. "I'm okay."

"Fuck, Scott. I was so scared." She kissed him, and buried her face in his neck.

"Me too. I woke up in the ER but they wouldn't let me see you until I'd had the scan. I'm all clear, no internal bleeding. Apparently, cuts on the head can bleed a lot, which makes them look worse than they are. I reckon I terrified the librarian who found me."

She shuddered to even think about it.

"Does it hurt?" she asked.

"It stings a little. They had to give me a couple of stitches. Do you reckon I'll have a cool scar?"

She smacked his chest. "Don't you dare make me laugh right now."

"The paramedics said I was lucky that I hit my head where I did. A few more centimeters to the left and I might have done some serious damage."

What if he's not so lucky next time? Dina thought. The hex was escalating, working hard to see that Scott was hurt. If she didn't leave now, it would surely kill him. She couldn't live with that.

Dina cupped his face, doing her best to memorize every feature. She kissed his cheeks, his eyes, his lips. She ran her fingers through his beard. Tears fell freely down her cheeks.

"Sweetheart, what's going on?"

She loved him so much—how was she supposed to do this?

"It's all my fault," she said, her voice muffled against his hospital gown.

"What is?"

"Why bad things keep happening to you. Why you keep getting hurt."

"Dina, it was just a rickety old ladder that some maintenance person forgot to fix. You certainly aren't to blame for any of that."

She looked up at him, and Scott brushed the tears away with his thumb.

"Please just listen to what I have to say," she whispered. Not willing to let go of him for a second, Dina tucked herself into his side, her arms curled tightly around his neck.

With a deep breath, she began speaking.

"When I was younger, someone hexed me. They didn't mean to, but they did. They hexed me so that everyone who falls in love with me will get hurt. Do you understand? All of this is because of the hex. All the accidents you've had since you met me. Since you fell in love with me"—her voice broke with a sob—"and it's never going to stop. It will only get worse from here."

Scott shook his head. He looked like he didn't want to believe her. She let him have a moment, watching as the truth of her words settled into his bones, his lips thinning.

"Can you reverse the hex? Or break it?"

"I've tried so many things. Nothing has worked."

He took a deep breath.

"Christ, Dina. Why didn't you tell me about this? How long does it last? Maybe it just runs out of power after a certain point. Did the others stay around long enough to find out?"

He was angry. He was mad at her for not telling him. She deserved that.

She hadn't considered it might run out of power before. But no, it was too dangerous to risk it. Besides, if it had lasted all these years she doubted it would fade out of existence the moment it had a chance to really get to work.

"I don't think so," she said.

"Is there a way to counteract it somehow?"

"That's what I tried, with the protection necklaces. And I've been reading your tea leaves. But it's getting stronger."

Scott's eyes softened, and he pulled her close for a kiss.

"We can figure this out, Dina, please don't give up. We'll think of something. What if—"

"There is something we can do," Dina broke in. She began to stand, pulling away from him.

"No. Come here," Scott said, his arms open. She shook her

head. "Do you want to go home? Or you can go to my flat for a bit, and bring Heebie?"

"I have to go, Scott. If I stay here, if I stay . . . with you, then you'll get hurt." Dina choked out a sob. "And I don't want you to ever, ever get hurt again because of me."

"Dina, sweetheart, what are you saying?"

"We can't do this anymore. Us."

"What do you mean? I don't give a fuck what some hex wants to do to me. I'll fight it, Dina. You're the best thing that's ever happened to me, and I'm not letting you go."

"You don't get to make that choice, Scott. It's my curse; it's my burden to bear."

Scott pulled her into a kiss. Her mouth opened eagerly, their lips crushing together, their bodies melting. Time stopped for a while, but when Dina pulled back, tears still shone in her eyes.

"I need you to know that I'm only doing this because I love you," she said in a voice that was too quiet, too final.

"Dina—"

"Please don't make this harder for me, Scott!" she cried. She moved back into the circle of his arms. "If you want," she said, her voice shaking, "I can make you forget about me."

Even the thought of it made him sick.

"Don't you dare," he growled.

"I love you," Dina whispered, and then she fled the room.

*S*now pelted him from every angle, but Scott didn't even notice it. He'd checked himself out of hospital the moment the doctor had said he could, ignoring the calls from his mums and Eric. He didn't notice the biting cold or the way his whole body was racked with shivers. His head ached, but he had to keep walking, had to drown out the roar inside him. Each step hurt. Nothing made sense; his mind and his heart were all jumbled, twisted, and broken. He loved her with every morsel of his being. How was he meant to live with this?

Scott placed one foot in front of another, not caring where he went, only that he went away from . . . from wherever he was. Nowhere could be far enough. These feelings would chase him everywhere.

She had even offered to make him forget her, and it had made him livid with anger. How dare she even consider removing herself from his memories? She was his *person*—he wanted no one else and would never want anyone else.

It was like he was back in the maze, only this time he was more lost than ever.

Scott rubbed at his cheeks, willing the tears that ran down them to disappear.

He was vaguely aware that people were staring at him— a grown man wiping tears from his eyes, marching down the pavement. He didn't have it in him to care.

He had lost Dina—fuck, he'd lost her. The look in her eyes when she'd tried to . . . what? Explain why she had to leave? Well, he'd almost crumpled. He'd almost said, *Let it kill me, I don't care. The past weeks have been the best of my life, and if I only have days with you then that's better than living without you.*

A cold hard surface slammed into Scott, forcing the air out of his lungs. He blinked, looking down to find a metal railing just above waist height. Ahead of him, the Thames surged, waves chopping at each other like steel knives.

Scott realized it was snowing, the delicate flakes melting on his skin and catching in his hair. By the looks of it, he was near Battersea. He looked down at his watch; it was nearly seven in the evening. He'd been walking for hours, the sky had already darkened into its evening shade of murky gray, the snow clouds showing no sign of clearing.

Tomorrow didn't feel real yet. How could he wake up without Dina in his arms tomorrow, or any morning after that? It all felt like a fathomless darkness. After what felt like hours staring into the darkening waves, his heart beating numbly in his chest, every thought of Dina's face, Scott turned around and began the long walk home.

Chapter 33

*D*ina was a walking thunderstorm, and anyone who stepped into her radius of destruction would feel her wrath. Except her wrath was more like deep, broiling grief, manifesting for passersby as dog poop under their feet, broken umbrellas, and gusts of wind that made their hair stick to their lip gloss. Dina wasn't trying to do it, but her magic was overflowing, cascading off her in waves of pain.

She didn't trust her magic not to cause several signal failures and bring down the whole tube network, so she walked all the way home, her feet aching as she made the final steps to her front door.

The moment she had the door closed, Dina threw herself onto the sofa, burying her face in the cushions. She choked out sobs, not even caring that her mascara would smudge all over the fabric. After a while she felt Heebie's tentative tail swishes and cautious sniffs around her cheeks. Dina shifted to her side so Heebie could crawl into the curve of her lap, kneading Dina's belly with her sharp little claws.

"What are you baking today, Madame Heebie?" Dina sniffed, tickling the cat under her chin as she kneaded. She liked to imagine Heebie in a little baker's hat and had once even tried knitting one—but Heebie had hissed when Dina had tried to dress her in it. She wasn't sure how long she stayed there, petting Heebie's soft black fur, but slowly the pain in her chest started to loosen, as if gentle fingers were prying open a stiff knot thread by thread. It wasn't gone, but it was a little quieter for now.

Heebie woke Dina up hours later, her living room bathed in the evening streetlights' glow. The cat meowed, butting her face against Dina's arm, and then going to stand by her food bowl.

"How inconsiderate of me. I slept through your dinner time." Dina's whole body ached as she stood, but she hauled herself into the kitchen and served up Heebie's dinner.

All the magic that had seeped out of her on the way home seemed to have taken its toll, and she felt utterly depleted. Although that could also just be the heartbreak.

Her phone buzzed, and without even looking at the caller she answered.

Immy and Rosemary's faces popped up on the screen.

"Dina, oh, Dina love, are you okay?" Immy said. Dina saw her tiny face in the corner of her phone screen: puffy, skin blotchy red and salt-stained.

"I fucked up," she croaked. Eric must have told them what had happened.

"You're okay, we're here for you. Tell us what happened," Rosemary said, her video a little slower, as she was calling from the States.

Dina took a deep breath and told them about the charms, and the accident, and how she loved Scott so much she felt her heart breaking.

*L*ate that night, Dina tossed and turned, sleep just out of her grasp.

"You have to tell your mum, Dina, I'm serious," Immy had said on their call earlier. "She'll know what to do."

"But what if she hates me when I tell her I'm bi?"

"Dina, she won't. But listen to us," Rosemary said. "You have to tell her anyway. And if it goes badly . . . Well. We love you, and we will be here for you until your mother decides to join us in the twenty-first century."

They'd spoken for a while longer, until Dina had felt exhaustion biting at her heels.

Her magic was too volatile right now, otherwise she would have bespelled herself to sleep. Instead, she stumbled bleary-eyed to the kitchen and made herself a cup of chamomile tea to take to bed. These flowers were from a batch she'd grown and dried last year on her very own windowsill. They didn't have quite the same strength as wild chamomile, but where was Dina meant to find and forage wild chamomile in London?

The tea was delicately sweet, and after a few long sips she felt her eyelids begin to droop. Sleep came over her at once, and when Dina next opened her eyes, the dawn sunlight was streaming in through her curtains, peachy pink.

There was a weight on her belly—Heebie sat there grooming herself, one paw outstretched.

"You should go home for a bit, Dina," Heebie said, in the voice of a classic Hollywood starlet. But that was preposterous, because Heebie couldn't speak.

"You're a cat," Dina mumbled.

"Indeed," Heebie replied drily, "but I'm your cat, so I can tell you what to do. You need to go home, Dina. To help heal your heart. To break the hex."

"I can't break it, I've tried everything. I made him wear protection charms, I checked his fortunes constantly, and it still fucking hurt him. I'm telling you I've tried everything."

Heebie looked at her with wise, knowing eyes.

"Not *everything*."

Dina snapped awake. The light coming into her bedroom was bleak and gray, like the clouds were sodden with rain. Heebie sat on her stomach, grooming the fur of her belly.

"Very funny, Heebie," Dina said. "You've been able to talk this whole time and only now you tell me?"

The cat looked at her, blinking once.

"*Mraaoww,*" Heebie said, as Dina tickled her chin.

"Oh, you've suddenly lost the power of speech?"

"*Mrraow.*"

"Hmmph. I don't buy it." Dream Heebie was right though: She should go home. The sleep, as frayed as it had been, had cleared her mind a little. Something like hope whispered in her chest. Her friends, and now her cat, had told her what she needed to do. And she was inclined to agree. It was time to come clean and tell her mother about the hex.

Chapter 34

"So let me get this straight: When you were in bakery school you put a fate spell on a guy you were dating, but it back-fired when he accidentally harnessed it against you and hexed you, so that everyone who falls in love with you will get hurt. And you and Scott have broken up because the hex was trying to kill him, and your mother is crying in the bedroom and making it snow inside the house because you never told her any of this. Does that about sum it up?"

Robert Whitlock leaned against the kitchen counter, a cooling mug of coffee in his hand.

If you forget the part where I'm also queer, then yes, Dina thought.

"That about covers it," she said instead.

Her father let out a long sigh, then came over to squeeze her shoulder.

"You know you can tell us anything, and we'd never judge you for it." Dina leaned her head against her father's arm as he patted the curls on the top of her head. She wondered if he was right. She'd arrived at her parents' house with the intention of coming clean about everything, but the way her mum had re-acted when she'd told her about the hex, not even specifying that Rory was a woman, made her doubt how the rest would be received. Nour had taken her daughter's secrecy as a personal affront.

Robert sighed and put his coffee down.

"I better go and see how Nour is doing. I'm sure she'll be fine in an hour or two."

Dina doubted that would be the case as she watched her father leave the room and climb the stairs.

She walked out into the courtyard of the house, watching snow fall onto the colorful tiles. The house had been pleased to see Dina, the kettle whistling excitedly the moment she'd unlocked the door, but the revelation of her hex had left her mother upset and the house confused. It was snowing, and a bitter chill hung in the air. At the same time, fire crackled happily in the hearth, scented like pine and cinnamon.

Dina was sure if she went up to her childhood bedroom she'd find the bed toasty and warm with hot-water bottles and the sound of rain pattering the windowpane—the only way she'd been able to fall asleep in her teenage years. Heebie prowled around her feet, knocking gently against her shins. Dina picked up the cat and cradled her like a baby, which Heebie endured like a penitent.

After some time, the snow stopped falling, and the magic sky above the courtyard, which was really just a roof, turned a deep violet speckled with stars. The shuffling footsteps on the stairs belonged to her father.

"She's asked to see you," he said, smiling weakly.

Dina would have been lying if she'd said she wasn't a little afraid of seeing her mother. Strong emotions made witches more volatile, and Nour wasn't exactly a calm person to begin with. But when she walked into her parents' room, she found her mother sitting cross-legged on the bed, holding an old book.

"Aji hdaya," Nour said. Come here.

Dina did as she was told, but the moment she sat down beside her mother she was pulled into a hug.

"Benti, I'm sorry," her mother said. "First of all, I'm sorry I never noticed it. I don't understand, my magic . . ." Nour looked helplessly down at her hands. "I should have seen the hex in your aura."

"It's okay, Mama. I have thought about that too. Part of me wonders if I hid it from you with my own magic."

Nour nodded slowly, considering the possibility.

"I've found something I think you will find interesting," she said.

A drawer opened and a pair of socks flew at Nour's head.

"Sorry, yes. The *house* found something," she corrected.

She tilted the book toward Dina. *Mother Agatha's Spell Compendium*, the title read. It was worn around the edges, the spine cracked and well loved.

"Who is Mother Agatha?" Dina asked.

"You know what, I'm not sure. It was in the attic when we moved in and I looked through it a few times, but whoever she was, her spells aren't really my style. There is one page, however, which I think we should look at."

Nour flicked her wrist, the pages turning to land on one. Dina sucked in a breath.

A spell to change your fate was scrawled across the top of the page in what was presumably Mother Agatha's handwriting. Underneath, Dina spotted many of the same components she'd used in her spell to bring Rory to her all those years ago.

"It's so similar . . ." she said, tracing a finger down the page.

"Look there," Nour said, pointing to a note in the margin.

"'Only witches of a strong bloodline will be able to effectively cast or counteract a fate spell,'" Dina read aloud. "'If the person upon whom the spell is cast should fall unconscious during the first month of the spell, it will no longer be in effect.'"

But that meant . . . ?

Dina looked up at her mother, who was smiling.

"But Rory did fall unconscious. And . . . Rory wasn't a blood-line witch, at least I'm pretty sure." All these years, she'd had it wrong. She'd assumed that Rory had harnessed the fate spell and turned it into a hex, pushing the magic onto Dina. But if the fate spell had dissipated before Rory had regained consciousness in the hospital, then there was no magic for Rory to harness. No way she could have hexed Dina.

Nour nodded. "The hex wasn't turned back on you, because it was broken the moment Rory had the car accident."

"But I *am* under a hex, Mama. Even if it wasn't the backfired fate spell, even if it wasn't Rory, I am definitely under a hex."

But if Rory hadn't hexed her, who had?

Chapter 35

*T*ogether, Dina and Nour drew a circle of salt in Dina's bed-room, placing a candle in the center. Nour had told Robert not to disturb them, as this was witchy business of the highest order, but he had made sure they'd eaten something before they went about performing magic.

"We need to get to the bottom of this, habiba," her mother had said. "If we stay up all night, we are going to find out who hexed you, and how to break it."

For the beginning of the spell, they washed both of their arms up to the elbows in rosewater, scenting the room with its floral aroma. It cleansed the magic, and would keep their work-ing true.

"Sit in the center for me, benti," Nour bade Dina. She let her mother walk her through this, as her magic was far more of the seer's kind.

Her mother handed her a lit pillar candle, and then sat down opposite her in the circle.

"How does it work?" Dina asked.

"When we're ready, we blow out the candle and in the smoke above it we will see the name of the person who cursed you. Now, be quiet and let me do my magic."

They sat in silence, rain pattering heavily against the darkened windows, the room bathed only in the warm glow of candlelight. Nour frowned, her palms facing upward, as she muttered a spell under her breath, too quiet even for Dina to hear.

Dina watched her mother's face, a mirror image of what Dina would look like in thirty years. Laugh lines crinkled around her brown eyes, age spots beginning to dot the tops of her cheeks. Nour had the ability to remove these of course, if she wished. But Dina's mother had always been one to age gracefully. She'd even kept the white hairs that now blossomed at her temples, saying they made her look distinguished and elegant.

Nour opened her eyes, and for a moment they glowed amber.

"Blow out the candle," she whispered.

Dina did so, the small trail of smoke curling into the air. For a second, nothing happened, and then letters began to form before her eyes.

"Ah, just as I suspected," Nour said gravely.

The letters hovered clearly above her before dissipating. There was only one name.

Dina Whitlock.

Chapter 36

"How the fuck did I hex myself? And how the hell am I supposed to break it?" Dina swore, sweeping up the salt circle into a jar with a cleaning spell. They wouldn't need its protection anymore since apparently the cause of all her problems was herself.

"It is uncommon for a witch to curse herself. But when it happens it can be very potent," Nour said, sitting on Dina's bed with Heebie curled in her lap.

"So what now? Do we do some kind of spell to undo it?"

Nour arched an eyebrow. "I thought you said you'd already tried cleansing spells on yourself before?"

"I have."

Nour shrugged. "That should have sorted it."

Dina was surprised at how calm her mother was being about this. Nour reached up and pressed her hand to Dina's cheek, holding it there.

"All these years, and you've been blocked from love. And Scott, I really thought . . ."

"Me too, Mama," Dina said, her chest constricting.

"It's in your power to fix it now."

"How?"

"Think about it, Dina. Really think about the intricacies of the hex. Anyone who falls in love with you will be hurt, forcing you to push them away for their own safety. It's just like the dream I had. You build this wall around you so that no one can get in, and anyone who tries is hurt. But what happens if someone gets through and loves you? They see inside. They see inside the fortress that you've built around yourself and they *see you*. What are you afraid they'll see?"

Dina wasn't sure when she had begun crying.

"Are you afraid that they will learn you're a witch and run away scared? Tell me, benti, did Scott run away?"

Dina shook her head. "He loves my magic."

"Exactly. And were you yourself when you were around him?"

"Yes."

"And he fell in love with you all the same. He fell in love with *you*, Dina, because you are worthy of being loved, and you deserve to love."

Dina lay her head on her mother's chest, and Nour stroked her daughter's curls. She felt so small, and so young.

There was one secret part of her left. A part that had always been there, that she'd wanted to share with her mother for so long.

She was so afraid. *Please still love me after I tell you, Mama.*

"There is something else, Mama. Something I've been keeping from you."

"Oh?"

"I never told you because I was afraid of how you'd react. Afraid that you and Dad might love me less if you found out." Dina inhaled a shaky breath. "I'm bi, Mama. I like both men and women. The first person I ever loved, Rory, she wasn't a man. And I've dated women, and been with women, so please don't say it's just a phase—"

Her mother cut her off, cupping Dina's face in her hands.

"My darling girl, my habiba. That's what you've been keeping from me for all these years?" Nour began to cry. "I'm so sorry I ever made you feel like you couldn't tell us, that I ever made you feel like I would love you any less. You're my daughter: There is nothing about you that I do not love."

The walls that Dina had built around her heart crumbled, and her mother held her, and told her she loved her until Dina was finally able to believe it. After a while, Dina stopped crying, and sat up to look at her mum.

"What do we do now?"

Nour thought for a moment. "There is something. It might help. A mother's magic is not something to be trifled with."

Dina thought of Scott, thought of the chance she now had to be with him, if only she could break this curse of her own making.

"Let's try it," she said. "What do I need to do?"

Dina waited as her mother went to the en-suite bathroom and emerged with a bowl scented with frankincense and filled with pre-mixed henna (the house had clearly known what her mother had planned).

Together, they spooned the henna into a bag and cut a small hole at the bag's corner.

"We're going to fix this, habiba." Her mother's determined voice filled her with a sudden flash of hope.

Dina became aware that her mother was singing softly under her breath. Ever since she was a baby, her mother had sung like this. Sometimes in Darija, sometimes in English, never in French. Nour took her daughter's right palm and began to apply the henna in a beautiful pattern.

Her voice lilted into a whisper and then back into song, the notes throaty and warm. Like hushed prayers.

Her mother tipped Dina's hand palm up, and drew a circle in the center, the henna scented with frankincense. Dina felt a tingling warmth where the henna was drawn, each stroke of the application stirring something in her core, in her spirit. Magic thrummed within her, its molten light flowing through her veins.

She looked down and saw in surprise an elegant pattern of flowers and vines that wove around her fingers, and in the center of her palm, an open eye.

"This is so you will see yourself as I see you," Nour said, her eyes prickling with tears.

Dina stood and turned to face the mirror. For a moment she did not recognize her reflection. That woman was beautiful, glowing, beaming a smile, kindness and joy radiating from her. That woman was Dina. *That's me.*

The hex had felt insurmountable, impossible to break, even once she had known she was the cause of it. It was one thing to be told she needed to love herself to break the curse, but quite another to do it in practice. But as Dina looked at herself, everything fell into place. Her family accepted her for who she was. And if she told herself that she was worthy of love, then it was true. And if it was true, there was no need for the hex anymore. No need for that wall that she had built between herself and others to keep them from seeing her as she truly was. Scott loved her, and she loved him. And they would be okay.

She shuddered in a breath as the insidious magic of the hex began to dissipate, like ashes blowing away after a fire's gone out. Then her ears popped, and the hex was gone.

Dina looked across at her mother, smiling through her tears.

"It's gone," she cried. "Mama, I'm free."

They collapsed into a heap of tears and laughter, Dina's father walking in and wrapping his long arms around both his wife and daughter, not knowing why they were happy-crying but just glad that they were.

After some time, Nour took Dina's face in her hands.

"We've fixed this for now, but I meant what I said. A witch cursing herself is a powerful form of magic, intentional or not. Loving yourself will feel easy some days, and other days it will be a mountain you cannot climb. Dina, habiba, I want you to promise me you'll see someone about this." She pressed a kiss to her daughter's cheek. "You know you can always talk to me—to us—about how you feel. But there are some things that magic can't fully cure, and you need to find someone you can talk to who will help you keep that wall from coming back."

Dina agreed.

"I'll speak to someone, I promise." She smiled.

"Well, then, what are you waiting for, benti? You have to go to Scott and tell him how you feel!"

The moment her mother uttered those words, Dina's bags appeared by the door, already packed. Heebie was stored away in her carrier, sleeping soundly. A train ticket even sat on top of Dina's bag.

She laughed. "Thank you, House."

Not bothering to go change or shower, Dina picked up her things. There was no time to waste. She had to go and gatecrash the opening of an exhibition.

Chapter 37

For the fourth time, Scott attempted to tie his bowtie. This time, it looked a little lopsided, but he couldn't be arsed to start from scratch. He stared at himself in the small mirror in his office, brushing hair out of his eyes. He hadn't slept well, and from the shadows under his eyes, everyone would know it.

"Thank you for joining us this evening to celebrate the opening of Symbols of Protection: The Mystical Art of Talismans from Around the World. I'd especially like to thank . . . Who the fuck do I want to thank again?" Scott turned around to check his notes.

Memorizing the names of the sponsors, benefactors, and the many museums around the world that had donated artifacts—only temporarily, of course—had taken him most of the afternoon. This was a big exhibition, and he didn't want to leave anyone out, or mess up any of his speech.

Dr. MacDougall was counting on this exhibition being a success. It would prove that she'd been correct to hire Scott, young as he was, to be a curator at the museum.

And if it was successful, he'd have a much easier time when it came to pitching his more outside-the-box ideas.

Nerves bit at him; there was a hollow, queasy feeling in his stomach. Scott was confident enough, but he hadn't given many speeches, and he certainly hadn't given many at opening-night exhibition galas before. His mums were going to be there, as well as Eric and Immy. There was, of course, one person missing—the person he wanted most to be there, and the only person who would not be.

Dina would have known what to say to calm him down. She would have pressed her lips against the crease between his eyebrows until his frown softened into a smile. He missed her tinkling laugh, and the way she scrunched up her nose when she smelled something bad—which in London was frequently.

The hollowness in his core expanded until a dull ache permeated his whole body. This was just how it was going to be now. Eric had told him the pain would lessen with time, but that hadn't started yet.

The weirdest part of it was that the longer he went without Dina in his life, the more certain he was that what they'd had was that once-in-a-lifetime kind of love. The "I want to grow old with you by my side" kind.

"Just get through tonight," Scott told his reflection, then placed his speech notes into the pocket of his navy blue suit jacket.

He could hear glasses of champagne clinking together as he walked down the steps into the main atrium. It was already dark outside, being November, but the glow of the lamps and the twinkling of chandeliers—which had been hastily installed earlier that day for the gala—gave the room a sparkling sheen. He had tripped on one of them earlier as it was waiting to be hung.

All the guests were dressed in black tie, with some in elaborate floor-length gowns in deep tones of emerald and vermillion. He shook hands with a few of the museum's trustees and sponsors, all important people who thought very highly of themselves and their contributions. Not that Scott would ever let them know how he felt.

Instead, he would continue to put on exhibitions, returning artifacts to their home countries and educating visitors about the strange and wonderful parts of their history. But there were quite a few hoops to jump through before he could get there—tonight being one of them.

"And this young man is the mastermind behind Symbols of Protection," said Dr. MacDougall, walking up to him with an unassuming man, neatly dressed, in tow. "Scott, this is Dr. Benhassi of the Musée d'Orsay."

Scott shook the man's hand, not quite believing that he was speaking to the head curator of one of Paris's largest art collections.

"It's an honor to meet you, Dr. Benhassi." Scott smiled. Dr. Benhassi had a kind, open face.

"It is you I should be thanking," he said, "since it's just been arranged that the d'Orsay will be hosting your exhibition when it begins its world tour."

Scott couldn't believe it. He glanced over at Dr. MacDougall who winked mischievously.

"Is that true?"

"Indeed it is," she replied. "It was the easiest agreement I've ever arranged."

Dr. MacDougall steered Dr. Benhassi away to meet more of the museum's curators, and that was a good thing, as Scott's mind was reeling. His exhibition—his *first* exhibition—would be going on tour.

And to the Musée d'Orsay in Paris. This was what many curators only dreamed of. He leaned against the cool stone of the atrium wall, sucking in a deep breath.

When the time came to give his speech, Scott was surprised to find that he was no longer nervous. He had spotted Eric and Immy in the audience. As they had slipped in a little late, he hadn't been able to chat with them beforehand. But seeing their familiar faces there grounded him, even as it also made him more keenly aware that Dina wasn't there.

He stepped onto the stage that had been erected in front of the entrance to the Reading Room, a large poster of the exhibition hanging behind him. The applause fell silent as Scott reached the microphone, and his heart began to thump traitorously in his chest.

"Thank you all for coming this evening to celebrate the launch of Symbols of Protection." They weren't quite the words he'd written on his speech card, but he wasn't intending to read them verbatim anyway. He continued thanking all the necessary donors, pausing now and again for short bursts of applause.

"Of course, none of our research could have been completed without the assistance of local historians and keepers of the oral history tradition of their homes. Throughout the exhibition you will hear snippets of recordings from interviews we held with these historians, because we should hear the stories straight from their sources."

That's when he saw her. Standing in the crowd, among so many others. His heart. She was beaming, her eyes shining with tears. Every second she wasn't in his arms left him aching, but somehow, Scott finished his speech. He didn't hear the applause; he barely registered the people shaking his hand and congratulating him as he stepped off the stage.

Dina, Dina, Dina, his heart hammered. But as he moved through the audience, he couldn't see her.

Someone grabbed his arm.

"She's over there," Immy said, pointing toward the Egyptian statues gallery.

Scott walked into the gallery, the sound of the gala growing quiet. All he could hear was his steps on the mosaic tiles. He turned a corner and there she was, waiting for him beneath a statue of Hathor.

Scott wanted nothing more than to hold Dina in his arms and never let her go. She looked radiant in a dark blue dress, made of some kind of slippery satin-like material that hugged her in all the right places. If he had to get on his hands and knees to grovel for her back, he would.

"I—"

Dina held up a hand.

"Please, let me go first," she said. She stepped toward him, and Scott caught a scent of orange blossom and cinnamon, his heart tripping over itself.

"I am sorry that I ever put you in danger. If that's enough to make you hate me, then I'll walk away now. But if—if you still want this, then you should know, I broke the hex."

His heart filled with hope.

"I had hexed myself without realizing it. The universe was out to get you, because of me. All those years, I was so afraid and insecure and that's how it manifested. But I'm learning to love myself. It will take some time, and it'll be hard, but if you could wait for me—"

"I don't need to wait." Scott pulled her into his arms, running his fingers along the small of her back. "Dina, I love you. I'm mad for you, surely you know that."

Dina looked up at him, tears shining in her beautiful brown eyes.

"Everything was real between us, wasn't it? You still . . . you still want to be with me?"

"Dina, I could live for a million years and that still wouldn't be enough time with you. Fuck, I was willing to risk it for only a few days when I thought the universe was going to murder me."

He laughed, tilting his face down to meet hers. Their lips met, arms wrapping tightly around each other like they were one body.

He would hold her like this, each day, for the rest of his life. He knew it then, knew it as firmly as he breathed in and out, his lips finding Dina's again and again.

"I should never have offered to make you forget me the other day. I promise never to use magic on you unless you ask me to." Dina looked up at him from the cradle of his arms, her curls flying in all directions, her cheeks stained with drying tears.

"No, don't say that. I love every part of you, Dina. And that includes your magic. Remember how you helped me in the maze? Who knows, we might have a few more mazes to go through."

She must have seen the sureness in his gaze, because she grinned, jumping up and hooking her legs around him. Scott's hands immediately found her ass, and he gripped her there firmly, a promise of what was to come later that evening.

He kissed along the length of Dina's neck and up to the curve of her ear.

"I forgot to ask, how did you get in without a ticket? Not that I mind you gatecrashing," he laughed, relishing the feeling of her body pressed against his once more.

"Oh, I put a spell on an old cinema stub so the security guard at the entrance thought it was a ticket for tonight."

They held each other for a while longer, until Eric popped his head around the corner of the gallery to let them know it was time to open the exhibition. The grin on his face told them he knew exactly what they'd been up to.

"You two look fucking adorable," he said, as they strode hand-in-hand back into the atrium. Immy high-fived Eric, both of them no doubt immensely proud of their successful matchmaking.

Dr. MacDougall smiled knowingly at them both too, glancing down at their entwined hands, as they walked into the exhibition gallery.

"You'll have to bring her round for dinner soon, so I can meet her properly!" she said to Scott, waving them inside.

The night was perfect, and the exhibition went down a storm. As they were getting ready to leave, a reporter from the *Guardian* found them, and congratulated Scott again, assuring him that he could look forward to a rave review in the paper.

When they climbed into a taxi, Dina turned to him. "Do you want to go home?" she asked. He nodded and gave the driver directions to Dina's flat.

When he sat back in the seat she was staring at him with a perplexed expression.

"What?" Scott asked.

"I thought you'd want to go back to your apartment," she replied.

"If I never have to set foot in that flat again I'll be a happy man. My home is where you are, Dina, and wherever that angry little cat of yours is too."

She tucked herself into his side, his arm shielding her from the chill in the air.

"Heebie isn't angry. She just knows what she likes," Dina mumbled.

When Scott looked down a few minutes later she had fallen asleep, a serene expression on her face. A fierce feeling of protectiveness flooded his senses, and he pulled her closer, draping his scarf over her lap to keep her as warm as possible. Lights glimmered outside the taxi window and all of London slipped into a gentle quiet as the snow began to fall.

Epilogue

The switching-on of the Little Hathering Christmas lights was not a sight to be missed. People from all the surrounding towns and villages flocked to the busy high street of Little Hathering for the lantern parade, and later for the grand switching-on of the lights, which began with the village Christmas tree and spread all the way down the street.

It was one of Dina's favorite nights of the year. The spiced scent of mulled wine and mince pies in the air, the slightly out-of-tune carol singers, and the glee of the small children showing off the lanterns they'd made at school. England was so dark in the winter; they needed these twinkling lights to keep them from falling into the gloom of the colder months and shorter days. All around her, people walked up and down the high street, stopping at the bakery to buy freshly baked gingerbread or cheering as they won a teddy bear at the "hook a goldfish" stand.

But Dina was a woman on a mission. In each hand she was precariously carrying two paper cups of hot chocolate from Mrs. Bailey's booth. It was the best in town—made from the good stuff: real shavings of dark chocolate with generous helpings of sugar.

She'd once recommended to Mrs. Bailey that she could try adding a pinch of cinnamon and a dash of orange oil to her festive hot chocolate blend, and now Dina was given free hot chocolates whenever Mrs. Bailey saw her, as a thank-you for the bump in business she'd had.

Dina didn't really think she had done very much at all to be meriting free hot chocolates for life, but she also wasn't about to complain about free hot chocolates for life either.

As she narrowly missed tipping a cup all over a child waving a sparkler in her face, Dina was relieved she'd cast a balancing spell on herself before she'd grabbed the cups. Scott had offered to help, but she'd told him to stay put, as he was securing them a spot near the large Christmas tree.

Her phone pinged in her pocket, and she wondered if that was Immy and Eric telling her that they'd arrived. Precariously pulling out her phone and resting the hot chocolates on a bench, she saw a message from Rosemary in the group chat with Immy and Dina.

Exciting news! They confirmed the start date to shoot the movie— I'll be in London soon!

Dina replied with as many excited-face emojis as she could with one spare finger. In the year since Immy and Eric's wedding, Rosemary had been over to visit a couple of times, but now with filming she'd be back in the UK for months. Dina couldn't wait to see her friend.

She did her best to hurry back, since she knew Immy and Eric wouldn't stay too late once they arrived: Immy was due in six weeks and no amount of spells could help her stay on her feet for too long. But then again, that wasn't so surprising considering she was carrying twins.

Dina smiled as she recalled when Eric and Immy had told them. She had felt overjoyed for them and knew instantly that she was going to be happy being the fun, eccentric aunt. Having children wasn't something either she or Scott wanted for themselves, though lately they'd been considering adopting a rescue dog. Of course, that all depended on whether Her Royal Highness Heebie was willing to share her love and affection, though she was growing more mellow in her old age.

Dina walked across the high street into the village square, the still-unlit Christmas tree standing more than nine feet tall at its center. She found Scott where she'd left him, now chatting with Eric and a very round Immy. Dina didn't think she'd ever get used to the feeling of seeing Scott smile at her. It was like her heart grew a little larger each time. The last year had been the best one of her life, and she couldn't wait for all the years to come.

"Four hot chocolates!" she announced, handing them around.

"I can't believe this is our last child-free lights night," Immy said, pulling Dina into a hug. "Do you think it'll be weird?"

"Not weird—just a good kind of different maybe."

"My kids are going to make the best fucking lanterns this village has ever seen though," Immy said.

"And they'll have the most competitive mother in the village too, by the sounds of it." Dina grinned, sipping her hot chocolate. Scott's arms wound around her and she rested her head against his chest, enjoying the warmth radiating from inside his coat.

"I have a surprise for you," he whispered in her ear, quiet enough that no one else would be able to hear.

"Oh yeah?" she said knowingly. She'd seen the box earlier that evening, as she strongly suspected Scott had intended her to.

He knew she wasn't a fan of big shocks or surprises, so that was his way of her finding out on her own terms. Inside the box was a ring—a perfect blue sapphire at its heart. She would have recognized it anywhere because it was her mother's.

"All right, everyone, let's count down from three!" the mayor of Little Hathering announced. The whole crowd chanted and the lights flicked on. A warm, colorful glow zipped up the tree, illuminating the square in buttery light. Dina heard the awed intakes of breath all around her and felt the joy of their wonder seeping into the air like magic.

"Would you rather have the surprise now or later?" Scott whispered, his beard grazing her ear, sending a ripple of antici-pation down her spine.

"Later, when it's just us," she said, and she kissed him without a care in the world.

Acknowledgments

Prepare yourselves: This is going to read like one of those bad Oscar speeches that goes on for too long, but, as they say, it takes a village, and I mean to thank everyone who had a part in making this book a reality. If my words seem calm and collected, know that I've cried three times while writing this.

First, to my incredible agent Maddy Belton, who took the mess of my first draft and was like, "I can work with this." You're a dream-maker, and I'm eternally grateful to have you fighting in my corner.

To everyone at Del Rey and Ballantine Bantam Dell for seeing the potential in *Best Hex Ever*, especially to Mae and Sam for your keen editorial insights, enduring patience, and mutual gushing when I send photos of hot actor fancasts to you over email.

From the U.S. side, a huge thank you to Meghan O'Leary, Taylor Noel, Emma Thomasch, Pam Alders, Anjali Mehta, Saige Francis, and Rachel Ake. And from the UK side, a big thank you to Issie Levin, Feranmi Ojutiku, Coco Hagi, Rachel Kennedy, Kirsten Greenwood, Rose Waddilove, Evie Kettlewell, Linda Viberg, Amy Musgrave, Rebecca Hydon, Lizzy Moyes, Meredith Benson, and, for the brilliant copyedit, Gemma Wain. This book wouldn't exist without all your hard work. To Valentina Paulmichl at the Madeleine Milburn agency for being so stellar at selling my international rights, Georgina Simmonds, Hannah

Ladds, and indeed to everyone at the agency for being such keen supporters of my filthy little books.

This book would have been hot garbage without my beta readers Aamna Qureshi, Antoinëtte Van Sluytman, and Frankie Banks. Aamna was the first person to read my second draft, and there were so many excited exclamation marks in your email that I thought: *Maybe I can do this.* Your enthusiasm kept me going. And Frankie, I'm not sure you know how great a compliment you gave me when you compared this book to a Taylor Swift song. To all the team at Orbit Books, where I work as a commissioning editor: You've been endlessly supportive of my writing ventures and I couldn't dream of better people to work with—Team Orbit for life.

Georgia Summers, can you believe we're here? Feels like only yesterday we were daydreaming about which agents we wanted to submit to on our Waterstones lunch breaks, and now we're debuting in the same year. Go us! A million and one thank-yous to Gyamfia Osei and to whoever put us on the same shift at Waterstones way back when. I'm continually awed by your work ethic and talent and I'm lucky to have you as a friend. To Lucie and Abbie, my found family. I wouldn't have gotten through those difficult years without your friendship. And to Rose, who understands that my love language is sending her twenty memes to look at when she wakes up. Laughing with you over the Orbit bench was a daily delight and I'm honored to have you as a friend (who else am I going to talk about orc romance with?!).

To all my family, I love you, don't read chapters nineteen and twenty and . . . Actually, let me just send you a redacted version. I hope I will be able to look you all in the eye next time I see you. To my Dad, you're the best. Thank you for all those trips to Waterstones and for always telling me that I could have as many books as I wanted, and for pretending you didn't see me adding romance books to the pile. I love you; I don't think I tell you that enough. Oh, and I'm going to beat you next time we play Scrabble. To Fitz, who can't read because he's a cat, so I'll speak in a language you can understand: pspspsps. To my beautiful Mama, even though you won't get to read this. I've dreamed about dedicating a book to you for as long as I can remember, and now we're here, there are no words that feel big enough. I miss you every day. I hope I made you proud.

Lastly, and most importantly, to Chris. My best friend, my love. You make me a better person, and a better writer (and you're smoking hot). I believe in HEAs because of you.

Read on for an excerpt from

Love at First Fright

NADIA EL-FASSI

On sale Fall 2025

Rosemary

Rosemary was ten years old the first time she saw a ghost. She'd been sipping a cream soda in the cozy, wallpapered kitchen of her grandmother's house, the overhead fan struggling to create even a feeble breeze in the sticky Georgia heat. Her parents never let her have soda, so that's how Rosemary knew, fingers tracing the strawberry pattern on the tablecloth, that her grandmother had passed away. This was something her teachers told her was likely to happen when people got older.

Not that she quite understood what it meant in practice. Characters died in books all the time, but that didn't count because you could just start the book from scratch and they'd be alive again. In real life she supposed it would be different.

But then Rosemary's grandmother walked into the kitchen. Rosemary looked up at her; she certainly didn't look like she was dying. If anything, there was more color in her cheeks, her hair wasn't parchment white anymore but a fiery red, just like Rosemary's own. Even the wrinkles etched around her eyes appeared to have shallowed and smoothed.

She might not look like the ghosts in the stories Rosemary read—there were no white bed sheets in sight—but there was a softening in the air around her grandmother, a sort of glowing haze that enveloped her as she reached out a hand and ruffled Rosemary's ruddy waves.

"Hey, honey," her nana said.

"Are you a ghost?" Rosemary blurted out. "Or an angel?" She'd been taught about angels in Sunday school, but she read books about ghosts and monsters when no one was looking.

Nana chuckled, looking down at herself.

"Well I don't have wings so let's say I'm a ghost. But listen honey, I don't have long before I go."

"Go where?"

"Somewhere good and peaceful, I think. Do you want to do a little cooking before I go? Maybe we make your mama some of my strawberry jam to cheer her up."

She pulled Rosemary out of her chair with much stronger arms than Rosemary remembered. Years—and many ghostly experiences—later, Rosemary would learn that this was because she had only died moments before.

Tying an apron around Rosemary, her grandmother instructed her around the kitchen to fetch some measuring bowls from the cupboards, and to grab a fresh pint basket of strawberries from the fridge.

"These ones still have little bugs on them, that's how you know they're fresh." Her grandmother pointed, then showed Rosemary how to properly wash and cut the strawberries.

They spent the next hour or so making a batch of her nana's strawberry jam. The air in the kitchen grew sweet with sugar and the tanginess of the fruit, and Rosemary licked sweet strawberry juice off her fingers.

"Half sugar, half fruit, and then a little bit of lemon juice just to seal it all up." Her grandmother explained, leaning against the counter as Rosemary stirred the bubbling concoction.

"I always loved this kitchen," Nana said, running a hand on

the wooden countertop. "I used to bake with your mama here all the time when she was as little as you."

"I'm not that little."

"Of course not, honey." Nana looked wistfully out of the window to the overgrown yard. "You see that tree? The short, stubby-looking one?"

"Mmhm."

"Every spring we'd get red-wing blackbirds coming to visit, and they would spend all morning singing in that tree. You could tell they weren't normal blackbirds because they had a badge of red and gold on their breasts. Such pretty birds."

Rosemary's grandmother had been a bit of an amateur ornithologist in her time, a hobby which Rosemary's mama thought was a little silly, but Rosemary secretly loved.

"Will we still be able to visit you?" Rosemary asked.

Her grandmother frowned.

"You can visit me at that tree, or at my grave, but I won't be here, not like this." Nana pressed a feather-light kiss to her cheek. "I wish I could have stayed longer to see you grow up into a young woman, but you're going to be fine, aren't you?" She gave Rosemary a knowing look. "And listen honey, I think it's best if you don't tell anyone about this."

"About making jam?"

"No, you can tell them about the jam. But people might not understand, some of them might not believe you when you tell them I helped you. I don't want you to get into any trouble, understand?"

Rosemary nodded and then asked, "Could you see ghosts too, when you were my age?"

"I could. That reminds me—unless you tell a ghost you can see them, they won't know. But many of them have interesting stories, especially the really old ones. I got this jam recipe from an old pastry chef that lived over in Keller." She grinned, Rosemary grinned back.

Tilting their heads over the pot, they sniffed the almost buttery sweetness of the jam.

"One final touch to make it perfect," her grandmother said, pulling a little brown glass jar out of a cupboard. "The trick to the perfect strawberry jam is a teaspoon of rosewater."

The heady scent of roses wafted through the kitchen.

Rosemary felt it then, a swoop in the pit of her stomach followed by a soft absence. Despite the summer heat, the kitchen felt colder. Nana was gone.

"Rosemary, what are you doing?" Her mother burst into the kitchen, hauling Rosemary off the stool she was standing on, switching off the gas.

"What were you—were you making jam?" Her mother looked at the pot and the pile of strawberry stems on the counter. She sniffed the air.

"Did you add rosewater to it?" She looked at her daughter, confusion and incredulity on her face.

"It was Nana's secret recipe."

At the mention of her mother, Rosemary's mum crumpled, and pulled her daughter to her.

"Sweetheart, I'm not angry about the jam. But there's something I need to tell you, okay? Why don't you come with me and we go sit on Nana's garden swing for a bit?"

Rosemary already knew what her mother was going to tell her. She stole a glance over her shoulder at the empty kitchen behind her, the steam rising from the cooling pot of jam, and knew she had just inherited a strange, but exciting, secret.

The ghost Rosemary was watching now was much younger than her grandmother's ghost had been, nineteen years ago. Unlike her grandmother's ghost, this one was graying at the edges, and had a semi-translucence to it. She'd clearly been around for a long time.

She was wearing a chunky knit cardigan that looked distinctly 80s to Rosemary's eye, though she couldn't be sure, and was reading a bodice-ripping Regency romance over the shoulder of another customer in the bookstore. Most ghosts have the ability to hold physical objects but avoid spooking the living folks around them (although not always). Rosemary would bet that when the store closed, the ghost would be here flipping through books all night. As afterlives went, it was a pretty sweet deal.

"I think we'll open up the floor to questions now, does anyone have anything they'd like to ask our terrifying trio here?" Max, bookseller extraordinaire and today's panel moderator asked the crowd seated in the horror section of Tickled Ink bookstore, snapping Rosemary back to reality.

Max had asked Rosemary to be on the panel to—in their own words—"bring the conversation into the twenty-first century," and she didn't blame them.

Tickled Ink was her local indie bookstore in Brooklyn and was perhaps Rosemary's favorite place on earth, aside from her writing beanbag chair. Thanks to Max, both the horror and romance sections—the two most important sections of a bookstore, if you asked Rosemary—were exceptionally well curated.

Her co-panelists, James Butler and David Marsh—two big names in the horror genre—had books coming out this month, only a few weeks from Halloween, and were adamant about doing an event at the popular bookstore. Max had only agreed to host if Rosemary would be on the panel too, convinced that she would bring in new and returning customers, compared to James and David, whose audiences mostly consisted of white men.

"I'd like to ask you all a bit about your writing process: Do you write every day, do you work toward a word count?" an audience member asked.

James cleared his throat. "I like to start the day with a run, it really clears the mind. Then I write from nine A.M. until one P.M., before stopping for lunch. On a good day I'll write six thousand words." He smiled smugly.

"For me, it's a little different. As a lot of you know, I don't follow a strict routine." David chuckled, running a hand through his thinning gray hair. "I'm more of an *ideas* man, so I wait until the ideas come to me and then I write like crazy until it's all on the page. I don't really go in for research beforehand." Rosemary knew he didn't go in for research as she'd read an early draft of his new book when his editor had asked her to provide a blurb.

If you're going to write a horror set during the 1870s Buffalo Massacre, you would think that you'd want to read up on the history of the period instead of just watching a few civil war era films. She hadn't been able to provide any kind of quote that a publisher would have wanted to promote the book with.

Finally, it came to Rosemary's turn to answer.

"I mostly write historical horror, with the occasional step into aquatic horror." A small whoop from a fan in the audience, waving a copy of *Julia*, the first novel she'd published five years ago, a deep-sea horror based on the "Julia" sound recorded by the U.S. Navy.

"I need to do a lot of research to make sure I'm presenting the era in the most authentic way. Since most of my books deal with sensitive themes like racism, transphobia, and women's hysteria, I like to find time to interview people who can help me make my characters as genuine as possible. Just last week, I had a phone call with a lovely archivist called Annie at the Merryweather Museum in England to discuss the strange obsession that the Victorians had with Egyptian mummies. One of the most fascinating things I learned from her was that they would have mummy unwrapping parties where they would place a mummified body on their dining room table and unwrap it like it was some kind of party game. The facts can be incredibly messed up but it makes for fantastic horror writing fodder." She laughed, before realizing that she was going down a tangent again, and had better get back to the point. "So I start my mornings with research, and then in the afternoon I'll write, as I'm very lucky that all you lovely people read enough of my books that I'm able to do this full-time. So thank you."

A few more questions were asked by the audience, and then a round of applause filled Rosemary's ears as the panel drew to a close. She thanked James and David for the wonderful chat, though her heart wasn't in it. They shook her hands but wouldn't really meet her eyes. A younger version of herself might have been hurt, but twenty-nine-year-old Rosemary was well used to this kind of behavior from a certain demographic of horror authors by now.

When Rosemary had arrived earlier to sign stock for Max, she'd overheard James and David—who definitely hadn't seen her come into the backroom of the store—talking about her movie deal.

"It's the same studio that optioned mine, but two guesses why they went with hers," David laughed, and through the stacks of books Rosemary saw him cupping invisible breasts.

Oh sure, her fantastic tits were the reason she got a movie deal, and it had nothing to do with the fact that *When the Devil Takes Hold*, her Victorian gothic horror, was one of the bestselling horror books of the last decade.

"You never know," James added, "she might have even found a different way of *persuading* the studio execs to take on the project."

Rosemary had rolled her eyes so far back at that point. These grown-ass men were standing in a corner, sniggering about how she's apparently sold her enormously-titted body in exchange for a movie. Well, whatever helped them sleep at night. They'd had their comeuppance later on when most of the fans had only shown up with copies of Rosemary's books for her to sign.

Now that the panel was over, Rosemary looked around to see if she could spot the ghost again. But they'd disappeared, probably to a quieter corner of the store so they could read in peace. Rosemary was tempted to venture into the back aisles of the shop to chat with the ghost—especially since she hadn't spotted them at Tickled Ink before—but she reminded herself that normal people didn't go around talking to invisible beings in public.

Max strode over, beaming from ear to ear.

"You were fucking brilliant, as expected," they laughed, pulling her into a bear hug that lifted Rosemary's feet off the ground.

"Do you want to wait around, we could go out for a drink after I close?" they asked, looking hopeful. Max and Rosemary had gone out for dinner a few weeks ago. Rosemary hadn't realized it was a date until Max had shown up with a bouquet of flowers for her. Not that she minded, Max was handsome in a Californian surfer kind of way, all golden bronzed skin and sun-kissed hair. And they made Rosemary laugh. They'd kissed at the end of the date, but Rosemary realized that with her upcoming trip, she wasn't really in the right place to start a relationship. She found Max attractive, but there'd been something missing in their kiss, a kind of vital spark. It wasn't the kind of kiss that kept you up at night, even if she wished it was.

"I wish I could, but my flight to London is tomorrow night, and I've only packed my book-case."

"Your bookcase?"

"Like my book suitcase, where I put all my books."

"You're single handedly keeping the ebook industry from taking over, I hope you know that. But hey, maybe we could get dinner when you're back?" They smiled, and it was so heart-achingly kind that Rosemary wished she felt different.

"Of course, I would love to," she replied. Max looked like they had been about to say something else, but then the bell at the till rang, and they both looked over, noticing the queue of readers eagerly waiting to purchase their signed copies.

"Well, that's my cue," Max said. "I'll see you when you're back from England. Have a lovely time, and don't murder the actors." They grinned wickedly before leaving.

Ah yes, the actors. One actor in particular. The actor that had been a bane of Rosemary's existence since she'd found out that he was going to be cast in her book to movie adaptation all those months ago. Hollywood heartthrob, and according to one very viral tweet, a certified daddy. Ellis Finch.

When Rosemary found out he'd been cast as Alfred Parlow, the leading man in her movie, she angrily googled his name. Sure, she'd heard of Ellis Finch before, and had been assured by her film agent that he was the shiniest of Hollywood actors, but he looked nothing like her character. Alfred was meant to look like a feeble Victorian gentleman. Google images showed her the photo of the devil that had haunted her dreams ever since.

Even in images it was clear he was tall, broadly built in a way that said he was muscular without being "gym-ripped." Ellis Finch was in his early forties, with a rakish grin and gray-blue eyes that pierced Rosemary through the phone screen. In some photos he was clean shaven, with an offensively chiseled jaw-line, in others he sported a gray-tinged five o'clock shadow. His dark brown hair curled a little at the ends and appeared to be graying at the temples. According to his Wikipedia page, he was born in Scotland but had lived in the UK for most of his life. Rosemary wondered if he had an accent.

Quite a few of the photos online were clearly paparazzi shots of him; sometimes at a café or a bookstore—and seeing him carrying a tall pile of books, shirt rolled up to display his muscular forearms, didn't elicit any strange feelings in Rosemary.

In fact, it made her stomach drop with what was *definitely* just acute dislike. And not to mention the photos of him parading around his latest girlfriends down the red carpet, a whole host of gorgeous, tanned models with dazzlingly white teeth, perfect matches for the action-man franchise he was famous for. Something about fast cars and explosions and hot women in bikinis.

Though she had to admit those all seemed to be from around a decade ago, and there was nothing about him dating anyone more recently. Rosemary told herself as she googled "Ellis Finch girlfriend recent" that it was all part of her research as a professional.

The odd thing was, when she looked at his face, she could almost understand the casting choice. He had clearly mastered a roguish expression that would have seen him perfectly cast as Wickham in a *Pride and Prejudice* adaptation. Or maybe Willoughby. There was just something about him that would make historical women act all wanton.

The fact of the matter was, he wasn't famous for period dramas, although he'd been in one years ago. From the list of movies Ellis had starred in it was clear he was better suited to action-packed blockbusters. Rosemary had no confidence that he'd be able to play Alfred as he should be played.

Rosemary unlocked the door to her studio apartment and surveyed the small mountain of moving boxes. It hadn't really been her plan to move out during the shooting period for the film. But the stars collided when she realized her lease was up within a week of the start of shooting. So into storage all her stuff would go.

It was strange seeing it all packed up, the walls empty of her vintage Hammer horror posters. Her whole life could be condensed down into fifteen medium boxes and a ten square-foot storage locker. She wasn't sure if she should laugh or cry.

She pulled on her comfiest sweatpants, which had once been cream but after a couple of accidental mix ups were now a pale pink color, and finished packing. Afterward, Rosemary sat on the sofa, now devoid of her many throws, blankets, and a particular tarot-card shaped cushion that Rosemary had made herself during a long stint of boredom in 2018, and opened up her laptop.

Perhaps she could get in a few paragraphs of her new book before sleeping. It was only seven P.M., but she had to be up at four A.M. for her flight, and Rosemary pre-dawn and pre-caffeine was not a good sight.

She'd just opened the word document when her phone buzzed. On the screen the caller ID photo popped up of her, Immy and Dina—her two closest friends who also both happened to live an ungodly distance away from her, all the way in England. Rosemary answered the group call.

"You're both up late," she said, by way of hello.

"It's the twins, they're struggling to sleep through the night, and it's my turn to check on them." Immy yawned. Immy had taken to motherhood like a duck to water, and Rosemary was glad she had someone like her husband, Eric, who very much viewed parenting as a fifty-fifty experience, and who also sent Immy off for a spa day every month.

"And it's a full moon tonight, so I'm waiting until midnight and then I'm going to do some moonbathing on the balcony," Dina said. In the background Rosemary could hear Dina's fiancé Scott call hopefully "will the moonbathing be naked?," followed by Dina's chuckling laughter. God, she missed her friends, she hadn't been back to see them since the twins were born nearly a year ago. She kept meaning to go back to England but between book tours and signings and working on her new draft, the best part of a year had flown past.

"Anyway, we wanted to check on you," Dina added, "how did the event go?"

"It was good, the other guys were exactly as expect—"

"—like shriveled up balls of misogyny?" Immy muttered.

"Screw them, you're tons more successful than both of them combined anyway. Where's their movie?" Dina said.

"Thanks for the pep talk guys, but I'm okay, really. I've finished saying my goodbyes to this old apartment and I'm psyching myself up to meet he who shall remain nameless."

"Ahh yes, the horrible and insanely hot actor. You know I think I've read a fanfic that starts like this . . ." Immy said.

"Well this isn't one of your fics, I'm not going to swoon the moment I see him," Rosemary said, picking at a piece of lint and avoiding eye contact even through the screen.

"Uh huh."

"Sure."

"You know it sounds like you two are trying to matchmake me, may I remind you that I'm not interested in that kind of thing. Besides, I don't think I'm Mr. Action Star's type."

Immy groaned. "But I'm so good at matchmaking! Look what happened last time."

Dina cackled, her engagement ring sparkling as she ran a hand through her curls.

"I'll tell you what," Immy persisted, "watch this clip—I'm gonna share it in the chat—and if you honestly tell me you don't think he's hot, then I'll shut my mouth and this is the last you'll hear from me about it. Deal?"

"Deal," Rosemary replied. How hard could this be?

Her phone beeped, and a moment later she had the video loaded on her screen, sharing it between the three of them.

Even with their faces tiny in the corner of the screen, she still felt the joy she could only get from friends seeping into her limbs, bubbling happily inside her.

"Ooh I've seen this clip already," Dina squeaked, and Scott popped his head into the call, waving hello.

"Is this the video where he kisses the living daylights out of that dairymaid?" he chuckled.

"The very one." Dina smiled, pressing a kiss to his temple before Scott ducked out of view again.

"You two make me all soppy," Immy yawned.

Rosemary rolled her eyes, and pressed play.

This clip was from the one period drama he'd been in, made a few years ago by the looks of it. Rosemary had never watched it, too scared to hate how he portrayed the character. The clip had been shared online millions of times, titled "Ellis Finch Best Movie Kiss Part 1."

"How many parts are there?" Rosemary asked, worried.

"At least ten." Immy grinned.

The clip was cut in such a way so that most of the dialogue was cut out.

It began with Ellis Finch, complete with button down billowing shirt that hinted at the packed muscle and dark hair beneath, striding boldly across a sunlit meadow. Wrapping a firm, tanned arm around the heroine's waist, he drags her close. Rosemary thought he would kiss her immediately, but that would clearly be too rudimentary for Ellis Finch, or rather, his character. Instead, he tucks a loose curl behind her ear, his thumb caressing her eyebrow, her cheek, her lips, before his hand strokes down to her neck and finally—*finally*—he kisses her. He kisses her like he is a man starved of all touch; like this is the final kiss before an execution (she hadn't seen the film, perhaps that was the case), like he'd never known love until he held her.

Heat shot through Rosemary and settled deep in her belly as

she watched the clip, transfixed. She was acutely aware of every minute movement of the kiss, of Ellis's rough grip around the dairymaid's throat—not aggressive, but carnal in a way that was possessive yet gentle. It made her shiver. For a split second she allowed herself to imagine what it might be like to be on the receiving end of a kiss like that. To have those hands pressed gently around her throat. To be faced with so much . . . *need*.

"Well, what do you think?" Immy asked.

Rosemary had to swallow, her mouth suddenly dry.

"She can't even answer, so clearly, she agrees with us." Dina smirked.

"Fine, fine," Rosemary stuttered. "I will admit he's hot. But in an earthy kind of way."

"Earthy. I'll take it." Immy laughed, her laugh quickly transforming into a yawn. "I think I'm gonna try and rest now. Sleep while the babies are sleeping and all that." She smiled.

They all said their "love yous" and "see you soons" and said goodbye. It would be barely any time before they were reunited in person anyway; Rosemary was going to stop by Dina's magical London café once she had arrived and checked in—Dina was a kitchen witch and had a bespelled herbal tea that was meant to cure jet lag.

As she lay in bed that night, her room emptied around her, suitcases finally packed, Rosemary was aware that this was one of those "big life" moments. Just like when she'd left Georgia to come to New York, now she was leaving her life here to fly halfway across the world to help produce the movie adaptation of her own book.

Getting a movie made of her book—and before she even hit thirty—was definitely one of those author pipe dreams. Similar to when she saw her book on the *New York Times* bestseller list; it didn't feel real yet. Rosemary wondered when it would. When they read through the script at the studios perhaps? Or maybe not until they arrived on set at the old English mansion where they were meant to be filming? Even with anxiety and excitement bubbling through her, Rosemary fell asleep, her dreams filled with Ellis Finch's face, the strength of his arms wrapped around her waist, pressing kisses to her neck, and lower.

Nadia El-Fassi is a half-Moroccan, half-Australian author of spicy romance and fantasy. She has an addiction to iced coffee, period dramas, buying D&D dice, and watching horror movies. They live in London with their husband and perfectly round cat. *Best Hex Ever* is her debut novel.

Instagram: @nadiaelfassiauthor
X: @chronicles_of_n

About the Type

This book was set in Berling. Designed in 1951 by Karl-Erik Forsberg (1914–95) for the type foundry Berlingska Stilgjuteri AB in Lund, Sweden, it was released the same year in foundry type by H. Berthold AG. A classic old-face design, its generous proportions and inclined serifs make it highly legible.